DOUGLAS WATT was born in Edinburgh   . Scottish History from Edinburgh Universi   . of historical crime novels set in late 17t   . investigative advocate John MacKenzie and   . Douglas is also the author of *The Price o   , a prize-winning history of Scotland's Darien Disaster. He lives in East Lothian with his wife Julie.

By the same author

Historical crime fiction:
Death of a Chief, Luath Press, 2009
Testament of a Witch, Luath Press, 2011
Pilgrim of Slaughter, Luath Press, 2015
The Unnatural Death of a Jacobite, Luath Press, 2019
A Killing in Van Diemen's Land, Luath Press, 2021

History:
The Price of Scotland: Darien, Union and the Wealth of Nations, 2nd edition, Luath Press, 2024

A Case of Desecration in the West

DOUGLAS WATT

Luath Press Limited
EDINBURGH
www.luath.co.uk

First published 2024

ISBN: 978-1-804251-38-6

The author's right to be identified as author of this book under the Copyright, Designs and Patents Act 1988 has been asserted.

This book is made of materials from well-managed, FSC®-certified forests and other controlled sources.

Printed and bound by
Ashford Colour Press, Gosport

Typeset in 11.5 point Sabon by
Main Point Books, Edinburgh

© Douglas Watt 2024

To Julie

List of Main Characters

John MacKenzie – advocate
Davie Scougall – notary public
Bethia Porterfield
Arthur Nasmyth
Ann Hamilton, Duchess of Hamilton
James Hamilton, Earl of Arran
David Crawford – palace notary
Patrick Grinton – local laird
Isabella Nasmyth – mother of Arthur Nasmyth
William Drummond – Arran's man of business
Sir James Turner – retired soldier
Hugh Wood – head gardener at Hamilton Palace
Andrew Wood – son of Hugh Wood
William Corse – Glasgow merchant
Margaret Corse – wife of William Corse
Robert Corse – student of divinity
Archie Weir – friend of Arthur Nasmyth
Jago O'Flaherty – harper
John Timothy – servant
Janet Dobbie – maidservant
Mary Scanlon – prostitute
George Harlaw – warrander
Alexander Cruikshank – regent at the College of Glasgow
Simon Gilly – chaplain in the palace
Margaret Cassie – nursemaid
William Dalziel – dominee

Prologue

Edinburgh, 5 September 1691

DAVIE SCOUGALL COULD not be described as a man who was comfortable in his own skin. A shy, nervous individual, he suffered from a list of anxieties as long as the fifth hole on Leith Links. His younger days had been afflicted by acute shyness which still bubbled to the surface now and again at times of stress as a stammer in speech or a sudden, uncontrollable blushing of the cheeks. Even as a grown man in his late twenties, he was crippled by nerves when he had to meet new clients or was summoned to Mrs Hair's office.

However, the ordeal he now faced was of an entirely different nature and he felt overwhelmed by it – almost paralysed. He hated, above all things, being the centre of attention and here he was in exactly that position. He could feel the sweat dripping from his oxters. His linen shirt clung to his back like a damp cloth. He rubbed his nape with a sweaty palm. He could not stop his legs shaking. His heart pounded inside his chest like a hammer bouncing on an anvil. What made things worse was that he had brought it all on himself. He recalled MacKenzie's surprise when he had broken the news over a bottle of wine in the Periwig, an Edinburgh tavern frequented by lawyers, a couple of days previously. He was not sure why he had felt compelled to tell his old acquaintance; perhaps he still craved his approval. MacKenzie had looked genuinely shocked by his revelation, before adopting a sneering tone. Why, of all the associations in Edinburgh, had Scougall chosen the one that promised the least fun and involved the most puffed-up poppy-cockery? There were dozens of clubs in the city, some dedicated simply to intoxication, some mixing strong drink with speculation in philosophy, and others of a clandestine nature, devoted to a particular political stance or vice.

But the Masons! Annoyed by his mockery, Scougall had replied that his own father was a Mason, indeed a member of the famous Musselburgh Lodge, and had benefitted from the craft by securing countless contracts for the supply of fish from various merchants. For Scougall, joining the Edinburgh Lodge would provide the same boost for his career – there were only a couple of Masons in Mrs Hair's office, including the lugubrious Galbraith, his main rival for promotion. Joining the craft would aid his rise inside and outside the office. When MacKenzie had pointed out that Mrs Hair's success had been achieved without shaking a Mason's hand or uttering the Mason Word, he did not take kindly to it. He had sat sullenly for a few minutes, sipping his wine, until MacKenzie, seeing he had taken his teasing badly, sat back and his expression softened.

'I only jest, Davie. There cannot be much harm in it,' he had said finally, before finishing his glass. MacKenzie had then taken out his pipe, filled it with tobacco, and was soon puffing away, laughing to himself. Davie Scougall never ceased to amuse him! 'You know, Davie,' he had continued after a short interval, 'a Highland clan is a bit like a club. It binds folk together for mutual benefit. The craft may do you some good. As a Lowlander, you don't belong to a clan. The Scougall family is a disparate, ineffectual group, a loose affiliation without glue.'

Scougall did not like the Masons being compared to a clan, which he considered an archaic social association best consigned to Scotland's past. 'Are you forgetting Archibald Stirling was a Mason, sir,' he had said, referring to MacKenzie's dead friend. 'I'm sure he would have viewed my initiation favourably.'

MacKenzie had nodded. 'You're right, Davie. He was constantly pestering me to join, arguing it would open up new avenues in society. Something always held me back. It's not that I'm against convivial company – you know I enjoy an evening in the tavern, or a game at the table as much as any man. It's all a bit too formal for me. There are enough strange, outlandish rituals performed every day by ministers and priests. Why devote your leisure to such business? However, I'm sure it will help you rise in the House of Hair!'

Thereafter the conversation had drifted onto less contentious subjects, such as the new golf club MacKenzie had purchased from Shield's stall in the Luckenbooths and possible names for Scougall's child; his wife, Chrissie, was eight months pregnant. They had left the tavern on reasonable terms after a couple more glasses.

Scougall now looked round the men seated before him in the chamber: the Masons were a grim band of worthies from all parts of society, an assemblage of nobles, lairds, merchants, doctors, tradesmen, artisans and, of course, lawyers. He looked up at the large eye painted on the wall above them, the all-seeing Masonic eye. It was somewhat disconcerting. He would have to be careful about how he behaved in public henceforth. But he was canny anyway, hating to offend anyone. Why did he need MacKenzie's approval? He was his own man now. He was married with a bairn on the way. He was rising well in the office. He was well regarded by Mrs Hair. Joining the lodge would cement his position as a man of consequence. A flash of ambition took the edge off his anxiety – who would take over her business when she was gone? She was an old woman with no heirs. She could not go on forever and Galbraith did not have the gumption to run the business. He, on the other hand, had a good head for matters of finance – 'Scougall & Hair' or 'Hair & Scougall' had a ring to it! A vision flashed through his mind of his middle-aged self, Sir David Scougall, Esquire, walking down the High Street dressed in a fine silk suit with silver-tipped cane in hand, his head resplendent in an expensive periwig.

Chrissie had reassured him over breakfast that morning it was a mark of honour. Her father also belonged to the Musselburgh Lodge. Being a Mason, she was sure, would do him much good and would not take up much time. 'What did they do anyway?' she had asked with a smile. Just a couple of meetings each year. It would allow him to mix with those above him in society. Scougall always felt reassured by her common sense. His doubts had faded and his confidence swelled – what did he have to be nervous about? He had closed his eyes and thanked the Lord, as he did every morning on waking and observing his bonnie bedfellow, for his good fortune in marrying Chrissie Munro. That morning he had placed his hands gently on her swollen belly and let them linger on the taught skin, feeling the little kicks of his unborn bairn. He had to think of his son or daughter. Becoming a Mason would provide security in an uncertain world.

'Please come forward, Mr Scougall.' The Master Mason's doleful words jolted him from his thoughts as if he had been caught sleeping in church. A sensation of terror seized him. He was being summoned to kneel before the gathered throng.

CHAPTER I

Claret at Holyrood House

MACKENZIE DESCENDED THE turnpike stair at the back of his lodgings and turned into Libberton's Wynd. He walked the ten yards to the Lawn Market, the broad section of the High Street of Edinburgh nearest the castle, avoiding piles of excrement with every step. Although it had been raining twenty minutes before, it was now a fine evening. The clouds had disappeared and the sky was a radiant blue above the high tenements of the city. The glistening cobbles were slippery underfoot and he proceeded carefully. He was still reluctant to take a stick, seeing it as a sign of decrepitude.

The request from Ann, Duchess of Hamilton had come out of the blue, as unexpected as a summons to the court of King William. It was a demand he could not ignore, or put off for a day or two, like one from a fellow lawyer, a judge or lesser noble. Duchess Ann was the country's premier noblewoman, the head of Scotland's most prestigious family (after the King and Queen) and she wanted to speak to him in her apartments at Holyrood House immediately. After more than thirty years in the legal profession, he was rarely taken aback, but this had caught him on the hop. He had put down his book, a collection of Dryden's poems, on the table beside his favourite armchair, finished his glass of whisky in one gulp, emptied his pipe into the hearth and shouted to Archie, his servant of many years, for his boots and cloak.

As he splashed through the puddles and avoided the piles of muck, he wondered what on earth she could want. He had no direct connection with her family. Indeed, except for a solitary meeting with her husband, the Duke of Hamilton, about twenty years before, he had had nothing to do with them. He wondered if he was simply required for a perfunctory legal request, the writing of a bond or instrument. He could not refuse such business, whatever it was. He had lost his lucrative position as Clerk of the Court of Session almost three years before, victim of the abrupt changes caused by the revolution which had unexpectedly made William and Mary king and queen. As a servant of the old regime, he had fallen from grace like many others. After being sacked, he had decided not to return to plead in court. Instead, he would look after the affairs of a long list of Highland clients. A job for Scotland's pre-eminent family could not be sniffed at, as long as she did not want to borrow money. He had learned from painful experience that lending to nobles was always a mistake – they never paid a farthing back.

The walk through the heart of the ancient city took about twenty minutes. It was too early in the evening for much rowdiness on the streets; a few hours later and the closes and wynds would be crawling with hundreds of drunken revellers. His mind wandered contentedly. As he passed Mrs Hair's office on the north side of the High Street opposite the Tron Kirk, he thought of Scougall and smiled to himself. Davie was no doubt already an apprentice Mason. The ceremony would have been an ordeal, but he would put himself through such humiliation. Passing the crowded Luckenbooths, the shops beside St Giles Kirk, he thought of his grandson Geordie. He must buy him a new toy before returning to the Hawthorns. Trips to his Edinburgh apartments were becoming rarer – one day he would sell them to cut costs. He also recalled that he needed new golf balls for a game against Sir John Foulis of Ravelston. He had lost a couple in the gorse on his last round on Leith Links.

As he reached the Canongate, he found himself thinking, as he did almost every day, of his late friend Archibald Stirling. A social creature to the core, Stirling would have relished the chance to meet the highest aristocracy. It was a shame he would never be able to tell him about it. A Gaelic aphorism came to him, bubbling up from his Highland core – a dead friend haunts you every day; he missed him with all his heart.

By the time he reached Holyrood Palace it was getting dark. He remembered that the new incumbents, William and Mary, had not yet visited their northern kingdom. Beyond the gates was the impressive palace façade, restored since being severely damaged during the last frantic days of the previous king's reign. James Stuart was now in exile in France and his chances of restoration fading. Only a few Highland clans held out for him; the rest had taken the Oath of Allegiance to the new monarchs. In Ireland, Jacobite prospects had been set back at the Boyne the year before and had crumbled after the bloody engagement at Aughrim in July. Despite this, King William's supporters remained paranoid and smelt a Jacobite conspiracy round every corner.

A palace guard, who was clearly expecting him, allowed him through the gates and led him across the courtyard to the noble apartments. As hereditary keepers of the palace, the Hamilton family's accommodation was the grandest except the royal suites. MacKenzie recalled the parties he had attended at the palace a decade before, when James, before he was king, held court there. It was a time fondly remembered by the wives and daughters of Edinburgh as an opportunity to show off their figures to a royal prince.

As he climbed the steps to the Hamilton apartments, he reflected that the present heir to the Hamilton patrimony – James Hamilton, Earl of Arran, the duchess's eldest son – was a very different character from his mother. He was a spendthrift, mentored in debauchery by the poet Rochester, who led the life of a rake in London. Arran had dabbled in Jacobite intrigue, resulting in a year's incarceration in the Tower of London. How the duchess had bred such a son was remarkable. She was known for good sense and devotion to the cause of Presbytery. But a hedonist fool often sprang from a puritan's womb.

MacKenzie was shown into a luxurious, high-ceilinged room by a servant dressed in expensive livery. A woman sat alone in a sumptuous chair by the fire. The servant announced his arrival in a cloying English accent. It was a long walk across the room to greet her. As she rose, he saw she was an unusual looking woman. In her late fifties, she was dressed in an opulent black silk dress which would not have looked out of place in the court of Charles I, sixty years before. A pearl necklace graced a long, thin neck. She had full lips, a snub nose and large, bulging eyes; her hair was dyed black and set in curls and ringlets, one descending onto her chest. She could not be described as bonnie, but her face was full of good humour. She told the servant to fetch some wine.

MacKenzie bowed and kissed her hand. 'It's an honour to meet you in person, your grace.' He had long experience of the obsequiousness required when greeting the aristocracy. The chiefs in the Highlands regarded themselves as no less than kings and demanded the same attention.

She nodded curtly and settled back in her armchair, indicating he should sit in the one across from her. She spoke quickly in an English accent, peppered by the odd Scots word. 'I'll get straight to the point, Mr MacKenzie. I've little time for pleasantries at my age. As you get older, each day is more valuable than the one before, so why waste them. Let me tell you first, you come highly recommended as a man of discretion, a rare virtue these days when few can be trusted on either side of the political divide.'

MacKenzie bowed his head even lower and returned her smile. 'I'm glad to hear it, your grace. May I offer my services as a lawyer of many years' standing.'

'You may have been surprised by my request that you see me. We have lawyers aplenty attached to our family – a flock of notaries, writers by the score, advocates of renown, a few judges who claim to belong to our interest – a gaggle of all sorts. However, I wanted someone unconnected to our kin. Someone outside the family. Someone who can look upon us with a clear, unbiased eye. I want to employ you for a particular task, Mr MacKenzie. It will require the application of sound common sense, a quality which I've found missing in most men, although I'm assured you have plenty of it.' She smiled mischievously.

MacKenzie nodded, returning her smile. 'I can advise your grace on any aspect of the law of Scotland or represent you in any court, if that's your desire.'

She shook her head and gave him a hard stare. 'It's not concerning a purely legal issue. It's something of a rather… different sort. A more delicate matter. I require your services in an investigative capacity.'

MacKenzie reflected that an investigation would be a welcome distraction from the run-of-the-mill work which filled his days, mostly procuring money for chiefs and managing their sprawling debts. He had done nothing of excitement since the tragic affair in Van Diemen's Land the year before.

'You'll be paid, of course. My notary David Crawford, will deal with the financial aspects of the business. All your expenses will also be covered.'

The servant reappeared and stiffly served wine. MacKenzie took a sip of claret and complimented the duchess on her cellar. She refused wine but took a glass of water. She dismissed the servant with a nod as if directing a sheep dog and waited for him to close the door before whispering in a conspiratorial way: 'My husband demands we take southern servants, Mr MacKenzie. A practice common, apparently, among Scottish noble families these days. I've little time for them myself. They are usually in an ill humour at being dragged north and look on Scotland as a country inferior to their birthplace. They look down their noses at the local servants and perpetually cry they cannot understand a word they speak.

There are continual battles over pre-eminence. They usually last only a few months before running back to London. Employing them is more trouble than it's worth, but fashion is fickle. Who could have predicted men would wear such absurd appendages on their heads or drink such a vile concoction as coffee?'

She put her glass down on the side table and her face grew serious. She looked down at her thin hands clasped in her lap and turned a jewelled ring round her finger. She inhaled deeply, then began: 'I must speak to you in the strictest confidence. My husband and children know nothing of what I'm to tell you, nor are they to be told anything, for the moment at least.'

MacKenzie nodded thoughtfully. 'Please tell me something of the case, your grace.'

She settled back in her chair and stared into the fire. 'I need to go back many years to explain. Some might advise me to leave things alone. Let a sleeping dog lie. I've lived in Scotland for almost fifty years now, so I regard myself as almost an auld Scots lady, although I do not sound like one and, by birth, I'm not Scottish. Like my servant in his fine livery, I was born in England. I cannot help it, as they say. I was born in the year 1632 in Chelsea Palace, my father's London house – so I'm a Londoner by birth. My memories of that great house on the Thames before the civil war are very happy ones. But the war ended much that was good in this world. You will know the story well. In the chaos of the times, I was packed off to Scotland for my own safety to live with my grandmother, whom I had never met before. I came to Hamilton for the first time in 1642 when I was a girl. It was a terrible shock to be sent north, although not as severe as losing my mother. I had never been to Scotland before. It was a distant, mythical place to me. I'd heard much about it as the centre of our family power. Three young English girls accompanied me north as my ladies in waiting – Marie Arthur, Sara Watkins and Rebecca Kimboll.' She stopped briefly and looked wistfully away for a moment. 'I've not spoken their names aloud for years. My three ladies – Marie, Sara and Rebecca. It was a long journey, a terrifying one for young girls, over two weeks in a cramped coach because of the distracted state of the country. The four of us forged a close bond. They, like me, had no choice in the matter. They accompanied me because my father requested it of their families and they could hardly refuse the Marquis of Hamilton. It's a descendent of one of my ladies, the granddaughter of Sara Watkins, that this... dreadful business concerns.'

MacKenzie sipped his wine and recalled that her father had been executed in March 1649, not long after the king himself. He was fourteen at the time, a student at the university of Aberdeen, devoting himself to the study of Cicero and improving his golf swing on the Links whenever he could escape the classroom.

'The move north was a harder wrench for my ladies,' the duchess continued. 'I see that now. I didn't consider it at the time. I belonged to the House of Hamilton. I had always known I would travel to our Scottish estates someday. However, they had no kin in Scotland and for them it was a strange, foreign land. They were just three young women, girls in fact, the direction of their lives dictated by my family – by me really, for I chose them to accompany me without a thought for their feelings. We all comforted each other on the long journey as best we could. They never saw England or their families again.'

The duchess was lost in thought for a few moments, staring at the fire, a tear appearing like a diamond in the corner of her eye. Finally, she shook her head and continued: 'My ladies remained loyal to me all their lives. They made Hamilton their home and married local men and, I think, after the shock of the early years away from their families, made good lives in Scotland and were happy. Sadly, they are now all dead. I've outlived them all. I commemorate their deaths every year. They all lie in Hamilton kirkyard. They were like sisters to me.' She paused again and took a sip of water. 'The case concerns Bethia Porterfield, Sara's granddaughter. Bethia was the daughter of Sara's daughter Agnes, who married a local man called Cornelius Porterfield.' Again, she looked lost for a moment, then took another sip of water. 'Bethia was orphaned at a young age, her father and mother taken by plague. She was brought up in my household thereafter, before setting up home in her parents' house in Hamilton about a year ago. She was like a daughter to me. A bonnie, happy girl; she reminded me so much of her grandmother. Then something terrible happened.'

MacKenzie waited patiently for her to continue. He finished his glass of wine.

The single tear ran down her powdered cheek like a raindrop on a windowpane. Her voice broke as she spoke. 'It was the morning of 14th of June, a few months ago, just after sunrise. I was awakened by shouts inside the palace. I knew from their urgency something was wrong. My maid came into my chamber in a fluster to tell me a body had been found in the river not far from the palace. Drownings in the Clyde are not uncommon, indeed a couple of our servants perished a few years ago during a drunken swim. I presumed someone had fallen in after a night of revelry. Then came word that Bethia had drowned. Her body was taken into the palace cellars. When I looked down on my dear girl, smashed by the rocks in the river, I was overcome by grief. She was only eighteen.'

It was not a simple legal matter after all, reflected MacKenzie. 'I'm sorry to hear that, your grace.'

'It's a terrible loss, Mr MacKenzie. I was responsible for her after her parents' deaths. She had everything to live for. She was recently betrothed to a young man called Arthur Nasmyth. He has just finished his studies at the College of Glasgow.'

MacKenzie leant forward, his eyebrows dropped and his face darkened. 'What do you believe happened to her, your grace?'

She shook her head. Another tear appeared in her eye. She took a silk handkerchief from her sleeve and dabbed it. 'It's said she was with child, Mr MacKenzie,' she whispered.

'Are you saying it's a case of self-murder? Bethia took her life because she could not face humiliation before the kirk session?' he asked.

The duchess looked away with an expression of anguish on her face. 'That's what is believed by some in the parish. However, I heard nothing about her pregnancy before her death. The sheriff's verdict is she killed herself because she was with child. She threw herself into the Avon Water, a tributary of the Clyde, upstream from Hamilton Palace. The river was in spate after heavy rain the previous day.' She stopped, then spoke more certainly: 'Knowing her as well as I did, I cannot believe this to be the case. I don't believe she would kill her own child, whatever the circumstances.'

MacKenzie thought for a moment. 'Why did she not just marry Nasmyth? It's a common enough tale. Lovers cannot wait for the marriage bed. After a few admonitions from the minister and elders, it would be forgotten.'

The duchess shook her head. 'I'm afraid there's more. Bethia spoke with me a few days before she died. She came to see me on, I think, the 10th of June. I could tell right away she was not herself. She appeared agitated, the colour gone from her cheeks, her usual cheerfulness departed. I comforted her the best I could and then, selfishly, I forgot about her. I now see she was desperate. I now see she made certain hints that all was not well. I stupidly ignored them.'

'What hints?' asked MacKenzie.

'Hints that something was amiss.'

'Are you saying you do not believe it was self-murder, your grace? You think there's another explanation for her death?'

'I feel something in these old bones. She told me she had learned something she wished she had never known. She did not know what to do. I begged her to tell me what it was. She was adamant she could not tell me.' The duchess looked up at MacKenzie and spoke forcefully. 'I want you to find out the truth about what happened to her. Whatever it is, I want to know, Mr MacKenzie.'

MacKenzie nodded, thoughtfully. 'What's happened to Nasmyth? What does he have to say about her death?'

'He's not been seen since her body was pulled out the Clyde. He fled Hamilton that morning. A search has been made for him across the southwestern shires and in Glasgow, where he was a student until recently. There's no sign of him. His mother, Lady Nasmyth, is at her wits' end. She fears the worst.'

'Fears the worst?' repeated MacKenzie.

'Fears he has done away with himself too,' she said forlornly, 'unable to face life without Bethia.'

MacKenzie pondered all she had said before replying. 'It's a troubling case, your grace. I will, of course, be honoured to help. I must tell you, however, that often the truth is painful. I might uncover things that would cause further anguish for you and your family. Do you understand, your grace?'

The duchess gathered herself and rested her hands on her lap. 'I need to find out for the sake of her grandmother. If you confirm Bethia was pregnant and killed herself, so be it. I want you to come to Hamilton as soon as possible. A legal matter will provide cover for your investigations, initially at least. You are overseeing the negotiation of a bond. I want the thing dealt with as soon as possible. I'm sure you have many more questions. When you reach Hamilton, you can make a thorough investigation in the palace and town. You can speak with those who knew her and know Arthur. I must return to Hamilton tomorrow morning.'

MacKenzie had not travelled to Glasgow since 1684, seven years before, when he had overseen the negotiation of a marriage contract. Before leaving, he would have to settle some business in town and cancel his game of golf with Foulis of Ravelston. Telling his daughter Elizabeth would be difficult; she would not be pleased. However, there was no question of refusing. 'I'm honoured you place such trust in me, your grace,' he said. 'I'll pursue the case as vigorously as I can. I only ask one thing, that I may be accompanied by my friend Davie Scougall, notary public in this city, in whom I have great faith. He often travels to Glasgow on the business of Mrs Hair, in whose office he's employed. I'm sure a detour to Hamilton for a few days will be a welcome change for him.'

CHAPTER 2

A Coach to Glasgow

THE HAMILTON COACH with six black horses was waiting for them at the gates of Holyrood Palace at seven o'clock in the morning. Scougall had never travelled in such luxury before. He was used to the dilapidated public vehicle that made its way back and forwards between Edinburgh and Glasgow. A puff of self-importance made him straighten his back as he took his place beside MacKenzie on the plush leather seat. They took off immediately up the High Street, turned down to the Pleasance and then went through the Cowgate and Grassmarket to leave the city by the West Port. Those citizens who were already on the street thought it was the duchess herself, or members of her close family, leaving the city rather than two dull lawyers.

'Was Chrissie alright with everything, Davie?' MacKenzie asked once they were outside the city walls and making their way along the western road.

Scougall smiled sheepishly. 'She's not pleased I'll be so far away with the bairn close. I had to emphasise the request came from the duchess. Her mother is staying in Edinburgh while we're away. She, at least, is delighted by the prospect of a few days in town with her daughter. How did you find Mrs Hair?'

'Friendly and sharp, as she always is,' said MacKenzie. 'She was going to send you to Glasgow on business in the next week or so anyway, so she needed little persuasion.'

Scougall was annoyed by the demand to accompany MacKenzie coming out of the blue. He liked to know about things in advance. In addition, he did not care for him interfering in his office. But now they were settled in the coach, he began to relax. He would be back in Edinburgh in a few days anyway. He loved travelling to Glasgow.

Once they were deep in the countryside, MacKenzie turned towards

Scougall and took hold of his hand, stroking it with his fingers. He could not help chuckling. 'How did you get on the other night?' he winked mischievously.

At first Scougall did not understand what he was referring to and removed his hand abruptly. 'Ah, you mimic the handshake. The initiation ceremony was somewhat daunting, but I think it went well. Obviously, I can't tell you anything about it. I've made a vow of secrecy. I'm now an apprentice Mason,' he said seriously.

MacKenzie smiled. 'Come now. I know everything Masons get up to, the handshake, catechisms, rituals. Do you think Archibald Stirling kept his mouth shut after a couple of bottles of wine? I even know the... Word.' He opened his mouth slowly as if about to utter it, then said, 'It's all complete hocus pocus of course, tripe of the first order. But if it makes you happy.'

Scougall was annoyed by the gentle ridicule and could not help showing it. He sat back and looked out the window huffily. MacKenzie laughed and turned to look at the Pentland Hills to the south as the coach sped along the Glasgow Road. He thought of Elizabeth and Geordie in the Hawthorns, nestled beneath the hills. Elizabeth was not pleased he had taken another investigation. 'I'm sorry, Davie. I only joke,' he said after a few minutes. 'I'm glad you're coming to Glasgow with me. I promise I'll mock you no more. There, are you out of your little sulk? I'll not mention the Mason Word again.'

Scougall nodded sullenly.

'Let me tell you something about the case,' said MacKenzie, changing to a business-like tone. 'All in the strictest confidence, of course.' He described everything the duchess had told him at Holyrood two days before. 'Attend your business in Glasgow first, Davie,' he continued. 'But keep your ear to the ground in case you hear anything about Bethia or Arthur Nasmyth. One of the merchants or lawyers you meet may know something. Her grace has promised a messenger can travel to Glasgow in an hour from the palace. We'll be able to keep in touch easily enough.'

The coach stopped at the burgh of Linlithgow, about fourteen miles west of Edinburgh, to water and feed the horses and allow the passengers to stretch their legs. MacKenzie and Scougall disembarked and sauntered round the elaborate stone fountain on the High Street of the busy town. 'How is Chrissie keeping?' asked MacKenzie.

'She's well now, sir. She was badly sick for the first couple of months, but now recovered. How is Geordie?'

MacKenzie smiled. 'A young rascal, Davie. The best thing to happen to me in years. You may have noticed a change in my mood. The melancholy lapses are less common. There's little time for dark thoughts with a screaming toddler in the house! I'm glad to say I'm well in mind and long may it last. He's the apple of my eye, indeed.' He repeated the phrase to himself in Gaelic, which seemed to amuse him.

'I'm glad to hear it, sir. And how is Elizabeth?' probed Scougall tentatively. As an admirer of MacKenzie's daughter in the past, he was now always hesitant to ask about her.

MacKenzie sighed. 'It's hard to bring up a child on your own. She forgets her loss sometimes, but it's difficult for her. She loved Ruairidh. I'll never understand why. But I didn't have to share a bed with him. There's still pressure from Seaforth.'

'Pressure, sir?' asked Scougall.

'Pressure for Geordie to be brought up in the Catholic faith, like his father and uncle.'

Scougall looked perturbed. 'I would hate to see Geordie raised...,' he searched for the right words to express his outrage, 'in the arms of the Whore of Babylon!'

MacKenzie looked disgruntled. 'I agree with you, Davie. Belonging to a faith despised by most Scots would not help Geordie's journey through life. It's my wish, and Elizabeth's, he be raised a Protestant according to the rites of the Episcopalian church, like his mother and grandfather.' MacKenzie shook his head at the hypocrisy of it all. He doubted the existence of God and thought religion a farce, but there were pragmatic considerations to be taken account of which would affect his grandson's future.

'Where is Seaforth now?' asked Scougall.

MacKenzie shook his head. 'At St Germain in exile, spending his tenants' money.' MacKenzie cursed in Gaelic. 'He could be stuck there for years, the rest of his life even. The cost of keeping him and his entourage in France is bankrupting the clan. Lands have been mortgaged and sold. The MacKenzie patrimony is being fragmented. Pressure is applied to the clan nobles, like my brother Ardcoul, to provide more and more money and, of course, to be ready with armed men if the royal standard is raised for James. It does nothing to encourage good relations between chief and people, indeed, it undermines it.'

'What right does he have to dictate Geordie's religion?' asked Scougall.

'He believes he has the right as chief. But the world changes. He's not a powerful figure like his grandfather, the famous MacKenzie of Kintail. He no longer has the respect of his people. He's not praised by clan poets but vilified as a man who worries more about the make of his periwig and cut of his silk jacket than the sharpness of his sword.'

MacKenzie and Scougall disagreed fundamentally about politics. Scougall supported the government of William and Mary which had come to power at the Revolution in 1688. He did not think a Stuart restoration likely, especially given recent military defeats for the Jacobites in Ireland. However, he did not want to fall out with MacKenzie, who was a Jacobite at heart, so he nodded and said, 'These are uncertain times, sir,' and, trying to change the subject, added: 'I hope the Glasgow merchants continue to prosper despite war with France. It's disrupted trade and caused the sugar price to fall. We must take account of these risks when we lend money to their ventures.' He nodded knowingly.

MacKenzie sighed. 'Mrs Hair hopes to fund the foreign trade despite the war, Davie?'

'She will provide loans for certain voyages. She says war increases the risk but provides opportunities. We take account of it in the rate of interest we charge.' Scougall emphasised the word 'we' to indicate his involvement in the decisions.

They climbed back into the coach and started westwards. 'I've heard sugar production in the Caribbean now relies entirely on the labour of slaves,' MacKenzie said. 'A few decades ago, indentured labourers worked the fields,' he said, shaking his head in disgust.

Scougall had given the subject little thought. 'In Barbados the planters follow the same practice as the Dutch and Spanish in the way they obtain sugar using slaves. It's not peculiar to that island.'

MacKenzie shook his head. 'I didn't say it was. How can enslavement be justified? It's an abomination. Men, women and children are kidnapped, incarcerated and traded for profit. It's an affront to morality. How does your Christian faith sanction such brutality?'

Scougall could not think of an argument in support of slavery. He had never been to the Caribbean. He had never met a slave. He had never seen a slave ship. He had only ever seen one or two black servants in the houses of nobles, as footmen, and a few in the port of Leith. He was not sure of their exact status in Scotland, whether servants or slaves. At last, he thought of a riposte. 'The Romans had slaves, sir. Even Cicero possessed some. It's said it is the natural order on earth that some races of men dominate others.'

'It's a stain on our nation! The Scots, you may remember, fought against the bondage of English Kings. The notion of freedom runs through our history. The sugar trade is carried out in the name of filthy lucre. To make money, we justify any sin. If it boosts trade and supplies men with work, it must be good.' MacKenzie stretched his legs out in front of him, put his head back against the luxuriant leather and closed his eyes. 'Wake me when we reach Glasgow.'

Scougall was glad the conversation was over. He would ask Mrs Hair about slavery when he got back to Edinburgh, how it affected lending money to merchants trading with the Caribbean, particularly Barbados, the centre of sugar manufacturing. He recalled the words of Exodus 1, 13–14: 'The Egyptians made the children of Israel to serve with vigour: And they made their lives bitter with hard bondage.' The Presbyterian faith claimed all God's creatures were equal and saved by faith alone. It made no mention of skin colour. He forced himself to think about something else. He wondered if Chrissie carried a boy or girl. But this thought caused a wave of anxiety. What if she died in childbirth like MacKenzie's wife? The thought of life without Chrissie appalled him. He closed his eyes and prayed with all his heart she would be delivered of a healthy child – that was all he wanted in this world. He would give up all the Mason Words and journeys to Glasgow in the Duchess of Hamilton's coach for a healthy wife and bairn.

Scougall's mouth lay open like a fish on the quayside and his head bounced gently against the window. He was slavering down his cravat and shirt. Suddenly he was being shaken awake by MacKenzie.

'I thought you were to wake me, Davie!' MacKenzie scoffed. 'You're dribbling on your jacket, man!'

For a moment, he could not remember where he was. He blurted out something about the sea. He had been dreaming of an expedition to a distant land, sailing on a mighty ship. Then he remembered they were on their way to Glasgow. Through the window on the right, he could see the steeple of the High Kirk as the coach trundled down the Gallowgate. He pulled himself up and wiped his cravat with his handkerchief. Glasgow was a pleasing place to the eye with many fine town houses and buildings. It was a smaller city than Edinburgh, about a third of the size. The River Clyde was on the left, sparkling in the late afternoon sunshine as they turned right onto the High Street and stopped outside a tavern. The tenements of Glasgow were smaller than Edinburgh ones – everything in Glasgow was on a more intimate scale. It was a place where you could relax, a pleasant escape from the frantic bustle of Edinburgh.

'Here you are, Davie,' said MacKenzie, pointing out the window. 'Gibson's Tavern. Await my instructions tomorrow. I'll write as soon as I have anything to tell you.'

An anxious landlord emerged from the inn. Expecting to see the duchess appear from the coach, or at least a member of her family, he was relieved to see Scougall descend in an ungainly fashion. 'Ah, it's you, Mr Scougall. I didn't expect you to arrive in such style. You've moved up in the world! The business of Mrs Hair clearly prospers.' He gave an exaggerated bow to Scougall and chuckled.

'I've accompanied Mr John MacKenzie, advocate. He's heading for Hamilton Palace in the duchess's coach. She provided us with transport to your good city.'

Gibson peeped his head inside. 'It's a pleasure to meet you, Mr MacKenzie. May I commend my humble establishment whenever you're in Glasgow,' he said looking up at him. 'We have a fine selection of wines and good fare at reasonable prices.'

'I look forward to enjoying your hospitality, Mr Gibson,' said MacKenzie, closing the door. A single knock on the roof informed the coachman to continue to Hamilton.

CHAPTER 3

Hamilton Palace

MACKENZIE CLIMBED DOWN from the coach and took in his surroundings. Hamilton Palace was an impressive building at the edge of the town of Hamilton set in extensive meadows and parklands. At either side of the three-storey structure was a tower surmounted by a balustrade. Over the principal doorway was a wooden balcony decorated with round wooden balls. The top half of the palace windows were made up of diamond-shaped pieces of glass.

A servant ushered him through the main door. Another servant, a black footman, was waiting inside a huge entrance hall. The walls were covered with a vast array of deer skulls and antlers, a testament to the family's love of the hunt. MacKenzie reflected that a few Scottish nobles now owned black servants, purchased from Caribbean merchants in London, aping the fashion of English aristocrats. He nodded pleasantly at him. 'John MacKenzie to see the duchess.'

The black servant, a tall man dressed in bright blue livery, smiled formally and bowed his head. 'This way please, sir,' he said in an unusual accent.

MacKenzie followed him up a wide staircase to the first floor and across a landing into a sitting room. Light streamed through three large windows giving a pleasant view of the woods to the north. The duchess was sitting at her desk, head down as she concentrated on her correspondence. MacKenzie was surprised to hear the music of the harp in the room. A grey-haired harper, dressed in a bright tartan jacket and trews, sat in a corner plucking a clarsach in the style of the Gaelic west. The music reminded MacKenzie of his boyhood in the Highlands fifty years before.

The duchess raised her head and smiled, offering him a seat in front of her desk. She put her quill down and finished sealing a letter. MacKenzie bowed his head and sat opposite her. The harp player, dismissed with a nod, rose stiffly and left the room like an old stork. The duchess turned to the black servant who remained standing, statuesque, at the door. 'Thank you for now, John Timothy.' He bowed his head and left, closing the door behind him. She turned to MacKenzie. 'Thank you for coming so quickly, Mr MacKenzie. A room is prepared for you in the east wing which should prove comfortable. You must have further questions.' She sat back and looked him in the eye.

'Is there any news about Arthur Nasmyth since we last spoke, your grace?' asked MacKenzie.

She shook her head. 'Still no word of him.' She thought for a moment then continued, her expression growing more serious. 'There's one thing I should mention. I only heard about it when I returned to the palace. An awful incident occurred when I was in Edinburgh. My notary David Crawford did not want to spoil my time away by telling me.'

MacKenzie waited for her to continue.

'It concerns Bethia, or rather, her body. We hoped to bury her close to the kirkyard. She could not be buried in hallowed ground because she was judged a suicide. She was laid to rest just over the wall. However, this infuriated the religious enthusiasts in the parish. One night a great stir arose. I'm sorry, indeed, disgusted to say her body was dug up, tied to the back of a horse and dragged through the town. She was hung from a gibbet on the High Street and all manner of ordure thrown at her. She was cut down, hauled back through the town to be thrown into a pit beside the river where she still lies. At times like these, I do not like to call myself a Scot. I remember I was born in London.' She shook her head and closed her eyes.

MacKenzie reflected that such treatment of a suicide's body was rare but not unheard of. It suggested a world devoid of empathy and reason. The same world which accused women of being witches, garrotting them and burning them at the stake. He nodded grimly. 'Emotions run high at the moment, your grace.'

'It's a great worry. The unscrupulous take advantage of such times. I thought the anger of livelier Presbyterians was assuaged since the Revolution. But the discontent continues. There's talk of heretics and blasphemers and, of course, witches. Bethia's suicide has inflamed passions.'

MacKenzie shook his head. 'I'll tread carefully in my investigations, your grace. I'll begin in earnest tomorrow.'

'You should visit Bethia's house where she lived with her maid, Janet

Dobbie. David Crawford will provide keys. At dinner tonight you'll meet my neighbour Patrick Grinton, a distant relative of Bethia's, and Lord Basil, my second youngest child and the only one left in the palace.' She stopped speaking to rearrange the objects on her desk. 'First, let me show you something of the palace. It's time I had my walk. I've had enough of business for today.' She rose and came round to MacKenzie briskly. 'My husband and I plan to make major alterations to the palace. Transform it into a building fitting our status. There's much to be done. The duke leaves all communications with the architects and builders to me while seeking advancement at court in London.' She gave him her thin hand, which he took, and they walked out of the room together.

MacKenzie enjoyed a leisurely tour of the palace, the duchess pointing out a series of halls, drawing rooms and dining rooms, as well as the library on the third floor. 'I've kept the best for last,' she said as they entered a long room running the entire length of the north side of the palace with round windows at each end. 'The Great Gallery contains our art collection.' The walls were covered with family portraits and old masters, including works by Van Dyk, Rubens and Correggio. Over the fireplaces were religious pieces by Raphael.

MacKenzie took his time appraising the pictures. 'A fine collection, your grace,' he said, standing before a portrait by Van Dyk. It was entitled *The Earl of Denbigh with a Blackamoor*.

'That painting was given to my father by Denbigh himself,' said the duchess. 'The works by Raphael were presented to my mother by King Charles I,' she added. 'My father was a fanatic for collecting. Sadly, many of his paintings had to be sold to pay the debts accumulated during the civil war.' She stopped in front of a large canvas which depicted a family group in the open air, Hamilton Palace and the River Clyde in the background. 'Here is my family, Mr MacKenzie. All sprung from my womb.' MacKenzie looked at the duke and duchess with their children. A fertile couple indeed. She pointed each out individually, naming them in turn: 'Arran, my eldest son and heir; Katherine my eldest daughter, married to Atholl; my sons Charles, Earl of Selkirk, John, Earl of Ruglen and George, Earl of Orkney; my daughter Susan, wife of Dundonald; my daughter Margaret, wife of Panmure. Basil, who you'll meet tonight, and Archibald, my youngest, away from home for now. My children are scattered around the country. These are my living children, of course,' she continued. 'The Lord has taken four others: Mary, William, Anna and Anna.' She moved to the next painting, a portrait of a man with an extravagant wig wearing a bright crimson jacket. 'And here is my heir. I do worry about him, Mr MacKenzie. You'll meet him when he returns to Hamilton soon.'

MacKenzie thought it remarkable that such a small woman had produced such a large brood. 'You are blessed to have such a sizeable family, your grace,' he said, carefully observing Arran's handsome features which hinted at haughtiness.

She smiled. 'Each is different. Each has qualities and foibles. I treated them all the same, but they all turned out different. The Lord must have a reason for it. Do you have children?'

'One daughter, your grace. My wife died after her birth twenty years ago.'

A child's scream suddenly took their attention. A tiny girl was running towards them from the end of the gallery, pursued by an exasperated nursemaid. 'Ah, my grandchild. Arran's daughter is being brought up here since her mother's death. A beautiful child, but a wild one. Just like her father. But we need a male heir, don't we, my dear, more than anything, we need a male heir. We need one or there will be trouble.'

The child stopped and curtsied to the duchess who patted her golden locks affectionately and introduced her and the nursemaid to MacKenzie. The child looked a couple of years old. The nursemaid, Margaret Cassie, was a dressed in a black frock and white bonnet. The child smiled up at MacKenzie then ran off down the gallery, squealing in delight, followed by the nurse.

'Quite a handful for an old woman,' the duchess smiled. 'I must rest now. Hugh Wood, my gardener, will show you the gardens. Ask for him in the courtyard at the west side of the palace called the Back Close. I've mentioned you're coming. He'll show you the main attraction of the palace. John Timothy, my black servant, will show you to your room. You can rest and wash before dinner. We dine tonight in the Great High Dining Room on the first floor.'

John Timothy had accompanied them on the tour round the palace at a respectable distance of a few yards. He indicated that MacKenzie should follow him. They passed down a staircase, up another and down a long corridor into a large landing area, finally coming to a room in the east wing. It was a comfortable chamber with a fire in the hearth, a four-poster bed and other pieces of solid oak furniture.

'You know we share something,' said MacKenzie as he looked round the room.

'What is that, sir?' the servant asked politely, remaining at the open door.

'We share the same Christian name. I am John also. Or in the Gaelic tongue, which is my first language, Iain, the Gaelic for John. In Gaelic, my name is Iain MacCoinnich or John MacKenzie in English. What's your full name, John?'

'My name is John Timothy, sir. That is the name given me,' he hesitated for a moment looking for his words, 'by the planter who bought me in Barbados.' John Timothy's expression hardened.

MacKenzie recalled the conversation with Scougall in the coach. 'How have you come to be in Scotland? It's a long way from the Caribbean.'

John Timothy hesitated. At first, he looked reluctant to speak but after a pause continued: 'I was a slave in Barbados, sir. I was sold to a merchant who took me to London where I was won in a card game by the duke. I served him in the city and then I was sent here. Fate decreed I come here, sir. If you do not mind me asking, what is the language you refer to?'

'Gaelic is spoken in the Highlands, the mountainous areas in the north and west. It was once spoken across Scotland, indeed it was at one time the language of our kings. It's similar to the language spoken in Ireland today. The ignorant and foolish, of whom there are many in the Lowlands, call it Irish.' MacKenzie smiled.

John Timothy came forwards a couple of paces but left the door open. 'I've heard the Highlands are inhabited by lawless barbarians, sir?'

'You should not believe everything you hear about the Highlands. Lowlanders have been full of prejudice against the place for centuries. How do you find life in Scotland?'

'It's easier than working in the sugar fields. Anything is better than that life of toil, although I preferred London. There are more people like me there. Black men and women. A small community. I do not know how long I'll be here. I hope I'll be sent back to London. It's hard being the only black man here.'

'Could you be sent back to Barbados?' asked MacKenzie.

John Timothy shook his head forlornly. 'I hope never to go back.'

'Are you married, John?' asked MacKenzie.

'We were not allowed to marry, although I had a woman.' He stopped again and looked down at his hands, held together in front of him. 'She was sold to a merchant and taken to New York. I don't know if I'll ever see her again. I don't know if she's still alive.'

'I'm sorry,' said MacKenzie. 'I lost my wife after the birth of my daughter.'

'My daughter also, sir. Sold at the age of nine. I know not where she is. I know not if she's alive.' A flash of pain crossed John Timothy's face and he dropped his eyes to the ground.

A shiver passed down MacKenzie's spine. The thought of Elizabeth being treated in such a way was appalling. He recalled his despair when she was missing in the Highlands a couple of years before. How this man had suffered. His life dictated by others. Glasgow competed in a vile trade. 'That's terrible, John. Do you have any word of them?'

He shook his head despondently. 'I pray… I hope… one day to see them again. I don't know if it will be in this world. If not, it will be in the next. I hope the next is a better place than this. I pray every day I may see them again. I know we'll all be reunited in Heaven. I'm told by Mr Wood.'

'Wood the gardener? He is to show me the gardens.'

'Yes. A good man. A friend, indeed, to all men.'

John Timothy turned to take his leave.

'Just one other thing. Did you know Bethia Porterfield?' MacKenzie asked.

John Timothy looked uneasy. 'Not well, sir. She visited the palace now and again to see the duchess. She was always kindly to me.'

'Were you here when she was found in the river?'

He nodded. 'I helped carry her body to the palace.'

'What about Arthur Nasmyth?' asked MacKenzie.

'I don't know him, sir. I've heard good things about him. They say he's a scholar.'

'What do you believe happened to her?'

John Timothy hesitated for a moment. 'I don't know, sir.' He bowed his head and turned on his heels. 'If you need anything, just ring the bell.'

MacKenzie went to the windows and looked down on the gardens. In the late afternoon sunshine it was like a scene from paradise. But, he reflected, evil always lurked somewhere in the garden of the world.

CHAPTER 4

An Evening Stroll

AFTER POSTING A letter to Chrissie describing the journey to Glasgow, eating a meal in Gibson's Tavern and drinking a couple of cups of ale, Scougall wandered the streets to clear his head. He knew the city quite well from recent visits. It was a small place after all, just a few streets bounded by the river to the south and fields to the north. He wandered up the High Street to the High Church where the famous General Assembly of 1638 had met, then along Canon Lane and Candleriggs Street to the Trongate and back down to the river. He stood watching the wide expanse of water in the gloaming. He did not miss the arrogant advocates and nobles who lorded it up in Edinburgh. Glaswegians were more concerned with making money than with status. His mind drifted to exotic locations. He had an itch to see the world beyond Scotland. He had never been to Glasgow until the year before and still had never visited England. A couple of journeys to the Highlands was as far north as he had ventured.

As he pondered future voyages, he made his way back through the town. The streets were full of merchants, tradesmen and artisans concluding business for the day, many heading off to inns for a few drinks. He stood taking it all in beside the Tolbooth, looking up at its seven storeys. It was a more regular structure than the Edinburgh one. He might stay up for another hour or so, read something in Gibson's snug, the latest pamphlet or news sheet or the book he had taken with him, and strike up a conversation with the other guests. It was important he keep informed about events in Ireland. He reflected with contentment on his personal situation. He had come a long way in the last year. Working for Mrs Hair was much more interesting than writing instruments of sasine all day in a tiny office. He was now a man of business, no longer a dull notary. A smile of self-satisfaction spread across his face. One cup or glass would be sufficient; he wanted to feel fresh for the next day's meetings.

He was just about to cross Bridgegate Street when he heard a commotion coming from his left, about fifty yards away. At first it was just a few raised voices, but it soon escalated into screams and yells. A small crowd had gathered outside a house. Scougall found himself gravitating towards the disturbance without thinking, his natural inquisitiveness taking over from his reticence. As he got closer, he realised the cries were being launched at those inside the house. He was surprised that the noise on the street was coming from well-dressed men and women: good Presbyterian sorts, not drinkers out to cause trouble after a bucket of wine. An uneasy feeling swelled within him. He stood directly opposite the house on the other side of the road and casually asked an old man leaning on a stick beside him what was happening.

The old man replied angrily: 'They are Quakers, sir. We've no need for such folk in Glasgow. What good do they do us? They are agents of the Pope! Blasphemers and heretics! They must be run out of town!' The man looked affronted. He raised his fist and shouted hoarsely. 'Get oot of Glasgow, ye Quaker bastards!'

'Quakers,' Scougall repeated to himself, not understanding what the man meant at first and then realising he referred to the group of religious dissenters. Scougall did not approve of any sect outside the national church. He thought the Quakers were troublemakers known for strange practices, such as not taking off their hats or swearing oaths. They disrupted sermons and wandered the streets in their shirts. They were an unwanted invasion from England, interfering with Scottish religion in the way Bishop Laud and King Charles had done in the 1630s, sowing the seeds of division just as the church question was finally settled and the Presbyterian system re-established.

The jeers increased in pitch. He crossed the street and peered over the shoulders of the protestors to see what was happening just as a man emerged from the door, dragging a woman behind him by her long, grey hair. She was screaming at him to let go. Another man and woman followed, pulling an old man out by the arms. They were marched off by their captors, suffering verbal abuse from the crowd outside. The number on the street was growing as the spectacle attracted the attention of revellers. The new arrivals were not well-attired churchgoers, but an assortment of artisans and apprentices spilling out of drinking dens to enjoy the entertainment and taking the opportunity to hurl abuse. The newcomers began to chant obscenities, which did not please the original demonstrators. A few stones were thrown at the Quakers. Scougall recalled that crowds could quickly deteriorate into mobs. He remembered the vast concourse swamping the High Street at the time of the Revolution which was swept up into a state of frenzy and transgressed the moral laws. The mob sanctioned any sin, including the killing of innocents.

Scougall was surprised to see two grim-faced women emerging from the house and dragging another old man up the street. The old man tripped as he was thrust forward and fell to the ground. The pair hoisted him back up roughly, grabbing him under the armpits. Scougall counted eight Quakers being taken out through the braying crowd to a storm of abuse: 'Blasphemers! Papist scum! Heretics! English shites!'

His feeling of contentment was gone. Hatred dwelled in the hearts of all men. 'What will happen to them?' he asked the old man, worriedly.

'A few days in jail or the stocks. After they've been pelted with dog shite! Glasgow has no need for such folk. They should fuck aff hame to England!'

Scougall realised that Glasgow was not a tranquil haven after all. It was no different from Edinburgh with its witch trials and angry mobs.

CHAPTER 5

A Conversation in the Gardens

MacKenzie found his way to the Back Close, a small courtyard at the side of the palace enclosed by outhouses including the bakehouse, brewhouse, dairy and washhouse. It was the beating heart of the palace and a hive of activity. He noticed an old man standing by a wooden shed, cleaning a garden tool. 'Are you Mr Wood?' he asked.

'I am Hugh Wood, sir. You are Mr MacKenzie, a lawyer from Edinburgh. The duchess told me to show you round.'

They shook hands warmly.

Wood was a large man with skin the colour of coffee from a lifetime working outdoors. He was slightly stooped, but his blue eyes sparkled. 'Are you a gardener yourself, sir?' he asked.

MacKenzie noticed Wood's large, gnarled hands resting on the handle of the spade he was mending as he nodded. 'I've a garden at my house outside Edinburgh. It was my favourite pastime, but I've sadly neglected it over the last couple of years due to the political upheavals. When things settle down, I'll get back to it. I might take a few ideas and perhaps some seeds or cuttings home with me, if we have room in the coach.'

Wood proved an enthusiastic guide round the extensive gardens. They meandered slowly in the early evening sunshine of lengthening shadows past numerous flowerbeds and herbaceous borders. In the Statue Garden, which contained painted sculptures among the beds, was an unusual sundial: a stone lectern supported by a stone pillar. 'It represents an instrument for telling the position of the sun, moon and stars. It was carved in 1648,' said Wood placing a territorial hand on it.

'I was 13 years old in 1648. I was attending college in Aberdeen,' mused MacKenzie.

'And I was a soldier in Oliver Cromwell's army. I'd never set foot in Scotland and never heard of Hamilton Palace,' replied Wood, smiling.

'Who would have thought I would spend my days here. You see, I wandered in my youth, Mr MacKenzie, strayed from the true path, until I found righteousness. God brought me to this beautiful spot and here I've remained. I serve Him by tending this garden.'

'We've both come far since those days,' added MacKenzie, looking back towards the palace. It was an idyllic scene, and for a few moments he forgot the reason for his journey and luxuriated in the beauty and tranquillity. 'This is a wonderful garden, Mr Wood. How long have you worked here?'

'Many years, sir. Since 1657.'

'I'm trying to place your accent,' said MacKenzie.

Wood smiled a toothless grin. 'I'm an Englishman, as you may have guessed. Born and bred in Yorkshire. But I've lived here most of my life. I now say I'm almost a Scot. My sons are certainly Scots, born here and speaking the local tongue. They regard themselves as Scots.'

'Not many of your countrymen choose to live in Scotland, or last many years in the north,' MacKenzie laughed.

'You're right, sir. Many dip their toes in Scottish water. Few last the course.'

'What's kept you here, apart from the garden?'

'My faith, sir. My religion. I'm a Friend, you see. There's a small community of us here since George Fox first preached in Scotland. I came north with him in 1657 and here I remained. He continued his travels.'

'Ah, I see. John Timothy mentioned you were a Friend. I didn't realise what he meant. So, you're a Quaker, Mr Wood?'

Wood nodded. 'We don't call ourselves that name, sir. It was given to us in mockery by a judge. We prefer Friends of the Truth.'

'How did you come to follow such a path?'

Wood sighed. 'It seems like another life. I was restless and unhappy in the army. Drinking and gambling and wasting my days on frivolous things. Then, one afternoon, I heard George preach in a field. I still remember the wonderful way he spoke to the crowd. It was so different from the priests in their steeple-houses. It was in words I could understand. I felt uplifted. I felt the turmoil inside me vanish. All the misery in my life melted away. I prayed to the Lord with all my heart. He told me to follow George, so I went with him, all over England and Scotland, to spread the word of the Lord. I liked it here and I've remained ever since, helping to sustain the community of Friends. I married a Scots lass, now taken by the Lord. All my family and friends are here. Besides, it's not a bad place to spend a few hours on an evening like this. There's nowhere I'd rather be. It's a paradise of sorts, as close as you'll find on Earth.'

They climbed a few stone steps to an elevated area of fishponds and fountains, and then wandered through the herb garden to the orchard beyond. 'The garden is famous for its fruit,' said Wood. 'We have peaches, apricots, figs, walnuts, chestnuts. All to feed the house. Visitors come from far and wide to see these trees. They are my pride and joy. I bring them on each year with the grace of God. They've always provided a fulsome harvest.'

At the edge of the orchard, a low boundary wall about three feet high marked the end of the formal garden. Beyond was a meadow and then woods. 'This is where the garden ends, sir. The woods go on for miles. It's where the duke and his family hunt. It's a beautiful wilderness, particularly in spring and autumn; if you have time, there are many paths to explore and clearings with fine views.'

In the far distance, to the left of the trees, MacKenzie could just make out a spire and a few towers on the horizon. It was the city of Glasgow. He thought of Scougall and wondered if he had learned anything about Bethia or Arthur. He turned to Wood and his cheerful expression disappeared. The time for pleasant conversation was over. He was in Hamilton for a reason. 'Did you know Bethia Porterfield, Mr Wood?' he asked casually.

Wood looked unsettled by the question. He nodded slowly, eying MacKenzie suspiciously. 'She was a lovely lass, sir. I'm heartbroken about what happened to her,' and then added sharply, 'I thought you were here on another matter?'

MacKenzie nodded. 'I'm advising her grace on various affairs, Mr Wood. Her grace mentioned her death to me in Edinburgh. I'm curious about it, as a legal man. The duchess is devastated. It's said Bethia was with child and killed herself. What do you think happened?'

Wood was silent for a few moments and brought his hand across his brow as he sighed deeply and shook his head. 'I know not if she was with child. I don't think she killed herself.'

'Why do you say that?' MacKenzie asked.

'I've known her since she was a child. She was the same age as my own grandchild and was in and out of our house as a girl. I don't believe she would take her life and she would never kill her own bairn! She cared for others. Besides, she had everything to live for. She was to be married in a few weeks. Why would she jump into a river on a dark night?'

'You mentioned your grandchild?' asked MacKenzie.

'The lass was taken to the Lord with my wife. She was Bethia's friend. Some bairns were told by their parents to shun us. Bethia was always a friend to us.'

'What do you mean shun you, sir?'

'Most folk have welcomed us since we settled here forty years ago. That includes her grace, who has provided us with employment. Others have not been so hospitable; it's the way of most places in the world. As you travel preaching the truth, some are receptive, others hate you for challenging their ways. We've faced persecution over the years. George has been abused on the road and in every town he came to. He's been thrown in jail countless times. I've received my fair share of beatings. I've spent days in the stocks and prison, but you must suffer to serve the Lord. Sadly, things have got worse recently. The Covenanters, the Presbyterians in these parts, despise us. When they were persecuted by the Stuart Kings, they ignored us. Now they have Presbytery restored, they turn to persecution themselves. They have turned on us.'

'What have they done to you?' asked MacKenzie.

'They invade our meeting places. They cast us violently onto the street. They assault and abuse us on the road. They spit on us. They throw stones at us. They strike us with sticks and clubs. They throw us in prison and put us in the stocks. Now they've desecrated our burial ground.'

'Your burial ground in Hamilton?'

'At Shawtonhill, up on the moor a few miles from town. All the Friends are buried there. The Covenanters attacked it a few weeks ago: knocked down the walls, burned the trees I planted myself, despoiled the ground, rode their horses back and forth churning up the earth, casting the bones of our dead everywhere. They were whipped up to a frenzy of hatred by their priests, called ministers in these parts, manipulative devils in their steeple-houses!'

MacKenzie recalled the small community of Quakers in Edinburgh. They were religious busybodies who possessed a thick vein of self-righteousness, like all religious sects. They could be troublemakers, loving to get under the skin of the official clergy who they harangued in their churches after sermons.

'Have the local magistrates investigated the attack?' asked MacKenzie.

'They've done nothing, sir. We'll have to rebuild it at our own expense. It will take years to restore it to its original state.'

'You should have redress for what you've suffered. I'll ask the duchess about it. I'm sure she'll look favourably on it.' MacKenzie took out his tobacco pouch and offered it to Wood. They were soon both puffing away on their clay pipes in the autumn sunshine. 'I'd like to know more about what happened to Bethia, Mr Wood,' said MacKenzie after a few moments' silence.

Wood sat on the dyke and looked MacKenzie up and down. 'Some say it's just a common tale of the fall of a young woman. She was a fine-looking lass and attracted attention. Men were interested in her, if you get my meaning. When she walked down the street, they looked at her. She didn't court their interest. It was not her fault she was bonnie, God made her that way. It was not just her looks, though. She had a bit of property left her by her father, some land and tenements in Hamilton and Glasgow. A tidy sum, I'd say. So, there was an added incentive to wed her. However, she only had eyes for Arthur Nasmyth. They were devoted to each other since childhood. It was no surprise they were betrothed, the day of the marriage set.' Wood stopped to take a deep breath. 'Then her body was pulled out the Clyde. At first it was thought a terrible accident. She had slipped in the dark when returning home late and fallen in. She had panicked in the water because she was not a good swimmer. It had rained heavily in the afternoon and the Avon was in spate. But soon the parish gossips were proclaiming she had been carrying a child. She could not face humiliation before the kirk session for fornication outside wedlock or the stool of repentance in their steeple-house. And so she ended her life and that of her unborn child.' Wood stopped again to shake his head and wipe his watery eyes. He turned to look directly at MacKenzie. 'I don't believe it, sir. It makes no sense to me.'

'What's happened to Arthur?'

'When he heard the news, he took off. He's not been seen since the morning she was found. Some say he was involved in her death, beyond fathering the child, which I don't believe; others say that he can't face the shame of bedding her when all he had to do was wait a few weeks, or that he's done away with himself, feeling responsible for her suicide. I've heard it said the child was not his and he can't face the betrayal. Whatever is said about him, he's a good, Godly boy. Coming from a well-to-do family, he wasn't after her money. I believe he loved her for herself.'

'Do you think she was pregnant, Mr Wood?' MacKenzie probed.

'I never saw any sign of it, nor heard anything about it until a couple of days after she died. It was then the story began to circulate. It's strange it didn't do so before. I saw her a few days before she died. She seemed happy as a lark, chatting away, looking forward to her wedding day.

The next time I looked on her bonnie face she lay in the palace cellars cold as stone.' He shook his head. 'I do not believe she committed self-murder. It was a terrible accident or...' Wood hesitated for a moment before adding, 'it was mischief.'

'Mischief?' repeated MacKenzie.

'Someone killed her for some reason.'

'Why would they do that?'

'These are strange days, Mr MacKenzie. Folk say Satan walks in this parish. They accuse us of being blasphemers. They pick on others like Egyptians and beggars. There's dread of witches, deists and Sadduccees. There's talk of secret meetings dedicated to debauchery and the worship of Satan.'

'What do you mean, Mr Wood?'

'Secret associations with the Devil, dedicated to sin and fornication. Witches glimpsed in the sky at night. Strangers seen in the parish; tall, dark men, well-dressed men, some say foreign men, who are associates of the Devil. They tempt maidens, debauch them and drag them off to Hell. Perhaps Bethia was snared and drowned by one.'

'Like a Masonic club of some kind?'

'No, sir. There are Masons in Hamilton. They are good, sober folk, usually. Not like that. It is rascals and rogues and hell-rakes, including, I've heard it is said (God forgive me, for I don't know if it's true) the duchess's own son Arran. It's said they meet secretly at night to drink and dance and swive and worship the Devil.'

MacKenzie recalled the portrait of Arran in the Long Gallery, the rakish features of the associate of Rochester. Had he transported his taste for debauchery back to Lanarkshire? It was amusing to think of Hamilton as a den of iniquity. But did it have anything to do with Bethia's death? 'Tell me all you know, Mr Wood,' he said, offering him more tobacco. MacKenzie judged the old man loved to smoke and chat.

'I've heard it said hell-rakes meet in the deserted places of the shire,' continued Wood. 'Places like the ruined Cadzow Castle, home of the duchess's ancestors. It's a dark, lonely place at night. One such association is called the Cadzow Kiss. A congregation of sinners who gather to perform shameless acts and take part in outlandish customs.'

MacKenzie thought it sounded like a typical drinking club. Such gatherings were usually harmless, a chance for men to let off steam. 'What does it have to do with Bethia, Mr Wood?'

Wood shook his head. 'The Avon Water, where Bethia drowned, flows below the castle. I can't think why she was there on the very night they congregated. I've heard the last meeting of the Kiss was the night she drowned.'

'Did she fall into the Avon near the castle?' asked MacKenzie.

'Yes, just upstream. Her bonnet was found beside the water. I don't know why she would be there.'

'Who found her bonnet?'

Wood sighed. 'O'Flaherty, her grace's harper. He came across it the next day. It may just be rumour, tittle tattle from the tavern. But there may be some truth in it. All I'm saying is I think there's more going on than a girl drowning herself.'

MacKenzie sucked on his pipe and pondered what Wood had said. 'Have you seen any strangers yourself, Mr Wood?' he asked.

'I have, sir, yes. I thought they were maybe foreign men, French soldiers perhaps. I think they were wearing uniforms. I saw them in the woods, the woods beside the Avon, a few months ago. What they were doing there, other than the Devil's work, I don't know.'

'Did you recognise any of them?'

Wood shook his head. 'It was dark. They looked like finely dressed gentlemen. I'm sure they spoke a foreign tongue.'

MacKenzie reflected that Wood was proving a good source of information – or was it just idle gossip? 'You saw her body in the palace?' he asked.

Wood nodded.

'Who found her?'

'The palace warrander, George Harlaw.'

'Where can I find him?'

'The Back Close across from my shed.'

'Can you tell me anything about her injuries after she was taken from the Clyde?'

'She was bashed up badly, sir. No doubt from hitting the rocks in the water. The rivers were high all over Lanarkshire. She was bruised all over... a terrible sight!'

MacKenzie realised it was getting late. The sun was down behind the trees and it was growing colder. He would have to change for dinner. 'I'd like to see where she fell into the water... and also your burial ground, Mr Wood.'

'I can take you to the Avon and the moor tomorrow, sir. It's not far by horse.'

CHAPTER 6

A Meeting in Gibson's Tavern

SCOUGALL SAT NURSING a cup of ale in the snug, a low-ceilinged room full of smoke and drinkers. 'This is all we have, Mr Scougall.' Gibson placed a pile of pamphlets and news sheets on the table beside Scougall's tankard.

'There was a disturbance on the street tonight, Mr Gibson,' said Scougall.

Gibson shook his head. 'Another one!'

'It's a regular occurrence?'

'Every few weeks there's some protest or altercation in this city. Who was it this time?'

'Some Quakers were dragged out a house and abused.'

'It's been going on for years. Even before William of Orange left for Torbay, Mr Scougall. First it was the Catholics who were misused. Effigies of the Pope burned on the street. Anyone deemed to have a Papist bone in their body had their windows smashed. Since King James was sent packing, they've picked on others: beggars, Egyptians, Quakers. Folk here are fed up with it, but they are scared to say anything. They don't want to upset the worthies responsible.'

'Who is responsible, Mr Gibson?'

Gibson smiled. 'I could not possibly say, Mr Scougall. At least not in public.'

Scougall took a sip of ale. 'Do you know anything about the recent drowning of a girl in the Clyde near Hamilton?'

'I've heard about it. A young maid carried a child and could not face the shame. It's a sad but common tale. I'm never in Hamilton myself these days. Too busy here. You'll have to excuse me, Mr Scougall.'

Scougall looked through the pile of pamphlets Gibson had left on the table. There were accounts of King William's progress in Ireland

and the war on the Continent, and the usual descriptions of miraculous cures and predictions about the end of the world. One sheet describing a colonial venture to the Carolinas caught his eye. He was about to take it up to read when the man at the table across from him leant forward.

'Did I hear you mention the death of Bethia Porterfield, sir?' he asked.

Scougall nodded nervously, suddenly self-conscious that he had spoken too loudly with Gibson. 'Did you know her?' he asked.

'I knew her but not well. May I join you? I am Simon Gilly.'

Scougall agreed and the man moved over to sit beside him, taking his glass and bottle of claret. Gilly had a thin, pointed face. He was dressed in the black garb of a minister but exhibited little of the usual grimness associated with the profession. Scougall recognised from his handshake that Gilly was a fellow Mason. A pulse of excitement passed through him as he realised joining the craft might prove beneficial to the case.

'I'm well acquainted with Hamilton,' said Gilly. 'I'm the chaplain at the palace. Until I get a parish of my own.'

'Have you been there long, sir?' asked Scougall.

'About a year. I serve her grace's family by conducting worship in the palace. It's not a very onerous position, just a few sermons now and again. Ah, I see you're reading about the venture to the Carolinas. The ship has already left Ayr. They were looking for a minister for the new community. I put my name forward but was not picked, no doubt because of my lack of experience. It's something I'd like to do in the future. See the world and be part of something new.'

'As would I, sir,' said Scougall enthusiastically.

'What's your profession, Mr Scougall?' asked Gilly as he poured himself a large glass.

'I'm a notary by training. I now work for Mrs Hair in Edinburgh. She lends money to merchants. I'm in Glasgow to meet potential clients.'

'The Carolina venture was looking for a secretary to manage the financial and legal affairs of the community. I believe a notary from Renfrew sailed on the ship. There will be other opportunities for men like us, I'm sure.'

'How was the attempt funded?'

'You'll see from the pamphlet they sought subscribers in the venture. Many came from Ayr, but also from Glasgow and the surrounding parishes, both merchants and lairds. Even a few ministers invested. They raised enough money for the ship and cargo, and provisions for a year. I would have subscribed myself if I'd had the money.'

Scougall decided to steer the conversation round to the reason for his journey west. 'You mentioned Bethia Porterfield. Have you ever encountered her?'

'I met her a few times at the palace when she came to see the duchess.' Gilly smiled with a hint of lasciviousness. 'She was a bonnie lass, indeed. Very bonnie.' He shook his head. 'Betrothed to Arthur Nasmyth. I'm acquainted with him. I would not have minded... wedding the girl myself.' Gilly looked like he was on the point of saying more but stopped himself. 'Nasmyth is a friend of Robert Corse who was a couple of years below me at college. Arthur has been a lucky and a very unlucky man.'

Scougall was surprised that a clergyman spoke in such a way about a young woman, especially one recently dead, but he smothered his disapproval and continued to question him. 'What kind of man is he?'

'I don't really know what she saw in him. He's a quiet one. Keeps himself to himself. Rarely out on the town with the other students. A gifted scholar, adept in Latin. He could have trained for the ministry but has no desire for it.'

'I believe he's disappeared?'

Gilly nodded. 'Robert has been in Glasgow looking for him a few times. You're interested in the case, Mr Scougall?'

'I travelled here with my friend John MacKenzie who is completing some legal work for the duchess. He described something of the case to me, having heard about it from her. I'm to join him at the palace for a few days of leisure when my work here is done. Did she kill herself because she was with child?'

Gilly shook his head. 'I don't know, sir. It strikes me as strange. She always appeared as quite strong willed. She was going to marry Arthur in a few weeks anyway, so why drown herself? I'm sure she could have put up with the censures of the kirk session. I'm forced to sit on the Hamilton session myself. It's a tedious business. We see numerous cases of fornication. Most of the maids and young men accept punishment for a few weeks. It is perhaps humiliating, but they are rarely driven to kill themselves. They sit on the stool of repentance for a few Sabbaths, then get on with their lives. They are forced to get married. The maids have their babies. I've known none to throw themselves into a river.'

'Mr Gibson says there's been unrest over the last few years in Glasgow,' commented Scougall.

Gilly nodded. 'That's one of the reasons I seek employment overseas. Certain ministers and their supporters among the laity are devoted to the ways of the past, to the Covenant. I don't share their strict interpretation of scripture. Many younger ministers are sceptical about the old ways. But some parishioners share the old Covenanting views. They are a minority, but they cause trouble. They are well organised and well funded. The Quaker issue has become a growing problem.'

'I had not realised how numerous they were in the west,' said Scougall.

'They are not really numerous at all. Just small groups living here and there, a few hundred all together. The radicals or enthusiasts, or whatever you want to call them, use their presence to get folk agitated. They decry the Quakers as blasphemers and Jacobites. I must tread carefully. It can be a difficult balancing act as a minister.' Gilly drained his glass and held up the bottle to check it was empty. 'Ah, my bottle is done, Mr Scougall,' he sighed. 'I must leave you to your pamphlet. Perhaps we'll meet again at the palace.'

CHAPTER 7

Dinner at the Palace

A SMALL PARTY of diners sat at one end of the long table in the High Dining Room. The opulent curtains were drawn as it was growing dark outside. Candles flickered round the room bringing to life the lions and dolphins on the huge tapestries covering the walls. MacKenzie sat on the duchess's right. Her son Lord Basil Hamilton, a gangly young man dressed in a maroon silk suit which was slightly too small, was directly opposite him. MacKenzie recognised the features of his older brother but thought Lord Basil seemed a less cynical figure. The other guest across the table was Patrick Grinton who resembled a relic from the past in his old-fashioned wig and jacket which had not seen a tailor's needle in years.

'Grinton holds the neighbouring estate,' said the duchess. 'He's a kinsman of Bethia's father, Cornelius Porterfield. He often dines with us at the palace.'

'I'm sorry for your family's loss, sir,' said MacKenzie to Grinton.

Grinton nodded vacantly without any hint of emotion; he seemed to be concentrating all his attention on his bowl of soup. After a few quick slurps, he put his spoon down and said: 'I'm the cousin of her father, Mr MacKenzie. The last surviving scion of the family; my mother was a Porterfield. It's a tragedy. An awful tragedy. The Lord is cruel. But he is also bountiful.' He looked lovingly at the selection of food on the table. 'You must visit me at Grinton, sir.' He began to sip his soup noisily again.

MacKenzie turned to Lord Basil. 'Have you completed your education, my lord?' he asked.

Lord Basil nodded. 'Yes. I attended the college in Glasgow a few years ago. Now I help my mother with the estate. I have a great desire to travel, however. I am desperate to see London and Amsterdam and Hamburg and further afield, the Americas perhaps. Have you travelled much, Mr MacKenzie?'

'A little, your lordship.'

'Then you must tell me something of the wider world. Which city did you find most appealing?' he asked eagerly, putting his spoon down and leaning forward enthusiastically.

MacKenzie smiled to himself as he remembered his own grand tour back in the 1650s. He had sailed from Aberdeen to Rotterdam, visited the Dutch towns of Amsterdam, Groningen, Leiden and Utrecht, then headed south to Paris and on to the wonders of Italy. How he would love to visit that beautiful country again. 'Venice has a special place in my heart,' he said, recalling long nights at the gaming tables in the company of beautiful contesse. He had spent a wonderful couple of months there. 'It's a delightful place... the buildings, the art, the vibrant colours... the warmth... and wine... and... I would love to return someday.'

'I must see it soon. Like my brothers. Can I not go soon, mother?' asked Basil eagerly.

'You must keep your mother company for now, Basil. Learn as much as you can about estate business. At least one of my children must know something about our patrimony,' said the duchess sternly.

'The others have travelled; the others have professions, while I am not allowed a tour.'

'You'll be allowed one in good time,' she replied. 'Arran's tour, as well as those of his brothers, cost a fortune. Each picked up bad habits, in particular a love of debt, in foreign climes. I would not like you to do the same. I fear you are the kind of man who might be... influenced by Italy. They are Papists there after all.'

'I'm bored here, mother. I need to see the world. Every young man should see something of the world.'

'I was lucky, my lord,' interrupted MacKenzie. 'Travel was much cheaper forty years ago. I spent a glorious year of freedom. But then I had to settle down to the law. That was very difficult, returning to the law after Italy. I cannot imagine two things more diametrically opposed!'

'Why tempt yourself with all that, my lord,' Grinton said, raising his head from an empty bowl like a tortoise and addressing Lord Basil. 'Better stay at home and save your money,' he added, dabbing his fat lips with a napkin. 'I once travelled to the kingdom of France. I was dreadfully unhappy and desperate to get home.'

'You did not find the country interesting?' asked Lord Basil, incredulous.

'I found it tedious, my lord. The French cuisine. The French language.

The French themselves. A tiring crew. It was a relief to return to Hamilton. I have everything I desire here.'

Lord Basil shook his head, infuriated by what Grinton was saying. 'Please tell me something of your time in Italy, Mr MacKenzie.'

'Mr MacKenzie is hungry after a long journey from Edinburgh. Let him eat and drink,' said the duchess.

When Lord Basil and Grinton had left the table, the duchess addressed MacKenzie, shaking her head. 'I'm sorry for my son. He misses the company of men. Soon I'll have to relent and let him go off somewhere. First I need to find a suitable governor. One who will not lead him astray. You would not be available for the task? Would a few months on the Continent not appeal?'

'That would be a difficult job for anyone,' said MacKenzie smiling.

The duchess suddenly clapped her hands and a figure emerged from behind the curtains at one of the windows. 'Play something, Jago,' she called across, 'so we may talk in private.' The harpist went to his instrument which rested against a chair and began to pluck the strings gently, filling the room with a haunting air.

'I have a few more questions, your grace,' began MacKenzie, 'before I begin my investigation tomorrow.' He finished his wine and turned to the duchess. 'You mentioned Bethia's house.'

The duchess nodded. 'She possessed a house in Hamilton where she dwelled before her death. She had lived in the palace after her parents died.'

'I would like to look around the property tomorrow.'

'David Crawford will give you the keys. His office is on the ground floor off the Back Close. I'll tell him to expect you tomorrow morning.'

'What about Bethia's finances at the time of her death?'

'Her father was a merchant who left the house and money for a reasonable tocher. He also owned a couple of tenements in Glasgow and a few in Hamilton. They provide a good rent. All in all, a healthy sum, maybe £2,000 pounds a year, Scots not sterling. She was comfortable enough.'

'Who will inherit the assets now?'

The duchess shook her head. 'There's some uncertainty, of course. If she is adjudged to be a suicide the crown will take the escheat of her moveable goods and sell them to the highest bidder. If we can establish she did not commit suicide, Grinton will inherit them, as well as the lands. As it stands, he will just receive the lands. I would describe it as a fair sum. Hardly one to encourage malfeasance. As you see, Grinton is a good-natured old thing, happiest at home with his dogs.'

'He's not married?'

'His wife died long ago.'

'What about Arthur Nasmyth's position?'

'He is heir to a substantial estate and fine dwelling place. Perhaps his mother might have hoped he would marry higher, but Bethia was a beauty which counts for something. Together they would have lived very well. Arthur's mother inhabits the house alone. His father, a soldier, is dead and there are no siblings.'

'Why do you think Arthur fled?' MacKenzie asked.

The duchess shrugged despondently. 'Perhaps he cannot face the shame of the death of his beloved in such awful circumstances. He's a sensitive boy, regarded as clever by the dominee in the grammar school. He may come back when he's come to terms with what's happened. It will be difficult for him. He may never return.'

'He may know more about her death than anyone,' added MacKenzie. 'What career is he to pursue?'

'The law has been discussed which makes sense to me. He's not suited for a military career like his father, although he has often talked about it. I've heard he was directed towards the ministry by his regent. I don't believe he is fit for soldiering or sermonising.'

'Why do you say that, your grace?'

'I've seen him sicken of killing a deer at the hunt. How would he stick a sword in a man on the battlefield? As for sermonising, only certain kinds of men are right for it.'

'What do you mean, your grace?'

'Men who like telling others what to do. Men who like judging the sins of others. I don't see Arthur in that kind of role.'

'Is there anything else you can tell me about the affair? Is there anyone else I should speak to?'

The duchess stopped for a moment and looked away, deep in thought. MacKenzie noticed the music had changed. He looked over to the harpist who was staring intently at him. Clearly a skilled player, he did not need to look down at his hands on the strings. MacKenzie felt his mood blacken. The new melody was a melancholic one. He looked out of the window behind the harpist where the curtain had not been drawn. It was almost dark, just a hint of grey in the sky. Two crows perched on the silhouette of a tree. He remembered dismal days. He had banished the bleak feelings since the birth of his grandson.

The duchess turned back to him. 'I almost forgot, Mr MacKenzie. I already told you she came to see me just before she died and would not tell me what she had learned.'

'Was it perhaps she was with child?' he asked.

The duchess hesitated for a moment. 'It might've been, of course. At the time, I thought something had happened. No, there was another thing I forgot. She told me a few weeks before that she'd received another offer of marriage. She would not yet tell me who it was from.'

MacKenzie raised his eyebrows.

The duchess rose from the table. 'You might speak to Arthur's friend, Robert Corse. He trains for the ministry in Glasgow. But I think he's back in Hamilton. And, of course, David Crawford who knows more about the affairs of Hamilton than most. The parish dominee, William Dalziel, also knows Arthur well. The school is on the High Street. Your associate, Mr Scougall, might talk to Arthur's regent at the College in Glasgow, Alexander Cruikshank, and also visit Sir James Turner, Arthur's godfather, who lives in the Gorbals.'

The duchess yawned and placed a hand on MacKenzie's arm. 'You must excuse me. It's been a long day. Sit a while and listen to Jago. Some say he's the best harpist in Scotland. John Timothy will bring you a glass. I'll see you tomorrow in my chamber, perhaps in the late afternoon. You can update me about anything you learn during the day.'

MacKenzie bowed as she took her leave. He watched her move slowly across the room and waited until she left. He took a chair by the window directly across from the harper. John Timothy served him a whisky. As he put the glass to his lips, the music changed again, this time becoming a rousing piece, mesmeric and triumphant. It spoke to him, not of the sadness of life, but the sweetness of childhood. He closed his eyes and was back in the Highland castle where he was raised. That world had changed much. Musicians like Jago who served the chiefs, as well as poets and doctors and breves, were disappearing. Some chiefs were now educating their sons in England. Their sons sounded like Englishmen. Soon they would have no need for Gaelic and the language would fade.

The music suddenly stopped. MacKenzie opened his eyes. He was not sure if he had dozed off for a minute or an hour, but he felt refreshed. 'What can I play now, Mr MacKenzie?' asked O'Flaherty.

MacKenzie smiled at the old man. 'You play with great skill, Jago. Sit beside me and talk for a while.'

As O'Flaherty walked stiffly over to him, MacKenzie thought there was something of the Egyptian in his swarthy complexion, lean face and wiry body. 'Jago is an unusual name in these parts,' he said as O'Flaherty sat and crossed his thin legs.

'You might say I'm a strange amalgam,' replied O'Flaherty. 'My mother was Spanish and my father Irish. I took my Christian name from her and my family name from him. I was raised in the north of Ireland among the Clan Donald. I learned the clarsach as a boy in the household of the great MacDonnell of Antrim. It's the only skill I have in this world, apart from soldiering.'

'How did you come to be here?' MacKenzie asked.

'I began serving the House of Hamilton after the civil wars, first at Brodick Castle on Arran, and then here. The duchess has a taste for my music, the duke not so much. I always intended to return to the land of my birth someday, but I've not set foot in Ireland since I left to fight for King Charles. That was almost fifty years ago!'

MacKenzie replied to him in Gaelic, saying that much had happened in Ireland in the last fifty years.

The old man smiled and replied in Irish, a similar tongue which they could both comprehend. 'I can understand you fairly well, sir. The languages are similar, but my Irish is rusty. I've hardly spoken a word in years. I don't often get the chance in Hamilton. I've not heard Gaelic spoken since I was on Arran. We get few Highlanders here. My first language is not Irish. It is the Spanish spoken to me by my mother.' He said something in Spanish and then reverted to English: 'have you read the wanderings of the knight of La Mancha, an amusing tale?'

MacKenzie smiled. 'I've read the translation by Thomas Shelton. A work of genius. The chiefs are no longer the force they were. They look south to London and spend all their people's money on luxuries and trifles. These are difficult days for harpists.'

O'Flaherty's face lost its playfulness and he nodded. 'The old world was broken by the wars. There were once harpists in every castle in Ireland and the Highlands, now hardly any. I have no son to pass my skills on to. It's the biggest regret of my life.'

'Why did you leave Ireland to fight for King Charles?' MacKenzie asked.

'I was young and foolish. I had a desire to go to war. I was only eighteen when I sailed with Alasdair MacColla to join Montrose. I was a hothead, eager for adventure. I left with a sword in my scabbard and my clarsach strapped to my back. I had no idea what I had let myself in for – the slaughter – clan against clan, country against country, king against parliament. I saw twenty Lamont lairds hung from a single tree by the Campbells. I witnessed the carnage of Inverlochy. When the wars ended, I vowed I would never raise a weapon again in anger. Instead, I devoted my life to the harp. I've composed more than a thousand songs. I've often asked myself why men kill each other when they could share music.'

MacKenzie nodded thoughtfully. 'That's a question philosophers have pondered too. I believe none have come up with a reasonable answer, other than man's nature is to wage war.'

'What brings you to the west, Mr MacKenzie?' O'Flaherty asked.

'I'm helping the duchess on a few matters, legal and personal. She's perturbed by the recent drowning of Bethia Porterfield.'

O'Flaherty nodded sadly and looked away. 'A beautiful lass. Everyone in the palace feels her loss keenly. I'm composing a lament in her memory. I'll play it to you sometime. I believe it's one of my finest compositions.'

'You knew her well?' MacKenzie asked.

'I knew her all her life. She was often in the palace as a young child and lived here after her parents' deaths. She loved to listen to the harp as a bairn. I was teaching it to her. She would have made a fine player.'

'What do you think happened to her?'

O'Flaherty looked at his reflection in the window. He was lost for a few moments. 'It's said by some folk she was with child and took her life.'

'Do you believe that?'

O'Flaherty shook his head. 'I don't believe she would kill herself or her child. Why was she out in the dark beside the Avon?'

'What do you think?' asked MacKenzie.

O'Flaherty shrugged his shoulders.

'Why has Arthur fled?' asked MacKenzie. 'He must know something about her death. Where do you think he is?'

A look of anger flashed across O'Flaherty's face. 'The lad's a coward! He's not been seen since she was pulled out the Clyde. He came to see her body, then ran off. He's either hiding in Glasgow or has taken ship for somewhere. Is it guilt or fear that's driven him away? I'm sure he must know something. An honourable man would come back and explain himself.'

'What can you tell me about him?'

O'Flaherty looked down at his hands. 'I thought him an unhappy young man. He was content enough as a boy. He became enveloped in sadness as he grew older.'

'How did Bethia cope with such mood swings?'

'She was used to him. She knew when to let him be. She knew how to coax him out of the pit.'

'Do you believe he would ever harm her?'

O'Flaherty shook his head. 'I do not believe so. I think he cannot face what's happened to her. He maybe feels responsible. Guilt has perhaps made him flee. I fear we'll never see him again in Hamilton.'

MacKenzie let the whisky swirl round his mouth, savouring its sharp taste. He swallowed it and waited for the burning sensation in his gullet. Then he asked: 'Was he the child's father?'

O'Flaherty shrugged again. 'I didn't know she was pregnant until a few days after she was found in the Clyde.'

MacKenzie finished his glass in another mouthful. 'It's a sorry tale indeed. The duchess is anxious to know the truth of the matter.'

'She was very fond of her.'

'Hugh Wood mentioned a secret association which meets in the parish.'

O'Flaherty smiled. 'He refers to the Cadzow Kiss. The Quakers are not invited to attend.'

'What is its nature?' asked MacKenzie.

'It is just a drinking club with a few peculiar customs... for certain men in the parish.'

'Have you attended it, Jago?'

O'Flaherty smiled again. 'A few times in my younger days, no longer.'

MacKenzie returned his glass to the small table beside him. 'It's time I retired. Where do you live, Jago?'

'The palace has been my home for years. I have a room here. It suits me well. I can compose my songs without disturbing anyone. I would be honoured if you would join me during your visit. We might share a glass or two of whisky and speak some more in the Irish tongue. I'll play you my lament for Bethia. You'll be the first to hear it.'

MacKenzie smiled warmly. 'It would be a pleasure, Jago. One final thing. I've been told you found her bonnet by the Avon?'

O'Flaherty nodded. 'I wanted to help the search despite being an old man. I know the woods along the Avon well. I found it in a bush beside the water. It must have fallen off when she went in.'

O'Flaherty bowed his head and returned stiffly to his harp. MacKenzie let the last drop of whisky drip into his mouth. The spirit had a different flavour from those of Inverness-shire and Ross-shire he was used to. In a few minutes, the drink began to relax him. He closed his eyes. When he woke, it was pitch dark outside. O'Flaherty had gone to bed. His harp stood beside the window. MacKenzie looked out the window into the darkness. He could just make out the lights of Glasgow in the distance and reflected that Scougall, an early riser, was no doubt already in bed.

CHAPTER 8

The Back Close

MACKENZIE ROSE EARLY the next morning and, after breakfast in his room, found David Crawford's office on the ground floor at the back of the palace. Crawford, a small, chubby man wearing spectacles and a wig, was already working at his desk. A white cravat tied tightly round his neck accentuated his double chin. He looked very much the dull lawyer.

MacKenzie knocked on the open door and put his head in. 'Good morning, sir.'

'Ah, Mr MacKenzie. Her grace told me you would drop in this morning.'

MacKenzie came into the office and looked round the small room crammed with ledgers and estate papers. 'I'm advising her on a number of matters, Mr Crawford.'

'Pulling together investors in Edinburgh for a heritable bond,' said Crawford, putting down his quill.

MacKenzie nodded. 'A small syndicate. Negotiations are almost complete. Things should be tied up in a couple of weeks. How long have you been employed at the palace?' he asked.

Crawford pursed his lips and replied with little enthusiasm. 'Almost thirty years. I served my apprenticeship as a notary in Glasgow, then came here. I've worked for the family ever since.'

'There must be little about their affairs you're not familiar with,' said MacKenzie with a hint of a smile.

Crawford did not respond immediately but eyed him carefully. 'Aye, I look after all her grace's financial affairs, everything concerning the estate. All money coming in and going out is accounted for by me. I record everything meticulously. I consider myself an important part of the House of Hamilton.'

'I hear you're being aided by Lord Basil,' said MacKenzie.

'I'm instructing his lordship in the art of bookkeeping. I fear his heart is not in the work.'

MacKenzie nodded at the humourless lawyer. 'Sound accounting does not always appeal to the young,' he said, then walked across to the window which looked out on the Back Close. The courtyard was already busy: horses being saddled, sacks of flour being unloaded from carts, provisions arriving from Glasgow. Crawford remained seated. After a few moments, MacKenzie turned and his mild expression dropped like a falling axe. It was time to get on with business. Crawford had taken up his quill again and was writing in his ledger. 'What do you think happened to Bethia Porterfield?' asked MacKenzie.

Crawford stopped writing and looked up, taken aback by the question. 'Why do you ask me?' he asked defensively. 'I thought you were here to examine the income of the estate.'

MacKenzie smiled benignly. He did not take to Crawford. He had dealt with a thousand such men in his long career. The law was full of small-minded, punctilious sticklers. 'I am, sir. My assistant, Mr Scougall, who will be on his way here soon, will examine the books and make copies. The bond will be signed when I return to Edinburgh and the money provided to the duchess. You may then account for it in your ledger. Bethia's case is a matter of concern for her grace. Why would a girl with everything to live for kill herself? It's a question which troubles me.'

Crawford shrugged his shoulders and continued to write. 'It's said she was with child and could not face the shame.'

'What do you think, Mr Crawford? Did you know her well?' MacKenzie asked, approaching the desk and standing directly in front of it. Crawford was forced to raise his neck to look at him. Crawford's cheeks reddened. He could not hide his anger. He took the spectacles off the bridge of his nose and placed them on his book, putting the quill in its holder. 'Of course, I knew her well. I've known her since she was a bairn and ran around the palace corridors. I lived here myself in the days before I owned a property in town.' He stopped for a moment, calming himself. 'It's all a mystery to me. Nasmyth and her seemed happy together. But affairs of the heart blow hot and cold in the young. Perhaps she suffered a fit of melancholy or temporary madness.'

'Did you know him well?' asked MacKenzie.

'Not well. He seemed... unremarkable to me. A quiet fellow. A good scholar, I've heard it said. Happiest with his nose in a book. I hardly noticed him to be honest. He didn't make a show of himself.' Crawford looked at his quill. He wanted to get on with his work.

'Do you have the keys for her house?'

'Why do you want them, Mr MacKenzie?'

'I've agreed to examine the matter for her grace. To make sure nothing has been overlooked.'

'Overlooked?' repeated Crawford.

'Fresh eyes see in the thickest mist, as we say in Gaelic. Look under a heavy stone and see if a snake hides beneath,' said MacKenzie.

Crawford reluctantly rose from his seat, revealing his corpulent and diminutive stature. He crossed to a press at the far side of the room and came back with a set of keys which he placed on the desk.

'Are you implying Bethia made a show of herself?' asked MacKenzie.

Crawford took his seat again. He did not reply immediately but ruminated in a way common to lawyers who are picking their words carefully. 'She was a livelier character than Arthur. Bright and sharp with a sparkle in her eye. Nasmyth was a dullard in comparison. I don't know what she saw in him to be honest. A reasonable estate, I suppose. A girl like her, a beauty like her, could have achieved a far better match, especially with her closeness to the family.'

'What do you mean, Crawford?' asked MacKenzie.

'She was close to the duchess, who was very fond of her, as the granddaughter of her lady-in-waiting. She might have obtained a match within the extended family, even one of the lesser children.'

'But no offer was made to her?'

'I don't know. I would only have been consulted on the financial terms.'

'You refer to Lord Archibald or Lord Basil?'

Crawford did not answer.

'Are you married, Mr Crawford?' asked MacKenzie.

'I am not, sir.'

'Did you ever have thoughts of wedding her?'

Crawford was annoyed by the question. His face beamed red again. 'I did not, sir.'

MacKenzie thought for a moment. 'Was she not too lowly in status to marry into the family?'

'Perhaps, but sometimes status can be overlooked.'

'Did she have other suitors?'

Crawford hesitated for a moment. 'I don't know who her suitors were, sir. She didn't have much time for the likes of me.'

'What do you mean?'

'I'm just a notary. An old one at that. She had no time for me.'

MacKenzie looked round the tidy room, lined with bookcases bursting with ledgers, estate papers and correspondence. A man who spent his life in such a room was hardly a catch for a young woman. It was the curse of employment in the law: a secure and monotonous profession, it provided a steady living, but was hardly filled with excitement. 'Perhaps it was just an awful accident,' he said. 'She was out at night for a walk and fell into the river. Hit her head on a stone and drowned.'

Crawford spoke gruffly. 'That's entirely possible. I don't have time to ponder such matters. Now, I must get back to my work. Take the keys,' he said impatiently, picking them up and holding them for MacKenzie. 'Return them when you're done.'

MacKenzie ignored him and continued to launch questions. 'Why would Nasmyth disappear within hours of her death?'

Crawford shook his head. 'I wish I could help you, Mr MacKenzie. I know nothing more about it... it's one of life's many tragedies.'

MacKenzie waited for a few moments, sensing Crawford's rising anxiety at being held back from his account book, before asking: 'When was Arran last at Hamilton?'

Crawford thought for a moment. 'Why do you ask?'

'I simply do my duty as a lawyer, as an investigator. I've promised her grace to examine the affair. That's what I'm doing, looking into the affair.'

Crawford put his quill down again and looked up to meet MacKenzie's eyes. 'Around the time she died. Arran was back for about ten days before he went to Edinburgh and then returned to London.'

'Arran was here when she died?' asked MacKenzie.

'What do you insinuate? That he was somehow involved in her death?'

'Not at all, Mr Crawford. I just want to build up a picture in my mind of all those in the palace at the time. Who accompanied him?'

Crawford shook his head. 'I must be getting on.'

'Who accompanied him?' MacKenzie repeated.

'William Drummond, his man of business. Adam Nisbet and Robert Pringle, his bodyguards. The earl returns here every few months, maybe thrice a year. His young daughter is being brought up by the duchess.'

'When did he leave?' asked MacKenzie.

'He was called to Edinburgh to see his lawyers a few days after the drowning. You'll know the family has a house at Kinneil on the Firth of Forth. He stayed there a couple of days and then a few days in the Holyrood apartments.'

MacKenzie nodded and moved to the door, suggesting he was on the point of leaving, but turned, unnerving Crawford as he spoke suddenly: 'What can you tell me about the Cadzow Kiss?'

Crawford's mouth dropped open in surprise revealing two rows of sharp little teeth. 'What do you mean, Mr MacKenzie?' he asked angrily.

MacKenzie remained where he was. 'I've heard the association mentioned in conversation. I want to know more about it, including when it last met.'

'I don't attend such an association,' Crawford said blankly. 'You'll have to ask someone else about it.'

'But you do not deny it meets from time to time in the parish?'

Crawford did not reply.

'As a man who knows everything about Hamilton, I thought you might know about it.'

Crawford frowned. 'I believe the last meeting was on the 13th of June. It's just a gathering of drunken fools. Not a serious association. It is, of course, an afront to the dignity of the parish.'

'That was the night she drowned?'

Crawford nodded.

'What exactly happens at the Kiss?' probed MacKenzie.

Crawford looked affronted. 'I've never attended it. It's not my cup of coffee, as they say. I'm an elder. I sit on the kirk session. I make decisions about the morality of parishioners. The Kiss attracts those who avoid the kirk on the Sabbath, drink late in the tavern and get mixed up in high jinks.'

'What is the nature of the meetings exactly. Is it just a drinking club?'

'I believe it's dedicated to pleasure of a kind. The exact nature of its business, I know not. There are rumours of debauchery. It was thought to have lapsed years ago, but it continues intermittently, sometimes not meeting for a few years, then reappearing. It seems to have made a resurgence recently. The parish would be well rid of it.'

'There have been efforts to suppress it?' asked MacKenzie.

'The kirk session has called for it to be disbanded as a Popish den of vice countless times. They have demanded it be suppressed by the sheriff. The problem is, no one knows when it meets, making it difficult to thwart. All those who attend are sworn to secrecy. The Godly in the parish are never invited, so it continues haphazardly, part of the old ways. It will fade as the country becomes more civilised, as Presbyterianism is embedded in this land. You should not judge us by its existence. I believe such associations exist everywhere.'

'I do not judge this parish by it,' replied McKenzie, 'and they do, indeed, exist everywhere there are men, in my experience. Would you know any of those who do attend it?'

Crawford looked increasingly desperate to end the conversation. 'I would not, sir. And I would not slander anyone by saying they did.'

MacKenzie nodded, then asked casually: 'What about Arran?'

Crawford looked upset. 'I don't believe the earl attends.'

'You do not believe it, Crawford! It was just a coincidence it met the last time he was in residence?'

Crawford did not answer.

MacKenzie went back for the keys which were lying on the desk. 'Thank you, Mr Crawford. I'll return these later. I was told I could speak to Janet Dobbie. Where might I find her?'

Crawford grumbled under his breath as he rose and left the room. MacKenzie returned to the window and looked out on the Back Close again. A few minutes later, Crawford returned out of breath. 'Come this way,' he puffed. MacKenzie followed him down the corridor and left into a larger room, which was clearly the servants' dining chamber. As they entered, two maids bowed their heads and scurried away. One young woman remained inside, standing nervously beside the long wooden table in the middle of the room. 'Here she is,' said Crawford and left without another word. MacKenzie shut the door.

MacKenzie could sense Janet Dobbie's anxiety and he tried to put her at ease. She was a young woman with a pale face and slightly crooked mouth. He smiled and asked her to sit at the table. He took the chair beside her and spoke gently to her. There was no need to deal with her in the rough way he had questioned Crawford. 'My name is John MacKenzie. I'm a lawyer from Edinburgh working for the duchess. I want to ask you a few questions about your mistress, your dead mistress.' He waited to observe her reaction.

She nodded nervously, looking scared. She crossed her arms over her chest defensively and looked down, not meeting his gaze.

'There's no need to be afraid, my dear. How long did you serve Bethia?' he asked.

She replied in a soft, timid voice. 'I've worked in the palace since I was a girl. When Bethia lived here, I tended her as her maid. She asked me to come as her maid when she moved into her own house.'

'So, you've known her for a few years?'

'About six years, since I left my father's house in Hamilton. I served her in her house for only six months before she died.'

'She must have thought you a good worker to ask you to attend her in her own house,' said MacKenzie affably.

Janet nodded. 'I liked her, sir. I liked her very much. She was good to me. I liked to serve her.'

'I can see that, Janet. So, you lived with her in the house for six months before she died. Was there anyone else living there at that time?'

She shook her head. 'No. Just me and her. I did everything: cooking, washing, cleaning, laundry, tending the fires. It's just a small place compared to the palace. I could do it all easily.'

'Was it a happy time?'

She moved herself, relaxing slightly and dropping her arms to her sides. 'Yes, sir. The best time of my life. She was good to me. She was kind, not like... well, you know... like others... in the palace. My duties were light. I tended the house. I worked hard to keep it clean. We had time to speak together in the evening after we'd eaten. We would sit beside the fire and chat before we went to bed. We would often laugh together.'

MacKenzie smiled. 'What did you speak about, Janet?'

She looked up, meeting his eyes for the first time, gaining confidence. 'We talked about everything, sir. The folk she met in town, or at the palace, or on her walks. How she missed Arthur when he was in Glasgow and what their life would be like when they were married. She wanted me to come with her to Nasmyth House as her maid. She told me I could marry myself and my husband would work as a footman there. I could keep attending her and help with her bairns, and when I had bairns, she would help me.' She looked away for a moment, tearfully. 'Now I will never live there. It's a pleasant place. Arthur's mother is a kind woman. I don't mean the palace is unpleasant. I'm lucky to have a position here, but it's different. It would've been a better life with her. It will be harder in the palace.'

'What about her state of mind just before she died. Would you say she was happy or sad?'

Janet hesitated for a moment. 'She was happy for all the years I knew her. But I think something had happened to upset her since Arthur returned from Glasgow at the end of May. Everything was fine at first, but she began to change. She was not herself. She looked ill at ease. She didn't speak to me so much in the evening. She retired to her chamber or disappeared for hours on walks. I tried to ask her what was wrong. I thought she had maybe rowed with Arthur. Such things are common among lovers, but I'm not sure if it was that. She would not tell me what ailed her.'

'You cannot guess what it might have been?' probed MacKenzie.

'I'm sure it was something to do with him. Something happened after his return. All was well when he was in Glasgow. Then something soured between them. Maybe it was his desire to be a soldier. She thought he should look after his estates. She wanted to be a laird's wife. She didn't want to live without a husband. Or perhaps he was spending too much time with his friends, Mr Corse and the others in Glasgow. I cannot remember their names.'

'How long would you say she was in this altered state of mind?'

'For a few weeks before she died.'

'Tell me about the last time you saw her, Janet.'

She closed her eyes to concentrate. 'In the morning, Arthur came to see her. I was busy with my work. They talked quietly for about half an hour in the living chamber and then he left. Then she went to the palace to visit the duchess. She was back in the house in the afternoon, attending her needlework, but not concentrating on it. She appeared distracted. Then after dinner, which she hardly touched, she left the house suddenly, taking her cloak and not telling me where she was bound. That was unusual. I just heard the door slam and she was gone. I sat in my room waiting for her to come back. I waited up late. She didn't return, even when it got dark. I was very worried. I didn't know what to do, so about three o'clock in the morning I woke Mr Wood. He roused his sons and organised a search for her. Then later, when it was light, I heard the terrible news she was found in the Clyde.' The girl began to sob.

MacKenzie took a handkerchief from his pocket and handed it to her. He waited while she wiped her eyes. 'How do you like Arthur, Janet?' he asked.

'I like him well enough,' she said. 'I don't know him as well as I knew Bethia. He is always friendly with me, maybe a bit shy, maybe a little ill-tempered sometimes. I thought them a fine pair though. They fitted together well, not like some who don't know each other and dread their wedding night. They were at ease with each other, mostly.'

MacKenzie thought for a moment. 'Some have said she was with child. Do you think that was the case?'

She shook her head vehemently. 'I knew nothing of that, sir. I would have known if she was with child. I lived with her. I would have seen some indication of it: sickness in the morning, tiredness. I saw none of that. Besides, I believe she would have told me.'

'It's said she was with child,' reiterated MacKenzie.

'How would they know she was with child? How would they know?' She looked angry.

'Who do you mean?' asked MacKenzie.

'The session. The religious men and women. How would they know she was with child, while all those who knew her well did not?'

MacKenzie nodded. 'How did you hear she was pregnant?'

She thought for a moment. 'I didn't hear it until a couple of days after she drowned. It was in this very room. Mr Crawford told the servants. By then the session had stated she was with child. I don't know how they knew. Mr Crawford said she had killed herself because of the shame. She had let Satan into her life by fornicating outside marriage. The next day all the servants were talking about it – everyone knew. That was the reason she killed herself.'

'Did Arthur look his usual self when you saw him that day?'

She thought for a moment. 'I let him in at the door. He was quiet, I would say, more subdued than usual, uncertain, fearful maybe.'

'As if he wanted to break off the marriage?'

She nodded, then shook her head. 'I don't know, sir. It could've been that.'

'Or she was telling him she was pregnant?'

She shook her head. 'I don't think so, sir.'

'Can you think of anything else that might explain why she died, Janet? Or anything else you would like to tell me?'

Janet looked down at her hands suddenly. She did not speak for a while but began to rub them together nervously. At last, she spoke: 'I don't know if I should say it, sir. I don't like to say it.'

'Please, Janet. It might be important.'

'She was troubled. Bethia was often troubled when she was in the palace.'

'Troubled in the palace? What do you mean?'

She looked towards the door and her voice dropped to a whisper. 'She told me men troubled her. It started when she was little more than a girl. They would not leave her alone. Men are like that. I know myself. Trying to touch you, demanding more. It put her off going to the palace.

She said she was scared to tell Arthur in case he caused a scene.'

'Did she name any of the men who were troubling her?' asked MacKenzie.

She hesitated again. 'I must be careful what I say, sir. I work here. I wouldn't want to get in trouble.'

'You can tell me in confidence, Janet. I'm investigating on behalf of the duchess herself. It may be nothing, but it might help us understand what happened to Bethia.'

She hesitated again. 'I can't, sir. I must think of my position.'

'It's very important Janet. It's possible one of them might be involved in her death.'

She began to speak but stopped herself. 'I cannot, sir!'

MacKenzie stood up suddenly and spoke angrily: 'You must tell me, girl. I'm investigating a death, for God's sake!'

'I cannot tell you, sir! I cannot tell you!' She looked terrified.

MacKenzie shook his head. 'I'm sorry, Janet. It's a common tale. A bonnie woman with no family to protect her. Did she say if any of the encounters went beyond a pawing? Was she ever assaulted or debauched?'

Janet took a few moments to gather herself. 'She didn't say. I don't think so. I think I would have known. I think the main thing was she was worried what Arthur would do if he found out. She felt she would be blamed. I said he would not blame her, but she was adamant she would be blamed. Women were always blamed, she said, so she must keep quiet about it. She would avoid them. All would be well when she was a married woman in her own house. When she was Lady Nasmyth, they would not dare treat her like that.'

'Is it possible she told Arthur and he didn't respond in the way she hoped?'

She shrugged her shoulders.

'What do you make of these men, Janet?'

'What do you mean, sir?'

'How have you found them yourself?'

She hesitated again. 'I'm scared of them, sir. All the maids fear the men in the palace. I try to avoid them if I see one approaching. I've been fondled... many times. They say dirty, evil things.' She stopped and looked down at her hands again.

'Think upon it, my dear. You can tell me more at any time. It's what Bethia would have wanted.'

The door suddenly opened. Two maidservants entered. Relieved, Janet took the opportunity to take her leave. MacKenzie stood for a few minutes looking out the window, deep in thought, then left the dining room. At the bottom of the corridor was a door into the Back Close. Another cart had arrived with provisions and was being unloaded. He asked a workman for the warrander George Harlaw but was told he was out in the fields. A passageway between two outhouses led to the driveway at the front of the palace. He walked down the long drive towards the town. The fine weather of the day before had given way to drizzle. A young woman who was cornered by men. Was the only way out to take her life? As he passed through the gates into the town of Hamilton, he had the feeling the duchess would not be pleased with what he was about to uncover in the west.

CHAPTER 9

A Glasgow Merchant

SCOUGALL ROSE EARLY, ate his usual breakfast of porridge and dressed carefully for his first meeting of the day. He polished his shoes, powdered his wig and dusted down his jacket. A rider had left Hamilton Palace at first light and reached Glasgow before eight o'clock with a letter from MacKenzie describing everyone he had met in the palace and asking Scougall to learn anything he could about the whereabouts of Arthur Nasmyth after his own work was complete. MacKenzie suggested visiting Alexander Cruikshank, Arthur's regent, and his godfather, Sir James Turner, in the Gorbals. Scougall wrote a short letter to Chrissie, telling her all was well, and a brief reply to MacKenzie describing who he had met. He checked his watch, a recent purchase which had cost him almost £20, the most expensive single item he had ever bought – more than any book or golf club – with the exception of Chrissie's wedding ring. He was devoted to the timepiece as he had an ingrained desire for punctuality.

William Corse's office was on Market Street, only five minutes' walk from Gibson's Tavern. Scougall was nervous about the meeting. Corse was a well-known figure in Presbyterian circles. He had been imprisoned on the Bass Rock, an island jail in the Firth of Forth where many of the Covenanting faithful were incarcerated under the Stuart Kings. Brought up in a Presbyterian family, Scougall had been raised on tales of the brave exploits of such men. Corse was known as a tough, indefatigable servant of the Lord, with a similar reputation in the sphere of business.

Scougall waited for a couple of minutes on the street outside the office to calm himself, then knocked on the door timidly. A young clerk looked up from a writing desk where he was scribbling in a ledger. Scougall introduced himself. Without saying a word of welcome, the clerk knocked hesitantly on the door behind him, opened it slightly and said something to the person inside. He then ushered Scougall into the room where William Corse was sitting at his desk. A gaunt man dressed in black, he had a face lined by age with tired, dark eyes under bushy eyebrows. Long white whiskers descended almost to his chin on both sides of his face. Corse put down his quill and rose to his feet. Scougall saw he was tall, perhaps approaching six feet (almost MacKenzie's height) but stooped with age. He greeted Scougall warmly. 'Ah, Mr Scougall. All the way from the great city of Edinburgh. I welcome you, sir, to Glasgow. A thriving metropolis, is it not? The Lord shines upon us. The Lord shines upon the city of Glasgow.' Corse's strong, resonant voice stood out against the physical decline evident in his sinewy body.

They shook hands. Corse held Scougall's hand for an unnerving amount of time and gave him a meaningful look. Scougall finally realised Corse was telling him he was a fellow Mason. He nodded nervously, before sitting at the other side of the desk, taking off his hat and placing it on a side table. He glanced round the office as he took out his notebook and pencil from his leather bag. The room contained no trappings of wealth, although Corse was a rich merchant and planter. It was a simple chamber with a desk surrounded by bookcases full of ledgers, books and papers. A large Bible sat on one side of the desk. There were no windows to provide distractions, no paintings to look at, nor pieces of plate to admire.

'It's a warm day,' said Corse, returning to his seat. 'Would you care for a glass of ale, Mr Scougall? I do not serve wine. Wine is the drink of the priests in the Papist church. Wine befuddles the mind and stokes the sin of lust. On the other hand, guid Scots ale provides clarity of the mind.'

Scougall nodded in agreement. 'A cup of ale will suffice.' He crossed his legs and placed his notebook on his thigh. 'How is business, Mr Corse?' he asked politely.

Corse filled two cups from a pewter jug, handing one to Scougall. He drank deeply and stared intently across at him. 'It goes well, although it could always be better. That's the way of business. How does the House of Hair prosper?'

'Well, sir. It goes well too. I'm a relative newcomer to the business, but Mrs Hair has long experience, decades of experience, in the lending of money. I've learned much in the short time I've worked for her.'

Corse coughed to clear his throat. 'You'll know from my correspondence that I returned from Barbados last year, leaving my sons to look after our plantations. I seek capital to fund one final voyage to the Americas before I retire from the trade. Most of my wealth is tied up in holdings in ships and longer-term loans. I am reluctant to call them in just now because of the war with France. I seek a little ready cash to fund the venture.'

Scougall nodded. 'Could you tell me something about it? What cargo will you carry?'

'As you know, I have long experience of the Caribbean trade. I'll take a variety of goods to the coast of Africa, fill the ship there with negroes, sail to Barbados and sell them for a good price. I'll load the hold with sugar from our plantations, return to Glasgow and sell to the Sugar Houses. I guarantee the profit will be substantial.'

Scougall recorded everything in shorthand. He would write up his notes later in longhand for Mrs Hair.

Corse filled his cup again and drank it down. 'Did you know I was imprisoned on the Bass as a young man, Mr Scougall?'

Scougall nodded. 'It must have been... a daunting experience, sir.'

'There were times I thought I would never leave alive,' said Corse. 'The cold was the worst. The long days of boredom. The hunger. But the Lord intervened. I was sent as indentured labour to Barbados where I had to work in the sugar fields. The early years of toil were the hardest in my life. But it was preferrable to the frozen lassitude of the Bass. We did the work now done by slaves, working every day, resting only on the Sabbath. I laboured my way out of servitude. I saved a little money and bought a little land, then a little more and a little more. By hard work and clean living, I prospered. I wasted none of my money on drink or debauchery – many in the Caribbean succumb to such sins. I spent twenty-five years on the island as a planter. I was thrice sick of the Barbados distemper and thought I would die each time, but the Lord preserved me. When I left the island last year, I was worth £10,000 sterling. I was a member of the island gentry. But I always wanted to return to Scotland to end my days here. I wish to buy an estate and live as a laird, now the Stuarts are gone. One last voyage and I'll sell my assets and buy land. I'll live as a landed man for as long as the Lord allows me.' He smiled contentedly and finished his cup.

Scougall was eager to ask more about his experiences on the Bass, but thought it would be out of place, so continued to question him about business. 'How much capital are you looking for, Mr Corse?'

Corse rubbed his chin thoughtfully. 'I'm looking for a substantial amount, Mr Scougall. That's why I sought the House of Hair, not some lesser lender. I seek £500 sterling. I believe we can make a profit of three to four times that. It's a large sum I request, but the rewards are great. The return for Mrs Hair will be significant.'

Scougall noted down the figures. The loan was larger than expected. 'It sounds an attractive return. May I examine your books?'

'Of course, sir.' Corse rose and walked stiffly to the other side of the room. He removed a ledger from the bookcase and placed it in front of Scougall. 'As you can see, I have sufficient cash from the quarterly payments of my debtors to easily cover interest payments on the loan.' Scougall made a cursory examination of the book and noted down a few figures. Corse went to a press and returned with another volume. 'And here's a list of my creditors and debtors.' It was a substantial list on both sides of the balance sheet. Scougall did not recognise most of the names, but a couple caught his attention – a sum of 10,000 merks borrowed by the Duke of Hamilton and £10,000 sterling by the Earl of Arran. Here was a link between Corse and the House of Hamilton. Scougall quickly added up the amounts in his head and noted that the debts owed to Corse were significantly larger than those owed by him. Corse seemed to be in sound financial health, although short of ready cash.

'Thank you, sir,' said Scougall. 'As Mrs Hair mentioned in her correspondence, this is an exploratory meeting. I'll need to obtain copies of these documents so she can examine them before we make a final decision.'

Corse returned to his chair and sat watching Scougall carefully. 'You'll know my reputation is a good one, sir. Reputation is everything in business. I'm a sound trader. I'm a burgess of Glasgow. I'm a man devoted to the Lord. A man on whom the Lord has shone. A man whom the Lord has chosen to be a shining light unto others. And a man who is closely connected by association... to you, Mr Scougall.'

Scougall realised he was referring to their shared membership of the Masonic craft. Corse would no doubt expect he would look more favourably on the request for a loan. Scougall reflected for a moment. He did not want to say anything that might prejudice Mrs Hair's decision. He decided to change the subject. 'The trade in slaves, Mr Corse? Is it a sound one?'

Corse smiled. 'There's strong demand for slaves in the Caribbean and America, indeed, huge demand. We'll sell them at an extraordinarily good price.' Scougall recalled the conversation on the subject with MacKenzie in the coach.

'Is it a... moral trade, sir? Is it a Godly one?' Scougall blurted out without thinking. He immediately regretted being so forward and spluttered: 'I mean... taking people... from their homes against their will… removing them from their families,' he added timidly, not wanting to offend Corse. He knew the merchant owned hundreds of slaves in Barbados.

Corse shook his head, then laughed. 'They are little better than beasts. They are not Christian folk like us. They are not civilised folk. I've lived among them for years. I know how they live. They are pagans who worship idols. The Lord created them to increase our wealth. We provide them with employment and discipline to improve themselves. They work well in the fields if directed with a firm hand. If the Lord did not sanction it, he would not allow us to reap such benefits from their labour.'

Scougall was now troubled by the trade, but he nodded to Corse. It was like a stone in his shoe. He had not given the matter any consideration before. He had accepted slavery as a natural part of the trading world, now it was niggling at his conscience.

Corse continued: 'I believe the Lord will shine upon us in this trade. He will protect the vessel from harm as He protected me during those years on the Bass. Who would have said I would've prospered if the Lord had not favoured me? You can tell Mrs Hair I have God's assurance of a fair wind for our ship. I guarantee it will deliver a healthy profit.'

Scougall nodded seriously, although he knew she would not look favourably on such assurances. Her first maxim in the business of moneylending was to trust no one. 'Of course, sir. I think I have all the information I need for now,' he replied. 'I'll consult with her when I return to Edinburgh. You seek a large amount of money, so we'll need to consider it carefully. Such a loan would make up a significant proportion of our capital. We'll have a decision as soon as we can.'

Corse looked offended. 'I thought as a fellow Mason, sir. You'll know these words, Mr Scougall.' He dropped his voice to a hoarse whisper, leant forward and stared at him intently: 'I say to you… the word "Jachin"… and the word "Boaz"… these words bind us together as brothers, Mr Scougall… I believe the decision will go my way.'

Scougall nodded nervously. He decided to try to change the subject again: 'I've heard much about Bass John. My family in Musselburgh are strong supporters of Presbytery. I would enjoy hearing your memories of incarceration with him.'

Corse smiled proudly. 'We must meet again in a more relaxed setting. It will do our business some good. I'll tell you something of my sufferings. I might introduce you to Bass John himself. He follows the trade of merchant in this city in these glorious days since the Revolution re-established Presbytery. He's a man as hard as flint in his devotion to the Lord. I'm sorry, I have another meeting now, but we can convene later.'

'It's a wonder Presbytery is returned to us... it's a miracle,' said Scougall.

Corse's face hardened. 'We have triumphed, but we must always remain vigilant. The Revolution terminated the rule of Pope-loving James Stuart. However, agents of Antichrist are still active in this land, even in this Covenanted town of Glasgow. Only last night we smote Satan on the High Street where hideous agents of the Papacy, called Quakers, worship openly. These Quakers plot with Jacobites and they favour that servant of the Whore of Babylon, James Stuart. But we taught them a painful lesson. We'll run them all out of town! They pollute Glasgow with their blasphemy. They are like rats feeding upon the cargo of a ship.'

'I saw it myself when I went for a walk,' said Scougall. 'What will happen to them?'

'They will not be punished adequately, unfortunately. A few days in the Tolbooth. A few hours in the stocks. These penalties are mild compared to the ones suffered by our people. We were cut down in the fields by the awful agents of the Stuart despots. We must cleanse the streets of this city if we are to continue to prosper. We must cleanse the streets of Glasgow. We must cleanse the places around this city in which they congregate. We must preserve the Revolution which returned our beloved church to the path of righteousness. We will countenance no English imposters defiling our Covenanted land. Glasgow is a Covenanted city, not one where any sect may worship. We'll not rest until the polluters are driven out.' Corse's fist came down on the desk with a thump.

Scougall noticed a glint of madness in his eyes. Like Bass John, there was stone in him. Scougall wondered if he should mention this impression to Mrs Hair. How was he to balance this with their shared Masonry. 'I know little about them, Mr Corse,' he said. 'I've had little to do with them in Edinburgh.'

'Then you are a lucky man, Mr Scougall. There are too many in Scotland. They are numerous in the parishes of Hamilton and Glassford. They multiply by fornicating with local women. The great folk show them protection. One of them even tends the gardens of the Duchess of Hamilton! Our nobles should not provide sanctuary for them. But we have seen nobles siding with Antichrist before. We will hound them out. It will be a hard battle, but we make progress.' He smiled benignly. Scougall nodded. He realised he was not brave enough to disagree with him.

'We'll give you a decision about the loan as soon as we can,' said Scougall. 'I don't see any major impediments. I must make a few calculations to reassure Mrs Hair.'

As Scougall went to take his hat, he remembered the reason for his journey to Glasgow and cursed himself for being so distracted. He had learned nothing about the case. 'Do you know anything about the death of Bethia Porterfield?' he asked casually as he placed his hat on his head.

'Why do you ask?'

'I overheard someone talking about it in the tavern last night. It's an awful tragedy for a young girl to die in that way.'

Corse nodded seriously. 'The ways of the Lord are mysterious. She drowned herself in the Clyde. She had lain with a man. She had fornicated outside wedlock and carried his bastard. She could not face the shame of it. She chose everlasting damnation by taking her life.'

'Who was the man she lay with?' Scougall asked, pretending not to know anything about the case.

'A student called Arthur Nasmyth who was betrothed to her. He could not contain his lust. A young fool, no doubt.'

'I heard he's disappeared. Do you know where he's gone?'

'I don't know him. I only know he hails from near Hamilton. I still own a little property in that town. I travel there now and again with my wife.'

Scougall was disappointed to discover so little. On the way out, he was shocked to see a familiar figure sitting opposite the young clerk. It was Dr Lawtie who worked in the Edinburgh morgue. Lawtie looked up at Scougall through thick spectacles and rose from his seat, just as surprised. 'My God, is it not Davie Scougall himself!'

'What are you doing here, Lawtie?' Scougall did not like the doctor, who he always found sneering and sarcastic.

'I aim to invest some of the hard-earned money I've accumulated over twenty years in the practice of medicine,' said Lawtie. 'Corse and other merchants are looking for investors in voyages to America and the Caribbean. The profits will be very great. Did you not know Glasgow is my hometown?'

Scougall shook his head.

'What brings you to the west, Mr Scougall?'

'Business, also, Lawtie. The business of Mrs Hair.'

'I keep hearing her name mentioned everywhere I go. She has engrossed the business of moneylending in the east of the country and now seeks to extend her influence in the west. Will she never rest?'

Scougall nodded hesitantly. 'She seeks a good return on her money, as any man does.'

'I could not work under a woman,' Lawtie added scornfully. 'It goes against the grain. I couldn't take orders from a woman.' Before Scougall could think of a riposte, Lawtie continued: 'Where are you staying in Glasgow?'

'Gibson's Tavern on the High Street.'

'Likewise, Mr Scougall. Then I know where to find you. Perhaps we might share a bottle in the snug tonight. About eight o'clock, unless you have other plans?'

The prospect of spending the evening with Lawtie was not appealing, but Scougall could not think of a reasonable excuse on the spur of the moment. He cursed himself for being a feckless fool on the way out. He had learned, however, one further thing from their meeting. Lawtie was also a Mason. There seemed to be no shortage of them in Glasgow.

CHAPTER 10

A Meeting at the Mercat Cross

THE GATES OPENED onto a short stretch of road which connected the palace to the town of Hamilton. MacKenzie wandered down the High Street finding his bearings. Hamilton was a typical Scottish burgh. There was a tolbooth acting as prison and council chamber, a kirk where the parish gathered to worship on the Sabbath, as well as shops and houses and taverns on both sides of the street. A stone cross indicated where a weekly market met. MacKenzie noticed a young man standing alone beside it. He was tall and thin, with his dark hair pulled back tightly in a ponytail. A leather bag lay on the ground beside him.

'Are you a visitor to Hamilton, sir?' the man asked in a friendly manner as MacKenzie approached him. 'May I help you with something?'

'I'm John MacKenzie, advocate in Edinburgh.'

'Robert Corse,' the man said. MacKenzie remembered the duchess had mentioned him as a friend of Arthur Nasmyth. Corse gave his hand to MacKenzie. 'What brings you to the west, Mr MacKenzie?' he asked pleasantly.

'A legal matter for the duchess. I hope it will be dealt with quickly. She's invited me to spend a few days as her guest once the work's done. As a keen student of horticulture, I'm excited by the prospect. There's much to learn from the palace gardens. I hope to take some seeds and cuttings back for my own garden. As many as fit in the coach. The fruit trees are famous throughout the kingdom and beyond. Are you a local man, Mr Corse?'

Corse nodded. 'Yes, I am, sir. I'm Glasgow born but moved to Hamilton when I was a child. I regard it as my hometown. I attended the burgh school across the road there. I now study for the ministry in Glasgow. I'm spending a few days in my family home.'

'Are you related to the ministers John Corse and Adam Corse, or the merchants Charles Corse and Hugh Corse?' MacKenzie referred to well-known Presbyterian firebrands.

A smile spread across Corse's face. 'Many share my surname in the west. Many are ministers; it's the family profession. I'm sure there are a few MacKenzies in the Highlands.'

MacKenzie chuckled. 'And many are lawyers in Edinburgh; it's our family profession. Only the Campbells have more advocates in the Faculty.'

'There are also many merchants in Glasgow with our name,' continued Corse. 'William Corse, well known in such circles, is my uncle. My father, William's brother, and my mother are dead.'

'I'm sorry, Mr Corse. Do you share your kinsman's enthusiasm for Presbytery?' asked MacKenzie seriously.

'His enthusiasm? I don't understand you.'

'I believe many of your name have suffered for the Presbyterian cause. William Corse was held on the Bass Rock. He's suffered much for his opposition to the Stuarts.'

Corse nodded. 'I share my uncle's devotion to the Lord. I'm not as enthusiastic as he, or other members of my family, in the sphere of politics. I'm more of a... moderate. Perhaps I enjoy too much the pleasant side of life: a little wine when the occasion allows, a song in the tavern, a poem or two, shared with a friend, a game of golf, a little skating, curling in the winter when the ice is good. These things do us little wrong, although some in my family frown on them as frivolities. My surname encourages people to think I follow a narrow, puritanical view. When I become a minister, I hope I can guide my parishioners through this vale of troubles and do a little good in the world. I've no appetite for the heat of politics or the anger and bitterness accompanying it. I pray such passion diminishes in this land as the years pass.'

MacKenzie smiled warmly. 'I'm glad to hear it, sir. We have a saying in Gaelic, Mr Corse. Wait until you hear the whole story of a man's life before you pass judgement on him. I'm sorry, you've found me guilty of prejudice, which I pride myself avoiding. Your surname evoked a strong reaction in the heart of an old Episcopalian. I took you to be one of the fanatics. Please forgive me.'

'Of course, sir. I take no offence.' Corse returned the smile.

MacKenzie turned to take in the High Street. 'Hamilton is a bonnie town. I cannot believe a young woman drowned herself here a few weeks ago,' he added.

Corse looked at MacKenzie with a pained expression. 'She was known to you, sir?' he asked.

MacKenzie shook his head. 'No. The duchess mentioned her death at dinner last night. A terrible affair. Her grace is deeply affected by it. She tells me the girl was brought up in the palace after her parents died. She's the granddaughter of her lady-in-waiting who came north with her during the civil wars. It has pricked my interest. According to her grace, there's uncertainty about the exact manner of her death, although the common view is she took her own life. Did you know her, Mr Corse?'

Corse looked almost tearful, his ebullience gone. 'Yes, I knew her, sir. I knew her almost as a sister. My dear friend Arthur was to be her husband. I've known them both since we were children here in Hamilton. The manner of her death is a terrible... stain on the parish.' Corse shook his head despondently.

'That she should kill herself and her unborn child?' MacKenzie asked. He did not want to seem too interested, but at the same time sought to learn as much as he could.

Corse looked flustered. 'Self-murder is a grave sin in the eyes of the Lord. God should decide the moment and manner of death, not man or woman, however desperate they are. They should not risk their eternal souls.'

'You believe it was self-murder?'

'I don't know, sir.' Corse shook his head.

'Was the child Arthur's?' asked MacKenzie sympathetically, judging Corse was upset.

Corse winced again. 'I don't know. Arthur never mentioned it to me, nor did Bethia,' he said vacantly. 'I only heard she was pregnant after her body was found. The thought of her death and my friend's disappearance affects me deeply. I'm sorry, sir.'

'I'm sorry too, Mr Corse. I didn't mean to upset you. Do you know what's happened to Arthur?' asked MacKenzie, patting Corse affectionately on the upper arm.

Corse shook his head. 'I wish I knew where he's gone. He fled the day her body was found. He's not been seen since. I find it difficult to talk about it, knowing them both so well.' Corse's head dropped.

'You have no inkling where he's gone?' asked MacKenzie.

'I've not seen him since that morning. He was in a terrible state. He'd been to see her body in the palace. I met him over there at the palace gates. I was on my way to see her myself. I believe he returned home to

Nasmyth House for a couple of hours, then rode for Glasgow. I heard he spent a few days in the city with a friend, then disappeared.'

'Who did he stay with in Glasgow?'

'Archie Weir, a friend from college.'

MacKenzie shook his head and sighed, before continuing to question him sympathetically. 'Who lives with him at Nasmyth House?'

'Only his mother. It's a huge worry for her,' replied Corse.

'Is the house nearby?' asked MacKenzie.

'A couple of miles west of Hamilton. It's only half an hour's walk.'

'I've been told he's a gifted scholar. He doesn't intend to follow you into the ministry?'

Corse shook his head. 'He has no desire to be a minister. It's been suggested by those who believe a college education only has value if it prepares a man for the kirk. I would say he's confused about his future. Troubled, even. Happy one moment, the next afflicted by melancholy. There are many who suffer similarly during these days of uncertainty. We can easily lose sight of the Lord, but we must trust in Him. If we trust in the Lord, all will be well.' Corse turned his head and looked down the street apprehensively, as if he wanted to escape the conversation.

'Did he confide in you?' asked MacKenzie.

Corse nodded. 'We are close. He's like a brother to me. We often talked late into the night about religion and metaphysics when we shared chambers in Glasgow. He's interested in the new paths of thought, such as Deism, which are now openly discussed. I've tried to direct him away from such heresies. I believe they undermine the authority of the Bible and Holy Trinity, and breed uncertainty in the heart. I argued we should trust in the benevolence of God. All that God has created on this earth is good and natural. During his worst moments he said he believed in nothing.' Corse hesitated for a moment. 'I've failed him, sir. I should have convinced him to stay in Hamilton that morning. I should have remained with him when he needed me.'

'I'm sure you have not, Mr Corse.'

'I thought he would return to Hamilton in a few days. But he's sent no message, not even to his beloved mother. We don't know if he's alive or dead.' Corse looked down the street again anxiously, before adding: 'Of course, he may have taken ship abroad. He often talked of joining a colonial scheme or regiment.'

'You shared apartments in Glasgow?' asked MacKenzie.

'We were at college for four years together. Since we were fourteen years old. He's a dear friend... you can see this is difficult for me, Mr MacKenzie.'

'I apologise, sir,' replied MacKenzie. 'I tend to ask too many questions. It's the old lawyer in me. When I hear about a death around which there is uncertainty, my mind starts spinning. I have an overpowering desire to learn the truth. I know the duchess will not rest until she knows exactly what happened. She doubts Bethia killed herself or was pregnant.'

Corse looked away.

'As his friend, where do you think he's gone?' asked MacKenzie.

'He had a desire to be a soldier like his father. He might have gone to London or the Continent. He could be anywhere. I've searched everywhere in Glasgow.'

MacKenzie smiled sympathetically. 'I hope there's word of him soon, Mr Corse.' He turned to go, then stopped and added: 'I can see you're keen to be off, sir. But before you go, on a different matter, Mr Wood, the gardener at the palace, has told me of a recent attack on the Quaker burial ground at Shawtonhill.'

Corse shook his head and grimaced. 'You must think this a barbarous back land. A fever pitch of hatred has been whipped up against the Quakers. They are accused of being friends of Papists and supporters of the old king, and of being guilty of transgressions of the vilest kind, such as blasphemy and heresy. I've tried to appease the passion of the enthusiasts, arguing the Quakers should be left alone to worship as they want. They are just misguided Christians who we should try to understand rather than abuse. But the desire to persecute runs deep within the hearts of some men and women in this land.'

MacKenzie continued: 'I intend to visit the burial ground myself later today. It has caused Mr Wood and his people great anguish. I promised him I would investigate the matter. The attack was clearly a violent riot. Compensation should be provided to repair the site and allow reburial of all the disturbed remains. The case should go before the sheriff of Lanarkshire. I'll provide Hugh representation in the sheriff court if need be. I aim to do a little good in the west.'

Corse smiled nervously. 'I'm glad of it, sir. Mr Wood and his people should be compensated for their losses. I pray every day the temperature of persecution will diminish. Perhaps when things are settled in Ireland, we may have some peace. Ah, here it is at last. The coach for Glasgow. I head for the city today. A little business to attend to. I hope I find Arthur or at least gain some news of him. Drop in to see me when it suits you, sir. I'll be back in Hamilton tomorrow afternoon. I live in the house on the corner of Pringle's Wynd. We might share a bottle of wine and talk of happier things, such as gardens and poetry, and the goodness and variety of life. I would enjoy hearing about the Highlands. I've never been north of Falkirk in my life.'

MacKenzie nodded enthusiastically. 'I would be delighted, Mr Corse. Perhaps one evening in the next few days. Oh, just one other thing. I've been told strangers have been seen at illicit gatherings at night. Do you know anything of such things?'

Corse shook his head as the coach drew up beside them. 'I would hardly know as a future minister. There are always strangers passing through the parish – drovers, pedlars and chapmen. As for illicit gatherings, we have the usual drinking dens, taverns, inns and howffs. I believe a little drunkenness is a good way for people to unwind.'

The coachman jumped down and opened the door for Corse. MacKenzie smiled and shook Corse's hand. 'I'm glad to see the kirk is training some enlightened ministers, Mr Corse,' he said. 'It bodes well for a more moderate age in the future.' He noticed that Corse's hand was shaking.

CHAPTER 11

The College of Glasgow

THE COLLEGE OF Glasgow was an impressive, three-storey building with a commanding tower and turrets only a couple of minutes' walk up the High Street, just past Blackfriars Church. Glasgow's university was a century older than Edinburgh's; scholarly learning had a long history in the city. The street outside was quiet, with no sign of boisterous students due to the summer recess. Scougall walked through the entrance into a courtyard and then through an archway into another courtyard where he found a college servitor who directed him to Cruikshank's room on the second floor. The scholar's chamber was a tiny, book-filled room with one small window looking down on the college gardens to the east. Cruikshank sat at his desk reading. He looked only a little older than a student himself, much younger than Scougall, with a mop of blonde hair – he wore no wig.

He indicated Scougall was to sit with a friendly gesture. 'How can I help you, sir?' he said, closing his book, removing his spectacles and raising his head to observe him.

'I'm Davie Scougall, a writer from Edinburgh. I'm helping my colleague, John MacKenzie, advocate, look for one of your students. We need to discuss a... legal matter with him.'

Cruikshank smiled and sat back, seemingly pleased to have a break from his reading. 'Who are you looking for, Mr Scougall?'

'Arthur Nasmyth,' said Scougall, and waited for a response as MacKenzie would have done.

'I've not seen him since the end of term,' replied Cruikshank, raising his eyebrows, 'when he graduated Master of Arts. Some hoped he might return to take a degree in divinity, like his friend Robert Corse. He certainly has the ability if he so desires. But he decided against it. The law in the United Provinces was also talked about, which should suit him well. However, I've heard he hopes to follow in his father's footsteps and become a soldier. Many are surprised by this choice.'

Scougall took out his notebook. 'Why was that, Mr Cruikshank?'

'He hardly fits the bill of a military man,' replied Cruikshank, 'if you know what I mean – he doesn't have the physique of a fighter.'

'How would you describe him?' asked Scougall.

'He's a good man,' said Cruikshank. 'A quiet, studious young man. He was never involved in any of the bother we often have from students – drunkenness, whoring, fighting, rioting, the usual list of misdemeanours of fourteen-year-old men given a little freedom.' Cruikshank shook his head. 'It's terrible what happened to his betrothed. A lovely girl.'

Scougall recorded everything Cruikshank said in shorthand. He was glad the regent needed little prompting. He was just the kind of person he liked to interview. When an investigation ran smoothly, his enthusiasm for it returned. He enjoyed learning about the lives of others. He would not describe himself as nosy, but interested in people. He would prove himself a skilled investigator acting on his own initiative. MacKenzie's ridicule of the Masons still rankled him. The thought of riding to Hamilton with Nasmyth, impressing the duchess and astounding MacKenzie, encouraged him. 'Did he have many friends in college?' he asked.

'A few close ones, I would say. He shared chambers with Robert, a friend since boyhood in Hamilton. I often saw him walking over the bridge to visit his father's friend Sir James Turner in the Gorbals. His other close friend is Archie Weir, you might speak to him.'

'Where can I find him?' asked Scougall.

'He's the son of Abraham Weir, a merchant who owns the Northern Sugar Works, just north of town at the end of Queen Street. You'll find it easily enough. Archie has started working there for his father.'

Scougall looked round the book-crammed room. A life devoted to scholarship would be a lonely one; he recalled his existence as a solitary notary writing instruments of sasine in a tiny office, day after day. 'Can you shed any light on his disappearance?' he asked.

Cruikshank sat back and observed Scougall carefully. 'I presume you've heard what happened to Bethia?'

Scougall nodded.

'It would be a terrible shock to a man like Arthur. Maybe grief has driven him away. He can't face the world after what's happened or, perhaps, he blames himself in some way. He's maybe overcome by guilt or...' he stopped himself for a moment.

'Or?' repeated Scougall.

'It's only hearsay, Mr Scougall. I don't like to gossip, as a rule. I like to base what I say on facts, like the ones in reliable texts, not idle rumour heard in the tavern. I'm a scholar, after all. I apply myself to the rigorous study of sources.'

Scougall waited, sensing that Cruikshank would tell him anyway. After a few moments, he continued in a lower voice: 'I'll tell you, then. It's something I heard in a tavern, where I go sometimes to relax after a hard day. It is only drunken banter. I heard it said...' again, he stopped himself but soon continued: 'I've heard it said... the child was not Arthur's.'

'Who was the father?' asked Scougall, surprised by the revelation.

'It's just idle gossip. All kinds of dross is dreamed up in the drinking holes of this city. I doubt there's any truth in it whatsoever.'

Scougall waited. He knew Cruikshank would not be able to help himself. Cruikshank leant forwards across the desk and his voice dropped to a whisper. 'I've heard it said the bairn was... the father of the bairn was... Arran himself,' he said conspiratorially. 'Of course, it's just idle chat. But sometimes there's truth behind such rumour.'

'Arran's bairn,' said Scougall under his breath, looking perturbed. It was the second time that day he had come across the earl's name. Its mention in connection with Bethia did not bode well, in his opinion. He knew about Arran's reputation as a libertine.

'The Earl of Arran,' whispered Cruikshank. 'The duchess's eldest son. The heir to the dukedom of Hamilton. It's said he had an eye for her as she grew into a bonnie creature in the house of his mother. He tricked her into his bed just after his wife died, using grief as a lure. I've heard many stories about him. I've heard him called a rake and blasphemer, Jacobite and devil worshipper, and that's just the good ones! If you believed them all, he would have swived every lass between Cornwall and Hamilton, and be a crony of Satan himself! It's said he spends most of his days in London fathering bastards. I don't know how the duchess puts up with him. Some mothers cannot see anything wrong in the wayward behaviour of their favourite child. And he's the man who will inherit the Hamilton patrimony. He'll no doubt squander it all!'

Scougall did not like to rely on drunken banter. He knew there was always gossip about the identity of noble bastards. However, he would pass on what Cruikshank had said to MacKenzie. There was sometimes no smoke without fire.

'Arthur cannot face the humiliation. He's fled to get his head straight,' continued Cruikshank. 'Where he's off to, I've no idea. It could be to join the army or seek his fortune in the Caribbean – there are strong links between this town and those islands. The truth, Mr Scougall, is that I've not seen him for months. He could be anywhere by now.'

'Is there anything else you can tell me about him?'

Cruikshank thought for a moment. 'He has a particular aptitude for the Latin tongue and a particular liking for the poetry of Horace, which I share. He composed some very adept translations of the odes. I never saw him doing anyone any harm. He was never any trouble in any of my classes, unlike his friends. Archie is a rogue at times. He was a bit of a joker in class. He's a man who likes a drink and sometimes gets into trouble. Corse is full of self-importance. He was always keen to be the first to answer in class. He is perfect material for the ministry. But I like him.'

'Just one more thing,' said Scougall 'I witnessed an affray last night. Quakers were abused by a crowd, dragged from a house where they worshipped and violently assaulted. I've heard their burial ground near Hamilton has been destroyed.' He recalled the vivid description in MacKenzie's letter.

Cruikshank shook his head. 'Aye, I've heard it too. I count myself a Presbyterian. I accept the Revolution and the return of Presbytery to this land. It does the nation good; puts it at ease with itself. Bishops are despised in Scotland, so why should we have them rule our church?'

'I share your views, sir,' added Scougall.

'I'm troubled, however, by the persecution of the Quakers,' continued Cruikshank. 'Someone is trying to stir things up.'

'What do you mean?' asked Scougall.

'Why are they persecuted when the zealots have all they want. They have achieved a church devoid of bishops. Presbytery is restored. The Presbyterian faction controls the government. They have attained their glorious revolution, so why are they continuing to kick up a stink?'

'I don't understand what you mean, Mr Cruikshank,' replied Scougall.

'Is talk of blasphemy and witchcraft and atheists and Quakers and Papists an attempt to cause a stir? Is it a way of whipping up the people, especially the gullible? I don't know who's behind it, the righteous or the unrighteous. But mark my words, someone is.'

'The righteous or the unrighteous?' repeated Scougall.

'This country is bitterly divided. The war in Ireland is still raging. The Highlands are a den of unruly clans. Politics is as dirty as a shit-filled midden, excuse my language. A little trouble in the west may benefit the government. They can step in to crush it. It may also benefit the Jacobites.'

'I'm confused, Mr Cruikshank,' said Scougall.

'If the Jacobites provoke instability in Presbyterian areas, it will suck in government troops to the west, improving the chances of a rising elsewhere. It's only a theory as an armchair politician. I prefer books and have no time for it all. I'm just pleased we now look to England and not Rome. God bless King Billy!'

Scougall had not considered the possibility of such manipulation. 'Jacobites could be encouraging the fanatics to persecute the Quakers?'

'It's entirely possible,' said Cruikshank. 'But I've not a jot of proof. Who knows when the French king will support another attempt to restore James? Ireland is a bog of troubles. A Jacobite army remains there, despite recent victories on the field by William. What will happen to those soldiers? Could some of them find their way to Scotland?'

Scougall shuddered at the thought of another civil war, especially as he was soon to become a father. He hoped for a swift conclusion to the campaign in Ireland and complete victory for King William. He thanked Cruikshank, told him he was travelling to Hamilton in case he thought of anything else pertinent to Arthur's disappearance or heard anything from him, and left deep in thought.

CHAPTER 12

Two Houses in Hamilton

MACKENZIE WATCHED THE coach trundle down the High Street and make its way towards the Glasgow Road. It was only a couple of minutes' walk to Porterfield House at the north edge of town, a small, two-storey dwelling in good repair standing in a little garden which was showing signs of becoming overgrown. He supposed it had not been tended over the summer due to the death of the mistress of the house. He opened the front door and entered a small, clean hall.

He stood for a few moments listening to the silence and recalling his conversation with Janet Dobbie earlier in the morning. This had been a happy household until a few months ago. He took a few deep breaths – there was a hint of perfume in the air, no doubt Bethia's. He entered the living chamber on the right, a wooden-panelled room with a few chairs and a dresser displaying porcelain and pewter. A couple of paintings on the far wall caught his attention. One depicted a man and woman, probably Bethia's parents before they died of plague. They appeared a solemn couple dressed in black. The other was of a young woman, surely Bethia herself. It was very different in style. The artist had skilfully brought her to life. She had a pretty face, large brown eyes, a full mouth and long, dark hair. Dressed in a light pink silk dress, she held a posy of flowers in her lap, probably picked from the garden in which she was painted. MacKenzie stood in front of the painting, trying to capture every detail in his memory.

At the back of the house, accessed from a door in the living chamber, was the kitchen and larder. They had been cleared, leaving only a slight suggestion of the smell of food. MacKenzie climbed the narrow turnpike staircase at the back of the house to a small landing on the first floor. Two rooms led off it. One was a small chamber, practically empty, where Janet Dobbie slept. Across the hall was the other, larger bedroom belonging to

Bethia. MacKenzie entered the room and observed it carefully. Everything looked in order, as if tidied away; nothing was out of place, except for the brown flowers in a vase on the windowsill and the reek of decay.

He stood thinking about a life lost at such a young age. Bethia was not much younger than his own wife had been when she died in childbirth. He went to the window and looked down on the garden behind the house. She must have often enjoyed the pleasant view and imagined her future as mistress of Nasmyth House. He pulled up the sash window and let in fresh air. He went to the press at the other side of the room. It had been emptied and all the drawers in her cabinet cleared. Some books were left in the small bookcase beside the bed. MacKenzie picked them up individually – a few French novels, an atlas and a Bible. He went through each methodically, flicking through the pages. A book collection could tell you something about its owner. He opened one of the novels and a folded sheet of paper fell onto the floor. He took it to the window to read in the daylight. He raised his eyebrows as he realised it was a letter to her from Arthur. Here was something no one else in Hamilton or the palace had seen before. It might provide some insight into Arthur's state of mind and their relationship before she died. He stood in the silence of the room and read the letter written only a few weeks before her death.

Glasgow,
15 May 1691

My dearest Beth,
I am sorry it has taken me so long to write since your last letter reached me, but I have been forced to attend to my studies. At last, I have some time to sit down before the fire and write back to you. I miss you as you say you miss me and, despite what you say, there is nothing I desire more than to be your husband.

I am not neglecting you deliberately. Once I have completed my degree, we will have plenty of time for our long walks and old haunts. We can discuss our plans for the future. I am still uncertain about which path to follow. However, you are wrong to assert I am already set on becoming a soldier. I have not decided yet.

Sir James believes I would make a useful military man. I know you desire me to remain in Scotland and live as a laird. I feel I must have a profession and believe soldiering would suit me well.

I would of course return home as often as possible. We could still make a good life together as man and wife, like my mother and father.

I was shocked to hear of the treatment of old Mr Wood and the Quakers. There is resentment against them in Glasgow and they are mightily abused by some of the hotheads.

I hear Arran will soon return to the palace. Let us hope he has not spent too much money or become involved in any other plots which will upset the duchess!

Robert is very well and sends his love, as does Archie. Robert is determined to follow a career in the ministry although I try to persuade him against it. He says he can think of nothing else as he has no appetite to travel beyond the shire. My other friends are well and Mr Cruikshank sends his regards. They try to encourage me out for a night in the tavern, but I will wait until my work is complete and then, perhaps, I will allow myself a bottle or two.

I was disturbed to hear the sad history you described of the black servant whom the duke has sent to the palace. He has clearly suffered greatly. I hope to make his acquaintance and hear about his life when I return.

We will soon be together again, my love. Do not worry. All will be well and settled when we are husband and wife.

Your loving friend,
Arthur Nasmyth

MacKenzie noted the uncertainties in the letter, the hints of Bethia's fears and Arthur's reassurances. Arthur clearly planned to take his own direction in life against her wishes. This could well be the source of the discontent between them. Did she fear it might involve breaking off the marriage? However, there was no suggestion of a pregnancy. Had she kept it from him or was it just a fabrication? There was something about the letter that puzzled him. It did not read like one written by a passionate lover. There was a certain coolness about it. Had Arthur's love for her waned?

MacKenzie read it back through again and examined the signature closely. There was a strange flourish under the 'y' in his surname. He put the letter in his pocket. He would study it again later. He left her room and wandered round the rest of the house to fix it in his mind. He returned to the living chamber to look at the paintings again. He stood before her portrait and noticed a few more details: the small dog at her feet and the ruined fortress on the wooded hill in the distance, surely Cadzow Castle above the River Avon. He saw she inherited her beauty from her mother. He thought of his own daughter, Elizabeth, just a bit older than Bethia, and wondered what life had in store for her as a young widow. Would she find love again and a marriage of contentment or did she face a long, lonely life like him? He opened the back door into the garden. It was a bright, pleasant place in the morning sunshine. The clouds of earlier had cleared. There was a wooden bench at the bottom under some apple trees. Bethia and Janet probably sat and chatted there. The apples had not been picked and had begun to fall onto the ground where they lay rotting in the long, wet grass. The garden had been well tended in the past by a keen gardener, but it had gone to seed. Just, perhaps, like the love between Bethia and Arthur.

MacKenzie, following the directions of Robert Corse, made his way along the narrow road to the west through gently rolling countryside. He passed through a couple of small hamlets and walked over a little bridge that spanned a burn. It was now another warm, cloudless autumn day. He took off his blue velvet jacket, slinging it over his shoulder and enjoying the warmth of the sun on his face, his mind drifting from the case for a few minutes as he relaxed and enjoyed the walk. It was good to be away from Edinburgh, away from the incessant bustle and stink of the streets. He missed the open spaces of the countryside and the hills of the Highlands. He remembered the excitement of walking to the higher pastures, or shielings, for the summer grazing as a boy. It was a season of pleasure, marking the end of winter, anticipating a time of plenty: weeks of feasting and stories and games, lasting all summer. He had a sudden desire to see his foster mother and father again, but they were long dead. It was strange to think he had both a mother and father, and a foster mother and father. His real father was a remote figure in his memory, dead so long ago, as was his mother, who had loved him with a sense of reserve. It was his foster parents who had loved him tenderly, especially his foster mother. He was the apple of her eye; she was happy in his very existence, overjoyed by any moment she spent with him. He spoke the words aloud in Gaelic, just as Geordie was now the apple of his eye. When he was fostered, she was much older than his own mother, nearer the age of a grandparent, and her own children were grown up. He had spent seven years in her house. It was a strange custom, fading now in the Highlands and belonging, like O'Flaherty's clarsach, to the past. He reflected that he himself belonged to two worlds, the old and new co-existing within him. Raised in the world of the past, he had moved far from it – to Edinburgh and the law, to black suits and powdered periwigs, rather than swords and targes. He had never contemplated fostering Elizabeth; sending her away for seven years to live with another family was unthinkable after his wife's death. The thought of fostering Geordie was out of the question. What had changed so much since he was fostered? The custom was not necessarily a bad one, but it now seemed irrelevant. He would, however, ensure Geordie knew something of the old world; there were good things about it, as well as bad. Elizabeth had rejected her Highland heritage. She had no liking for Gaelic and had made no effort to learn any. He had floundered when trying to raise her on his own, neglecting his own language in the tunnel of grief he passed through after his wife's death. He would make sure his grandson spoke the tongue.

Nasmyth House was a substantial dwelling beside a ford over a burn, little more than a trickle in the autumn sunshine. The house's size indicated Arthur's wealthy background. An impressive building, similar in style to the Hawthorns, it was a three-storey structure with crow step gables, red roof pantiles and sash windows, surrounded by fine gardens. It exuded comfort and stability. Arthur clearly came from a family of means. He would be laird of Nasmyth himself when he was twenty-one.

A woman in a long, sky-blue frock was tending her roses in the garden. She turned as the gate screeched open. MacKenzie greeted her, doffing his hat. She had a spattering of freckles on red cheeks and bright blue eyes which matched her dress, but a strained, taught look on her face.

'A fine day, madam.'

She looked across at him nervously.

'Don't worry,' he continued. 'I'm sorry to alarm you. I'm John MacKenzie, a guest at the palace. I'm a lawyer from Edinburgh here on business.'

There was a trace of a smile on her face which quickly disappeared. 'Isabella Nasmyth, sir. I'm glad to make your acquaintance. How can I help you?' she said turning from her task and setting her cutters down in the basket of roses at her feet.

'Your blooms are very fine, madam.' MacKenzie inhaled the perfume of a white flower hanging over the gate.

'Are you a student of horticulture?' she asked, the tone in her voice softening.

'I grow roses in my own garden. I see you have Maiden's Blush… Blush Belgic… Rosa Mundi. You have a fine collection.'

'My favourite is this one, sir. The Musk Rose. The scent is exquisite.'

MacKenzie's face grew serious. 'The reason for my visit, madam. I wish it was to see your roses. It is not. I wish to speak to you on a matter of concern to the duchess.'

Isabella nodded her head. 'May I offer you a glass of wine in the house?' she asked, seeming to relax.

MacKenzie followed her down the path, through the open front door and across a large hall into the living chamber. She rang a bell and an old maidservant appeared, before disappearing and reappearing with a tray. The maid poured them both a glass of wine and handed one to him. Isabella sat on the chair opposite, taking hers.

MacKenzie observed her carefully. 'Your good health, madam. *Slàinte*, as we say in Gaelic!'

'You are a Highlander, Mr MacKenzie?' she asked, bemused.

'From Ross-shire, the MacKenzie lands in the north. My father held the estate of Ardcoul. My elder brother Simon is now laird, as you would say in the Lowlands. As a younger son, I was sent south to earn a living in the law – I had no choice in the matter – I was expected to work for my clan in Edinburgh, sorting out all the bother they got into. I trained as an advocate and rose to be Clerk of the Court of Session, but I lost my position during the late political upheaval. I've lived in Edinburgh for many years, but still regard myself as a Highlander. Gaelic is my first tongue, the one spoken to me by my mother and wet nurse when I supped at her breast. It's the one I'm most at ease speaking and which I converse in after a bottle or two of wine, when I stumble in the Lowland tongue,' he laughed.

She smiled at him, thoughtfully. 'I've never been to the Highlands, sir. I've only been twice to Edinburgh in my whole life. I've never travelled out of Scotland,' she mused distantly.

'Why would you leave such a beautiful garden?' said MacKenzie. 'Although, contrary to general opinion, there are many fine gardens in the Highlands. It's not all banditry and rebellion as the government would have us believe.'

She smiled coyly. 'It's my treasure. There's little else brings me joy in life. It helps me forget my troubles. My husband is dead. You may have heard my son is missing.' She sipped her wine greedily.

MacKenzie drank deeply, savouring it. He had a thirst after the walk from Hamilton. 'I want to speak to you about your son. I'm deeply sorry about what's happened.' He broke off for a moment trying to find the right words. 'I've been asked by her grace to investigate Bethia's death.' Isabella's head dropped.

'I'm sorry, madam. I see it's difficult for you.'

She began to cry. She took out a lace handkerchief and wiped her eyes, then took another sip of wine, and another, then looked up at him. 'Excuse me, Mr MacKenzie. I cannot sleep a wink at night. I pace the house in a distracted state. I only find a little slumber after drinking wine. When I do sleep, I suffer awful dreams. My beloved Arthur, my only child, is gone! I've not seen him in weeks. He's sent no letter or message. I know not if he's dead or alive. I fear the worst. Terrible thoughts keep invading my mind!'

MacKenzie waited for her to gather herself before he continued. 'There are outstanding legal matters from Bethia's death, madam. She had property in Hamilton and Glasgow with no direct heirs of her body. The duchess wants to find out what happened to her. She wants to clarify matters from a legal perspective. She's employed me as an independent counsellor. A decision of self-murder affects the dead's disposal of assets. It's important we locate your son as soon as possible. He may be able to shed some light on her demise. You've heard nothing from him since he left the parish?'

She shook her head. 'Not a word in ten weeks.'

MacKenzie sat back and took another sip of wine. 'Please tell me about him, madam. The more I know, the better my chance of finding him.'

The hopeful words seemed to rouse her. She sat forward, put her glass down and looked at MacKenzie intently. 'Arthur is a fine boy. The best scholar in the burgh school. A good student at the college in Glasgow. Diligent in the Latin tongue, I'm told, although I know little of it myself. Although a student, he lived a quiet life in Glasgow. He was happy with a few friends and dedicated to his studies. However, since completing his degree, he's been at odds with himself, unable to settle, unsure about his future, thinking of going in one direction, then changing his mind. Some have encouraged him towards the ministry, others to the law, which I myself favour. Of late he's adamant he wants to follow in his father's footsteps as a soldier. I believe he has no aptitude for such a life.

However, he worshipped his father. Sir James Turner, a retired soldier in the Gorbals who my husband served under, has unfortunately fed his mind with tales of the military life.'

'How long is your husband dead, madam?' asked MacKenzie, noticing her hands were shaking.

'He's long dead, sir. More than ten years. He was hardly ever at home. When he returned from campaigns, it was always a special time. Arthur loved his stories and the presents he brought back.' She hesitated for a few moments. 'Arthur does not have the constitution for a military life. He's not like his father, who was a skilled swordsman and horseman. My husband died on the battlefield, hacked to death by the Turks. I don't want my son to suffer a similar fate. Bethia did not want him to be a soldier.'

'I'm sorry, madam. Then we have that in common. My wife was taken from me more than twenty years ago. It's hard bringing up a child on your own.'

She smiled at him. 'I'm sorry, Mr MacKenzie.' She took another sip of wine, finishing her glass and filling it from the bottle that had been left on the table beside her. 'I'll tell you all I can. If it helps find him. I'm glad someone is looking for him.' She turned and pointed at a painting on the wall behind her. 'That's Arthur. Painted earlier this year, not long after their betrothal. There's one of Bethia painted at the same time. It's a good likeness of him.'

MacKenzie rose and went to the picture. It was identical in style to the one in Bethia's house and painted by the same artist. Nasmyth had dark brown eyes and black, curly hair with a slightly protruding chin and a small, curved scar on his cheek. He was dressed in a smart, green silk suit. Painted in front of his bookshelves, he rested his hand on a pile of books on the table beside him. A sword hung from his side, hinting at military ambitions. In the background was a painting which looked like the one of the famous general Montrose in black armour. 'He was dedicated to Montrose, madam?' asked MacKenzie, remaining beside the painting.

She nodded. 'He was always talking about his campaigns with his father.'

MacKenzie returned to his seat. 'Tell me about Bethia, madam,' he said gently.

She looked down at her hands and shook her head in despair. 'I loved her like my own daughter. I've known her since she was a child. She played in this house when she was a bairn. They were betrothed a few months ago, just after Easter,' she continued. 'It was always expected they would wed. The jointure and tocher were agreed; the day set for the ceremony.' She paused for a moment and looked down at her trembling hands. 'I will never recover from the shock of hearing the news of her death. It was like being told my own daughter was dead. It was a greater shock than learning of my husband's demise. As a soldier's wife, I was always expecting it. I had imagined it many times. Bethia, on the other hand, had her whole life ahead of her. It came out of the blue, in an unimagined way. I'll never forget the forlorn look on Arthur's face when he told me. He had been out all night looking for her. He told me she had fallen into the Avon and her body was dragged out the Clyde. He had seen her lying dead in the palace. He was in a frantic state, almost out of his mind. He sat staring into the fire, drinking brandy after brandy. He rode off although I begged him to stay. I thought he would be back later that day. I waited up all night for him. But he didn't return. He's all I have left, sir.'

'I share your pain, Mrs Nasmyth. I'm told by everyone she was a tender, gentle girl. Loved by all.'

'She was a happy, bonnie creature. He doted on her and she on him. They were firm friends, which is not always common in those who marry.'

'When did you last see her?'

She sipped her wine and thought for a moment. 'It was a few days before she died. She came here looking for Arthur one afternoon. But he was out riding. She wanted to leave him a note in his chamber, so she ran upstairs. I returned to the living chamber. Then, a few minutes later, I heard her leaving. I shouted farewell, but she didn't reply. I saw her closing the gate and making her way quickly down the road to Hamilton. That was the last I ever saw of her.'

'Was it unusual she did not say farewell?'

Isabella nodded. 'She always came in to chat with me. I think she had never done that before. Something was wrong, although she had seemed fine when she appeared at the door.'

MacKenzie put his glass down. 'I'm sorry to ask this, madam. It's a difficult question, but I must. Did you know she was with child?'

Isabella shook her head and began to sob. 'That's what breaks my heart. I knew nothing until I heard it in town a few days later.'

'This is also a difficult question. Do you know whose child it was?'

She shook her head. 'No one in the parish will speak to me about it. I presume it was Arthur's.'

'Do you know anything about the arguments over her burial?'

She shook her head despondently. 'The fanatics have used her death as an excuse to riot.'

'Tell me what you mean, madam,' said MacKenzie.

'Her burial in holy ground was forbidden because she was judged a suicide. She was guilty of the sin of self-murder and murder of her bairn. As a compromise, she was buried just north of the churchyard, beyond the wall. This did not assuage them. One night they dug her up and dragged her behind a horse through the town. They hung her on a gibbet and abused her body. Cut her down, dragged her to the shore and dumped her in a hole. I hope she and the poor dead bairn within her cold womb find some peace. They say they are men of God. But they are vile devils surely!'

'Can you think where Arthur's gone, madam?'

She shook her head. 'When he didn't return in a couple of days, I sought Robert Corse, his friend who shared rooms with him in Glasgow. He had no word either and was worried sick. I believe he's often been back to Glasgow to look for him. His other friends have done the same, as have the servants of Sir James. After a few days, I went to Glasgow myself. I searched everywhere – the college, his chambers on the Trongate, all the inns and taverns in the town. No one knew anything or would tell me a thing. I did learn from Archie Weir that he stayed a couple of days with him but then left. He had heard nothing else from him. I asked his regent, Mr Cruikshank, but no word. On the way back I visited Sir James. He had heard nothing and was very worried. He said he would get his servants to search in Glasgow and the local villages. He's too infirm to travel. Sir James fears Arthur has run off to join the army and blames himself. If that's the case, I might have some relief. At least he would still be alive with the prospect of returning when he's overcome his grief.' She broke down in tears. 'A bad thought keeps invading my mind, sir. One which will not leave me. I fear I'll never see him again. I'll be left alone to live out my days with no grandchildren to bring me comfort. I fear he'll never return to me... alive.'

MacKenzie took another sip of wine and waited for her to calm herself. 'What kind of man is Robert Corse?'

'A kindly one. An old school friend who studies for the ministry. They've known each other most of their lives.'

'What of Archie Weir?'

'A friend from college. His father is a rich merchant who owns the Northern Sugar Works. I don't know him so well. I've only met him a few times. He appears a good man with an engaging smile. He's always laughing about something.'

'What of the regent, Cruikshank?'

'He's mightily fond of Arthur.'

'Where does Cruikshank hail from?'

'Hamilton, too. A few years older than the others.'

MacKenzie put down his glass and refused her offer of more wine. He needed to keep his wits sharp. She filled her glass again. He could see a slight sheen over her eyes, the first hint of inebriation. 'My assistant, Davie Scougall, a notary public from Edinburgh, is in Glasgow on business, madam. He's a perceptive young man who will search rigorously for him. Davie may turn up something that's been overlooked.' Despite trying to sound positive, MacKenzie had a sense of foreboding. He was pondering Arthur's role in Bethia's death. Had he found out she was pregnant with another man's child and killed her in a fit of rage? Had he drowned her himself in the Avon? He could not dismiss this entirely. It seemed out of character, but any man could be transported by a fit of madness. And if she was pregnant, who was the father? He looked back at the painting on the wall. Arthur did not look like a killer, but who did in their portrait? 'There's just one other thing, madam. May I examine his chamber in case there's something that might help us, that might suggest where he's fled?'

She nodded. 'I don't see any harm in it. Come this way, Mr MacKenzie.'

As they climbed the staircase, he noticed she was swaying slightly and had to support herself on the banister. They entered a room at the front of the house. It was a large chamber full of fine furniture, bookcases and a strange assortment of military artefacts. 'My maid will show you out, Mr MacKenzie. I must rest. Please let me know as soon as you learn anything.'

MacKenzie observed the portrait of Montrose on the wall. It was a copy of one by Gerrit van Honthorst. On a desk lay an assortment of books and papers. On the bookcase were works of poetry and philosophy, as well as books on military history. MacKenzie opened one and read the inscription inside – it was a gift from Sir James Turner. There was a work in Spanish by Cervantes and an Italian work, *L'amorosa fiammetta* by Giovanni Boccaccio.

The collection of weapons was spread across the room: an assortment of swords, daggers, knives and guns of different types, some attached to the walls by brackets, others lying on the floor. He lifted up an old gun from a corner. He thought it was a piece called an arquebus. He had known men who were fascinated by weapons. For some they were mere artefacts of decoration, antiquarian oddities which fired their imaginations; for others they indicated an unhealthy obsession with violence.

CHAPTER 13

An Afternoon in the Country

MACKENZIE RETURNED TO Hamilton and ate a slice of venison pie and drank a cup of ale in the tavern on the High Street, a warm, inviting inn. After lunch, he met Hugh Wood at the Back Close. On horseback, they took the road southwest from the town following a winding path through the woods along the Avon Water. The ruins of Cadzow Castle soon came into view above them. After they passed under the castle battlements, the Avon turned sharply south. Half a mile further upstream, Wood stopped his horse and dismounted in a small, open area beside the river.

'This is where Bethia went in, Mr MacKenzie,' said Wood.

'The water looks harmless today. You'd struggle to drown in it,' replied MacKenzie.

'It's gentle enough now. Just a couple of feet deep,' continued Wood. 'However, it was in spate that night. There had been a downpour in the afternoon. It would be difficult to get out, especially in the dark,' Wood said grimly. 'Her bonnet was found in the bushes over there by O'Flaherty. A search was made along the Clyde and its tributaries on the day she was found. She was swept downstream and pulled out near the palace.'

MacKenzie looked at the bare patch of ground. It was about four yards square with a sheer drop of three feet into the river where a pool extended for a few yards surrounded by large rocks. He looked into the brown water and caught the flickering movement of fish, probably young trout. In the bright afternoon it was an innocuous place to dawdle in the dappled sunshine. However, in the dark, it would be disorientating if you fell into the cold water. He imagined the scene on the night of the 13th of June: darkness, the roaring of the water over the rocks, the curtain of tall trees above. A sudden panic due to the cold; then the water sweeping her downstream and smashing her on the rocks. But why was she here that night? Perhaps she chose to end her life on this spot. Perhaps she had come with someone. The path was back in the cover of the trees, a fair distance from the river – perhaps five yards away, he judged. Why would she come down to the water's edge in the dark after a deluge? She would surely have heard the water. Or did she simply take a wrong turn?

'Why do you think she was here that night, Hugh?' asked MacKenzie.

Wood shook his head sadly. 'I don't know, sir. I've no idea why she was here. Why would anyone come here at night?'

'Was she meeting someone? Was she with someone?' MacKenzie mused.

Again, Wood shook his head.

'I suppose it's the kind of place a person might kill themselves,' said MacKenzie. 'Where was Nasmyth on the night she drowned?'

'I've heard he was with his friend Robert Corse in town. They were seen on the street in the late afternoon. He joined the search for her. Janet came to tell me Bethia had not returned home. She was in a terrible state. I've heard he searched high and low all night, along the Clyde and its tributaries, until he came back to town at dawn and heard her body was found near the palace.'

'What time did Janet come to you?'

'I don't know the exact time. It was the middle of the night. Maybe two o'clock.'

MacKenzie lifted a small, flat stone from the ground and tried to skim it across the water, a favourite childhood pastime. It bounced a couple of times, then sank into the water. 'If she was being pursued, she might have panicked. She might have come off the path and ended up in the water, if she was scared and lost her way,' he pondered.

'She knew this stretch of the Avon,' replied Wood. 'She would know to avoid going close to the water after heavy rain. She was a clever girl, not a fool. There must have been a reason she came off the path.'

MacKenzie picked up another stone and skimmed it across the water. It was possible she had come here to kill herself. But something did not fit. 'Was there anything else indicating this was the spot, apart from the bonnet?' he asked.

'I don't think so, sir.'

They went back to the horses and returned the way they had come, then took another road southwest of Hamilton for about five miles. They passed through the small townships of Meikle Earnock and Haspielaw before climbing up into the moors, a wild area with few dwellings, inhabited only by sheep and blown by the wind. They rode a couple of miles further in the open countryside. Wood stopped his horse and dismounted near a dilapidated stone wall on the top of a rounded hill. The place afforded views across the counties of Lanarkshire and Ayrshire. To the north, the spires and towers of Glasgow could be seen and beyond the Kilpatrick Hills and Campsie Fells. The mountains of the Highlands were just hazily visible in the far distance. They walked up to the wall. The Quaker burial ground opened out beneath them on the downward slope of the hill.

MacKenzie was shocked by the scene of utter devastation. The wall had been smashed in places. The graveyard looked like it had been ploughed by a team of oxen. The trees outside the wall had been set on fire, leaving their charred trunks rising like black quills against the sky. Graves had been dug up, leaving gaping holes and piles of earth. The contents of coffins – skulls and bones, along with a few decayed body parts of the recently interred – were scattered everywhere. MacKenzie had never witnessed the aftermath of a battle, but an image of the hellish field of Inverlochy came into his mind as described in a poem by Iain Lom. Such bitter destruction could only be carried out in the name of religion – the worst atrocities always had a sacred element: Cromwell's slaughter of Catholics in Ireland, the St Bartholomew's Day massacre of Huguenots in Paris, the butchery of the civil wars in the Highlands.

MacKenzie shook his head in disbelief and turned to Wood. 'My God, Hugh. I'm sorry your people have suffered such abuse.' He cursed in Gaelic.

Wood shook his head forlornly. There were tears in his eyes as he looked over the burial ground. 'It is desecration, Mr MacKenzie. An affront to all Christian folk. We've buried our dead in this place for forty years. Dozens of our people lie here. I knew them all. I've shared food with them all. I've worshipped with them all. Many of the bones belong to children, taken early by the Lord. My wife was buried beside the south wall over there. I know not which bones are hers now. Two of my daughters, taken as children, lie there also, their tiny bones mixed up with all the others. We'll have to dig one large pit and put them all in together, maybe with a small headstone, although it's not our custom to have stone monuments. This is how Satan acts under the cover of God's name.'

'Why did they do this to you?' asked MacKenzie solemnly.

'For one simple reason. They want us to leave the parish of Hamilton.

They hate us as deeply as they loathe James Stuart. They'll persecute us until we're driven back to England or take refuge in America. Then they'll turn on someone else. Their faith is constructed on a foundation of hate. Their notion of purity tolerates no difference. It's Presbytery or nothing for them.'

'Do you know who's responsible for this, Hugh?'

Wood sighed. 'Most of the community do us no wrong. But a small number whip up the gullible who follow like sheep. I've heard there's a few leaders, men like Bass John and William Corse in Glasgow, Arthur Renwick and Archibald Cameron: diehard Presbyterians. They were no doubt in their beds that night. Their lackeys did this. The villagers in Meikle Earnock said it sounded like a cavalry charge coming up the road. The riders carried halberds and pikes and maces, as if they rode to Rullion Green or Bothwell Brig. Instead, they used them to smash the bones of our dead.'

MacKenzie climbed through the broken wall and wandered gingerly, avoiding bones with every step.

'They dug up Bethia later that night,' continued Wood, following him into the burial ground. 'After they had been here, they galloped back to Hamilton, dug her up, dragged her through the town and hung her on a gibbet.'

MacKenzie shook his head. Dropping to his haunches, he found a tiny skull half submerged in the earth. He picked it up and held it for a moment before returning it to the soil gently. He wondered if the destruction was linked to the death of Bethia. They returned to the horses in silence. 'The case should be taken to court,' MacKenzie said after mounting. 'Justice should be done. You should be compensated so the ground can be restored and your dead reburied. Can you think of any connection between Bethia and this desecration?'

Wood shook his head. 'I don't know. Perhaps they were in a state of frenzy and sought another easy target.'

CHAPTER 14

The Northern Sugar Works

SCOUGALL WALKED DOWN Queen Street and out into the rigs to the north of Glasgow. It was only five minutes' walk to the Northern Sugar Works, an assortment of warehouses, storerooms and offices around a central courtyard. He observed a merchant and workman in conversation beside a pile of barrels.

The merchant, a ponderous man in a black silk suit, noticed him as he entered through the gate. 'What can I do for you, sir?' he asked.

'I'm looking for Archie Weir,' said Scougall, hesitantly.

'I'm Abraham Weir,' he replied. 'Archie is my son. He's in the office over there. He should be working on my books.'

Scougall thanked him and left the pair to their conversation. He crossed the courtyard and entered the office. A young man looked up from a desk, happily returned his quill to the stand and observed Scougall expectantly. Archie Weir had a friendly, beaming face with strands of red hair poking out from his wig. 'How can I help you, sir?' he asked. 'An order of rum? We have a new batch just distilled. Fine and strong. I've tasted it myself. Or a consignment of sugar?'

Scougall smiled and shook his head. 'No, I'm not here to buy anything. Are you Archie Weir?'

The young man nodded.

'I'm Davie Scougall, a notary from Edinburgh. I work for Mrs Hair. You may have heard of her; she has a moneylending office in the city.'

'She's well-known, even in the west,' said Weir. He sat back and beckoned Scougall to sit across the desk from him.

'I'm looking for someone, Mr Weir,' said Scougall. 'My associate, John MacKenzie, an advocate from Edinburgh, has been asked by the Duchess of Hamilton to find him. I was directed here by his regent, Mr Cruikshank. I'm looking for Arthur Nasmyth.'

Weir's friendly expression disappeared. He looked at Scougall suspiciously for a few moments, then asked: 'Why is an Edinburgh notary looking for him?'

'Mr MacKenzie wants to speak to him on a private legal matter. I've to encourage him to return to Hamilton. I know no more about it than that, sir.'

Weir pondered for a few moments. He looked like he was weighing things up, then his face lightened and he replied calmly: 'Would you care for some wine or something a little stronger, Mr Scougall?'

Before Scougall could answer, Weir jumped up from his desk. He was short in stature, about the same height as Scougall. He went to a press and removed a bottle of rum. He held it lovingly for a few moments, cradling the bottle in his hand, before pouring himself a large glass which he emptied in one go. He filled another and took it back to the desk 'You'll not join me, it's fine stuff?' He finished the glass again and poured some more. 'It's a terrible tale. The death of Bethia. The disappearance of Arthur. I'm desperate for news about him myself. He's a dear friend. I've seen nothing of him, nor heard anything, for weeks now.'

Scougall shook his head, declining the offer of a drink. 'It's too early for me, Mr Weir.'

Weir looked guiltily through the window to where his father was still deep in conversation, before beginning earnestly. 'I saw him last about ten weeks ago. He came here on the very day Bethia was found in the Clyde. He'd ridden all the way from his mother's house. He was in an awful state, as you can imagine – distracted, raving, completely overwrought by despair. He looked like he might end his own life like her.'

'What did he tell you had happened?' asked Scougall.

'I sat him down where you're sitting now, Mr Scougall. After he'd taken a glass of rum and another, he calmed a bit. He told me she'd killed herself by jumping into the river. He'd searched for her all night after hearing she was missing. All he wanted to do was to borrow a little money to flee overseas. I tried to persuade him to change his mind or at least give the matter careful reflection. What about his poor mother left alone in the world? But he was adamant, so I gave him the money and we toasted his future. I said he could stay in my chambers in town until he found a ship, but he was worried about being seen in the city. Then I suggested a secret room used by my father to hide Covenanters in the days of their persecution. That's where he remained for a few days.'

'A few days?' repeated Scougall.

'I had to leave for Ayr on business the day after he arrived. When I returned a couple of days later, he had gone. One of our men, Elijah Bannerman, the fellow out there speaking to my father, saw him leave. Arthur left a short note telling me he was going and thanking me.'

Scougall was pleased to have found out something. 'Do you still have the note, Mr Weir?'

'No. I burned it as he requested.'

Scougall thought for a moment. 'Have you no idea where he went?'

Weir shook his head. 'I don't even know if he did depart on a ship. I hope he contacts me, wherever he's settled.'

'Where do you think he's bound?'

Weir thought for a moment. 'He always had an itch to travel. He could've gone to Ireland or even the Americas. He said he would write to me. But there's no word from him yet.'

Scougall thought for a few moments. 'Could you show me the chamber where he hid?'

'Come with me, Mr Scougall.' Weir finished his rum and took his jacket from the back of his chair. Scougall followed him out of the office. Weir shouted across to his father that he was showing a potential customer, Mr Davie Scougall, round the Works.

They entered a large warehouse full of barrels of rum and sugar. 'How is trade, Mr Weir?' asked Scougall.

'It's been badly affected by the war and higher taxes. Sugar prices have fallen over the last few years. We still make a reasonable profit, though not as good as a decade ago. We really made a packet then. That's how my father built all this.'

'Where do you buy your sugar from?' asked Scougall.

'Mostly from Barbados, although now also from St Kitts and Nevis, as well as Jamaica.'

'Do you buy from the plantations of William Corse in Barbados?' asked Scougall, remembering his meeting with Corse and endeavouring to gain some more information about his business.

'Yes. Among others. We buy from many planters on the island. It depends on price and quality. Corse has long experience of the trade, but he's a hothead in religious matters. He can be prickly to deal with, so we don't rely on him for all our supply. I've heard a ship in which he had a substantial share was recently lost.'

Scougall was shocked by the news. Corse had not mentioned it at their meeting. 'Do you know any more about it?'

'Not much, Mr Scougall. I heard it went down with a cargo of negroes on board. All of them lost.'

Scougall followed Weir through stacks of barrels to the back of the warehouse where a door led into a storeroom. Behind a dirty awning, another door led into a narrow corridor. At the bottom of it, another door opened into a small, dark, windowless chamber. Weir lit a candle to illuminate the sparse interior. There was a damp, musky smell in the room which contained only a tiny desk, a straw mattress, a heap of bed linen and a few bits of paper on the floor beside the mattress. Scougall picked up a couple of pages and identified them as news sheets dating from a couple of months before. He got down on his haunches and pulled the mattress up. Another crumpled piece of paper was underneath – a pamphlet advertising for volunteers for a colonial expedition to the Carolinas on a ship leaving from Ayr. Scougall carefully searched the rest of the room as MacKenzie would have done, committing all the details to memory, including the names of the pamphlets. As Weir left, Scougall slipped the one about the colony into his pocket.

'How many days was he here?' asked Scougall when they were back in the warehouse.

'At least three. Elijah saw him leaving the day before I got back.'

'Perhaps we might discuss the sugar trade more fully some time,' said Scougall, 'so I can brief Mrs Hair on its prospects.'

Weir agreed readily. 'We might also share a few glasses, Mr Scougall,' he added.

Once they were outside in the courtyard again, Scougall thanked Weir and was just on the point of leaving when he asked: 'Do you know anything about the venture to the Carolinas?'

'Indeed. I had some hopes of going myself. But my father objected. He did subscribe £100 in the venture.'

'Is it possible Arthur is bound there?' asked Scougall.

Weir nodded. 'He didn't mention it to me, but it's possible. The ship left weeks ago. It should have made land in America by now. We should have news of its success or failure soon.'

On his way back to the centre of the city, Scougall noticed the man who had been talking to Weir's father across the road from him. He gradually crossed the street to overtake him.

'Good afternoon, sir. Did I see you at the Sugar Works just now?' Scougall asked.

The man nodded, then recognised him. 'Ah, it's... Mr Scougall... I heard Archie calling to his father. I am Elijah Bannerman. I'm employed at the Works. I'm glad to say my work for the day is done.'

'I'm a notary from Edinburgh through on business. I'm looking for someone on a legal issue... Arthur Nasmyth.'

Bannerman stopped and turned to Scougall. 'I've heard he's missing.'

'Mr Weir, Archie, that is, told me Arthur was hiding at the Works for a few days. He told me you saw him leave.'

Bannerman nodded. 'Indeed, sir. I provided Arthur with victuals when Archie was away. I was not to disturb him, nor let anyone know he was there. That's what Archie told me. Arthur left a few days later.'

'When did you see him go?'

'I was in the office in the late afternoon. I looked up from the desk. I saw two figures making their way across the courtyard.'

'Two figures?' asked Scougall.

'One was Arthur Nasmyth. I saw him clearly. I didn't recognise the other person. He was wearing a hooded cloak.'

'You're sure it was a man?' asked Scougall.

Bannerman nodded. 'I think it was a man. He was wearing breeches. They were past the window in a moment. I went outside to see if Arthur wanted to leave any word for Archie. By the time I got out, they were moving quickly and were already at the gates. What was strange was they didn't turn left towards town. Instead, they took the road to the north. When I reached the gates, I could see them about a hundred yards away, then I lost sight of them. I found that Arthur had left a note for Archie when I checked the chamber. I gave it to him the next morning when he got back from Ayr.'

'What did Arthur do in the chamber all day?'

'Nothing much. I brought him a few pamphlets and news sheets to read. Just ones I had lying about. He sat on the mattress looking despondent most of the time. No wonder, given what had happened to Bethia Porterfield.'

'Did you give him a pamphlet looking for volunteers for a venture to the Carolinas?'

Bannerman thought for a moment. 'No. That was an older one. It was published a while back. The ones I gave him were all hot off the press.'

'Did you know Bethia?'

He shook his head. 'Never met her. I'd never spoken to Arthur before. Only shared a few words with him in the Works. He looked like he was haunted by grief.'

Scougall thanked him for his time. 'May I buy you a cup of ale for your trouble, Mr Bannerman?' They were now standing outside Gibson's Tavern.

'No thank you, sir. I must get home. My wife is due a baby... any day now.'

'As is mine,' said Scougall sheepishly. He felt guilty for not being able to comfort Chrissie back home in Edinburgh.

CHAPTER 15

The Return of Arran

IT WAS LATE in the afternoon by the time MacKenzie returned to the palace. After washing his hands and face from the porcelain bowl in his chamber, he changed into a fresh shirt and breeches for a meeting with the duchess.

She sat at her desk in the sitting room on the first floor. Two men were standing beside her looking out the window. Their expensive velvet suits, long wigs and knee-length black boots made them stand out as not belonging to the local community. They held wine glasses in their hands.

The duchess beckoned MacKenzie forward and he bowed to her. 'Mr MacKenzie has come from Edinburgh to advise me on a few matters, James,' she said dryly. 'My son, Arran. And his man of business, William Drummond.'

MacKenzie bowed his head to the new arrivals. As Arran came forward, the extravagance of his attire was fully revealed. He wore a magnificent scarlet coat with gold trim. MacKenzie recognised the handsome face he had seen in the portrait the day before, although the earl was probably ten years older and showing the first hints of middle age. Self-importance dripped from every pore. He eyed MacKenzie suspiciously before downing his glass and saying facetiously, 'You must excuse me, sir. I spend too much of my time in the company of lawyers as it is,' then turning to his mother: 'It's been a long journey, mother. I must rest before dinner. We can speak about the marriage business later.' Arran spoke in an unusual accent, influenced by years in England but with the odd Scottish inflexion breaking through now and again, revealing his local origins and early education at the burgh school of Hamilton.

MacKenzie was used to the condescension of the nobility. He nodded affably. There was one indisputable law in the world: power and status encouraged haughtiness. He nodded at the other gentleman, who smiled weakly. Drummond was dressed in a more subdued dark blue suit. He had a ruddy, pock-marked complexion. 'I'm pleased to meet you, sir,' said MacKenzie, shaking his hand.

'It's good to be back on Scottish soil after a long sojourn in the south,' said Drummond. 'I breathe more easily the further north I get. Only when I see the mountains of the Highlands do I finally say I'm home.'

'Where do you hail from, sir?' asked MacKenzie.

'Perthshire,' said Drummond. 'My brother is Drummond of Glenlix. He has a small estate near Crieff. As a younger son, I had to fend for myself, so to speak. I serve his grace as secretary and adviser.'

'Then we have something in common, Mr Drummond. I am also a younger son who had to make his own way. Do you have the Gaelic?' asked MacKenzie.

Drummond replied in Gaelic, saying that he did speak the language but not in front of those who did not understand it. He then repeated this in English for the benefit of Arran and the duchess.

Arran bowed his head slightly and made to leave the room.

'James, listen to me.' The duchess spoke sternly, clearly angered by her son's impertinence, forcing him to stand to attention and turn towards her. 'I've asked Mr MacKenzie to investigate a particular matter. It's something of importance to me. The matter of Bethia's death,' she said.

Arran looked peeved and shook his head. 'Is it not best to let things rest, mother? Stirring things up is surely unwise. Her death is tragic, of course, but hardly uncommon. A wench has lapsed. She could not wait until her wedding night. It's a common weakness among the lower orders in every corner of this land. She could not face the stool of repentance. How could she reveal herself as the parish strumpet?' He turned to MacKenzie: 'The Presbyterian divines hold such a severe view of human nature. It drives folk to extremes, going as far as ending themselves. I prefer a philosophy which holds man in a realistic light. In my book, man is a flawed creature, sometimes prone to good, often driven to bad, while all the time serving his own interest.'

'James, enough of your nonsense metaphysics!' the duchess turned on him angrily. 'And do not speak that way about Bethia! I want to get to the bottom of it,' she said with a trace of bitterness in her voice. 'I owe it to her. I owe it to her mother and grandmother, my beloved friend, who came all those miles with me in 1642.'

'Very well, mother.' Arran turned to MacKenzie. 'Tell me where you stand, Mr MacKenzie. Are you a Presbyterian?' he asked.

'Episcopalian, your grace. There are few Presbyterians in the MacKenzie clan,' said MacKenzie provocatively. 'Many Episcopalian clergy have been ill-treated in these parts. They find themselves homeless for supporting the old king.'

Arran eyed him closely. 'I agree the rabblings have gone too far. We're providing support for those who've lost their livings. But it's a complicated matter. Many of their tormentors are our own tenants who sought revenge for the atrocities committed by Dundee in the name of King James.'

The duchess interjected. 'I did all I could. I advise my son to be cautious in all he does, politically, especially at this juncture. As things are not set in stone and William has only been on the throne for a couple of years, it would be advisable to take no rigid position, one way or the other.' She stopped to emphasise what followed: 'To commit to the Jacobite side would be a serious error of judgement, James. The gravest of errors. Would you not agree, Mr MacKenzie?' She looked at Arran sternly.

MacKenzie realised she was warning her son. He knew Arran was rumoured still to be in contact with the exiled king, while courting King William at the same time. He had already paid for his duplicity, suffering a stint of imprisonment in the Tower of London. Many noble families were playing a similar double game, an insurance policy of sorts. Open support for either side would be limited until the outlook was clearer; either William's position became unassailable, or King Louis of France backed the old king with money and troops. There was, of course, a further consideration, not spoken of directly, but intimated in the earnest expression on the duchess's face. The Hamilton family's historic claim to the Scottish throne. Who could predict the turn of events? Who would have guessed William and Mary would now sit on the thrones of Scotland, England and Ireland? What if James died suddenly, his Catholic heir was unpalatable to Protestants in Scotland and England, and then William was killed? Jacobite assassins were known to be trying to murder him. Who would then be king? MacKenzie smiled to himself as he observed Arran. It was just possible he stood before a future monarch. He made a mental note to record his impressions of him when he returned to the Hawthorns – it might make an interesting account for a future historian. He had a strong feeling, however, that Arran would not make a successful king, following in the footsteps of the inept Stuarts.

'I'll make sure your son commits neither way, your grace,' said Drummond with a suggestion of a smile on his face. 'I recommend caution in all things. We both recognise the importance of the time. The situation in Ireland is in flux, as it is in the Highlands, where a few chiefs still support the old king. The position of the French King is unclear, as ever. We must do nothing to prejudice the rights of the House of Hamilton.' Drummond's words appeared to appease the duchess.

'Don't worry, mother. Rest assured there's only one interest I follow,' said Arran. 'It's not the Jacobite or Williamite one, but our own.' Turning to MacKenzie, he continued: 'I must do nothing prejudicial to our rights in case I'm called upon by the people to intervene at a crucial juncture. I would never put myself forward, but if friends requested it, if the people of Scotland demanded it, I would be ready to rule. Besides, I have other things to worry about. There's always the issue of money. The bane of the nobleman! Life in London becomes more and more expensive. I cannot appear parsimonious before the English nobles. The Hamilton family is regarded as the most honourable in Scotland and now Britain. That's a position I must retain. A favourable marriage will help much. It's vital to our interest. Another English bride is essential. A poor Scottish lass will not do, even a bonnie one!' Arran hesitated for a moment and his expression lightened. 'Perhaps,' he continued, 'when you have a moment, we might discuss the subject of money, MacKenzie. You might provide advice, as a man well versed in such matters, on how to secure a bond substantial enough to see me through the winter at court.'

MacKenzie had no intention of lending Arran a bawbee, but he gave him his most equivocal expression. He might use the opportunity to gain some information from him.

'Mr MacKenzie did not come all the way from Edinburgh to fund your dissolute life, James. I want him to concentrate on Bethia,' said the duchess sharply.

'Of course, mother. I only meant I would happily entertain him for a few hours. Perhaps a ride in the woods. It would be fine leisure and provide the opportunity for him to question me more fully about her. I would be happy to share all I know with him.'

MacKenzie sensed Arran was on the defensive and took the opportunity to continue to question him. 'Did you know Bethia well, your grace?'

MacKenzie noticed an uneasiness as Arran replied. 'Of course I knew her well. I've known her since the day she was born. As I said, it's a tragedy. Nasmyth is robbed of a beautiful wife. But such things happen in life. When our servants drowned in the Clyde a few years ago, no one cried mischief, no one went running for Edinburgh advocates to pour over the case. They went swimming after a few drinks and were caught in the current; it can be a dangerous river at the wrong time. These things happen for no rhyme nor reason. We are best to let the matter lie. Do you not agree, Drummond?'

Drummond smiled urbanely and addressed the duchess. 'Indeed, your grace. We should not stir up a hornet's nest, especially when the future of the government is uncertain. We don't want instability just now on our estates.'

'There, you see, mother, Drummond recommends caution. I in the sphere of politics and you with Bethia. Allow emotions to settle. Inaction is often the wisest policy. Let others act and make mistakes.'

'What about Arthur, the young man who's disappeared?' asked MacKenzie, determined to learn as much as possible.

Arran sighed impatiently. 'A promising lad. A good scholar. Taken with the life of a soldier. He came to speak to me the last time I was in Scotland about a military career. He wanted my help to get a place in a regiment, although his mother desired a more placid profession for him, like the church or the law,' he scoffed. 'Something sedentary and unexciting.'

'What advice did you give him, your grace?' asked MacKenzie.

'I said I would look into the matter. I spoke to his mother. I told her soldiering was an honourable profession. I believed the boy was suited to such a life. He will certainly be better off, after recent events, making his way outside Scotland.'

'He would not make a minister?' asked MacKenzie.

Arran shook his head and scoffed. 'He's not suited for such a rigid life. I think it preposterous he was pointed in that direction.'

'Why is that, your grace?'

'Arthur's not the kind of man who could tell others how to live their lives. I could not see him sitting on the session judging sins, like fornication or witchcraft. He's a quiet man who will take orders from his superiors and ride into battle when he's told to and not question it. He would make a reasonable military man. I could not see him preaching in a kirk, thundering about damnation, hunting out blasphemers or fornicators.'

'What did Bethia think of him becoming a soldier?'

'She was against it, of course. Everybody was against it. Except me and old Sir James, his father's friend. Now I must rest. We can talk more about it on our ride tomorrow. A couple of hours' exercise in the morning will do us all good. It's a grand place to ponder things. You can ask your questions then.'

MacKenzie raised his voice and continued as Arran made his way out: 'There's just one other matter, if you'll allow me, your grace. I wanted to bring it up with you both.' He turned to the duchess. 'I've learned from Mr Wood of the terrible destruction wrought on the Quaker burial ground. I visited the site myself this afternoon. I was shocked by the devastation. It's been razed to the ground as if struck by artillery. Bones and body parts lie everywhere.'

The duchess shook her head. 'The treatment of Hugh's people troubles me greatly. But you must understand, Mr MacKenzie, it's a difficult balancing act for us as the main landowners in the area. Some of the enthusiasts despise the Quakers, whom they view as incomers with blasphemous beliefs. They seek to persecute them as they were persecuted in the so-called Killing Times. I've supported Hugh and his people for years. I've given them employment and in return they've worked hard for me. They are good, honest people, if a little misguided in religion. This has made me unpopular with some of my tenants – not all, just a vocal minority who are influential. If I condemn the enthusiasts too vocally, I may encourage unrest, even violence, on my lands, such as rioting or rebellion. Many are still armed after the Covenanting struggles. Weapons are hidden away ready for use again. I want to avoid bloodshed at all costs. I support Hugh and his people as far as I can go, but I cannot be seen to side with them completely. That would alienate my tenants and destabilise the area. We don't want to go back to the days when Lanarkshire was in a state of armed rebellion and government soldiers were sent to quell it. I'll see the burial ground is tidied up quietly when things settle down, and then restored, maybe in a little time, with a minimum of noise or fuss.'

MacKenzie nodded knowingly. 'The destruction goes beyond a dislike of the Quakers. It reveals a visceral hatred. It's an attempt to obliterate them. I fear the next step will be a lynching or killing. I've heard from my assistant Mr Scougall of another attack in Glasgow last night.'

'Sometimes the best policy is to let the temperature fall,' said the duchess. 'If I was seen to provide compensation now, it might make a fragile situation worse. If I gave them armed protection, it might encourage further attacks. Pour oil on the flames. But as I said, we'll tidy things up when we can. Hugh knows I'll look after his people.'

'Let me look into it, mother. I might send a couple of men to clear the ground and begin rebuilding the walls,' said Arran. 'And in return Mr MacKenzie might provide me with some... financial advice,' he smiled. 'Tit for tat, as they say.'

'Should the case not go to the sheriff court or privy council?' asked MacKenzie.

'As my mother says, such action would inflame things. It's best dealt with using a little... local knowledge. I'll speak to you again when I've made some enquiries, MacKenzie.'

As they were leaving the room, O'Flaherty came in. MacKenzie took him aside as the duchess, Arran and Drummond departed. He spoke to him in Gaelic: 'I would like to take you up on your invitation, Jago. How about a dram tonight?'

'Of course, John. It would be a great pleasure. I'm taking my clarsach back there now. I look forward to it.'

CHAPTER 16

A Dram with Jago O'Flaherty

JOHN TIMOTHY SHOWED MacKenzie to O'Flaherty's chamber at the top of a narrow staircase in one of the palace turrets. There was a bed in one corner, an old settee, a couple of chairs, a large press and a few books in a bookcase. A variety of stringed musical instruments were scattered about. Sheets of music were strewn across a small desk. Although it was getting dark, the curtains were not drawn, giving a fine view over the gardens to the west.

'Whisky?' asked O'Flaherty.

MacKenzie nodded.

O'Flaherty filled two glasses generously from an earthenware jug and they toasted each other.

'It has a different flavour, the taste is... unusual,' said MacKenzie appreciatively.

O'Flaherty smiled. 'Irish whisky. When I hanker for the taste of my homeland, I can buy a bottle or two in Glasgow.'

'You have comfortable chambers, Jago,' said MacKenzie. 'The view is a sight for sore eyes. Have you ever thought of returning to Ireland?'

'I've lived here too long now. My parents are dead years ago. If I went back, I'd be disappointed. The country is still volatile after all these years. I don't think it would offer an old man much comfort.'

'You've never married?' asked MacKenzie.

O'Flaherty sipped his whisky before answering. 'There was a woman once, years ago. It didn't work out. She's long dead. I'm set in my ways now.'

MacKenzie took another sip and savoured the flavour. 'A dead friend of mine wrote a book about the civil wars,' he said. 'He left me the task of editing it. I cannot get round to starting. He would have loved talking to you about Montrose and MacColla.'

O'Flaherty smiled. 'Montrose inspired his men with fine words before battle. MacColla was a killer without remorse, though the poets called him an honourable warrior.'

'Civil wars with a religious flavour are always the worst,' added MacKenzie.

O'Flaherty nodded. 'Thank God the years since have been relatively peaceful. At least the recent revolution did not result in a long period of bloody conflict in Scotland. A little trouble in the Highlands, perhaps. Dundee made good use of the Highlanders at Killiecrankie. I find it difficult to support the Jacobite cause enthusiastically anymore, although I fought for it in the past.'

'I find myself taking a similar view,' said MacKenzie. 'Scotland has suffered too many foolish kings. We've been let down by the Stuarts. I just can't get used to having a Dutchman on the throne.'

'Then we must toast the return of a better king. When that will be, God only knows!' laughed O'Flaherty.

'I'll toast the return of a wise king,' said MacKenzie.

'Have we ever had a wise king!'

'Some say James VI was the wisest fool in Christendom!'

They both laughed and drank more whisky. O'Flaherty rose stiffly to fill their glasses and stoke the fire. Once he returned to his chair, MacKenzie decided to move the conversation back to the case at hand. 'I wanted to ask you more about Bethia, Jago. The duchess has asked me to investigate her death.'

The harper nodded solemnly and settled himself into the couch.

'I've heard you discovered the bonnet which identified where she went into the water. How did you come to find it?' asked MacKenzie.

O'Flaherty sipped his whisky and sighed. 'After her body was found, all the servants in the palace were sent to look along the streams and burns that flow into the Clyde for evidence of where she went in. I was told to search the Avon with John Timothy. I know the area well. I've walked the woods there for thirty years. About half a mile beyond the castle, on the north side of the river, is a small open area a few yards from the path. Children go there when the weather is warm to swim in the river. There's a pool of reasonable depth, perhaps a few feet, although the river is usually shallow there.'

'I was at the clearing this afternoon,' said MacKenzie.

'You'll know the water is about five yards from the path. As I stood at the edge, a piece of material in a bush caught my eye. It was stuck in the undergrowth between the path and river. A bonnet was caught in the thorns.'

'How did you know it was hers?' asked MacKenzie.

'Her initials were embroidered on it. Let me show you. I still have it.' O'Flaherty rose and went to the press. He took something from a drawer and handed it to MacKenzie. It was a white, slightly soiled, bonnet with the initials 'BP' embroidered inside in red thread. 'There's no doubting it's hers. Her initials were added to all her bonnets in the same way,' said O'Flaherty.

'Did you see anything else there?' asked MacKenzie.

O'Flaherty shook his head. 'Nothing of interest,' then paused for a moment. 'Except some footprints at the water's edge.'

'Footprints around the spot she fell in?'

'I believe, so. I think at least two sets, maybe more. Small ones and larger ones.'

'So, she was there with someone else?'

'It's possible. If the smaller prints belonged to her… that's not certain. They could have been made at different times.'

'Did you tell anyone about the footprints?'

'I told the sheriff at the inquest. He seemed little interested. He thought I was an old fool and had come upon my own footprints. I know I did not stand near the spot before. I believe he had already made up his mind. She had killed herself and her child. The worthies in the parish had decided. I've not said anything more about it until just now. You're the first person to ask me about them.'

MacKenzie pondered what O'Flaherty had said for a moment. If the harper was correct, it suggested someone else, or more than one person, could have been with Bethia when she went into the water. Or did someone else stand there later, after she'd gone in? Nasmyth was supposed to have searched all night after hearing she was missing. Did he come there later? Or was he there with her when she fell in? 'Have you heard anything more about Arthur?' asked MacKenzie after a few moments.

O'Flaherty shook his head. 'Nothing.' He sighed and filled their glasses again.

MacKenzie sat back and smiled. He spoke in Gaelic. 'This is good whisky, Jago.'

O'Flaherty replied in Irish. 'It's good to share it with a fellow Gael.'

They sat in silence for a few minutes. MacKenzie stared into the fire, thinking about Bethia.

Finally, O'Flaherty spoke. 'I forgot to mention, John. I've received some intelligence you might find of interest. I got a message in cypher today. The Kiss is to meet in two nights' time at the old castle. I no longer attend, as I told you, but I'm still informed of meetings in case I change my mind. It's no doubt connected to Arran's return.'

MacKenzie thought for a moment. 'I would like to observe proceedings for myself. Is that possible, Jago?'

O'Flaherty smiled. 'There is a place to watch from. Once the drinking starts, no one will notice us. Meet me at the Back Close at eleven.' O'Flaherty went to his clarsach. 'Now, I said I would play you my lament for her.' He began to pluck on the instrument.

MacKenzie sat back and sipped his whisky, letting his mind wander. It was a haunting air of intense sadness. The music encouraged his mind's eye to follow the Avon Water upstream from the Clyde, all the way to the small, flat platform beyond the castle. He saw the dark shape of Bethia on the bank on the open area of ground. He could hear the roar of the water. He could hear her deep breaths. He could smell her fear.

CHAPTER 17

A Ride in the Woods

THE NEXT MORNING, a party made up of MacKenzie, Arran, Drummond, a ghillie and Arran's two men mounted horses in the Back Close and took the track across the gardens, passing through a gate in the boundary wall into the trees of the deer park. Arran and Drummond rode in front, both looking resplendent on their fine horses, gentlemen of the court indeed. After a pleasant trot of about half an hour through the large trees, they came to a clearing of grassland. The ghillie raised his hand for them to stop. About a hundred yards away, at the edge of the trees, was a stag, his long antlers revealing he was a good age. Arran indicated with a nod that MacKenzie should take a shot at him. MacKenzie turned his horse sideways and removed a gun from the holster on his saddle. He was no marksman and had no desire to kill the creature. Taking aim, he fired wide deliberately, missing by yards and sending the beast running off into the undergrowth.

'I'm a bit rusty, gentlemen. I spend little time hunting these days,' he said, smiling. 'I've no doubt scared every deer in miles.'

Arran manoeuvred his horse alongside MacKenzie and handed him a small, fur-covered flask. 'I prefer brandy to whisky, MacKenzie,' he said.

'My second favourite spirit.' MacKenzie took a swig and it was handed round the rest of the party.

For another half hour they trotted through the magnificent trees. It was early autumn and the leaves had begun to change colour to bright yellow and deep red. At about midday they dismounted at the top of a small, treeless hillock. The palace looked like a toy castle miles away in the sea of trees. They sat on blankets and were served food and wine by the ghillie.

'Tell me how your investigation proceeds?' asked Arran as he munched on a chicken leg. 'My mother is driven by her fondness for Bethia.'

MacKenzie filled his pipe with tobacco and lit it before replying. 'I must admit I'm confused, your grace,' he mused.

'Confused?' repeated Arran.

'Everyone I've spoken to describes her as a kind, happy young woman. Why would she take her life? Because she carried Arthur's child? I hardly think so. Because she carried another man's child? Perhaps, but it seems doubtful. No one had any knowledge of her pregnancy until a few days after her body was found. Arthur is described as a sensible and serious man, but he's fled, taking no responsibility for any of it.'

Arran shook his head, disgruntled. 'I share your concerns, MacKenzie. But I must say one thing before you continue. Bethia was not quite the angel you describe.'

'What do you mean, your grace?' asked MacKenzie.

'I don't like upsetting my mother, so I say little about it in her company. Bethia knew she was a beauty. She knew she attracted the attention of men. And she enjoyed it. She flirted. She flirted with me. She would lead me on with her eyes. Then when I placed my hands on her, seeking only a kiss or slight touch, no more than that, repelling me.'

'Have you seen this side of her, Drummond?' asked MacKenzie.

'I've seen her being forward with my lord, sir. Perhaps she has lain with more than one man, who can say,' Drummond replied coldly. 'Perhaps she didn't know whose bairn she carried. Perhaps that's what tipped her over the edge.'

MacKenzie wondered why their descriptions were so different from everyone else's. Instinctively, he did not trust them an inch. Courts attracted rogues, whether in the Highlands or London. Why would they seek to blacken her name?

Arran glugged his wine and blurted out: 'She killed herself. There's nothing more sinister at work. Arthur is a weak man, unable to come to terms with her demise. I don't think we'll see him in these parts again. As for my mother, she's obsessed with the past. Obsessed with that journey north with her three ladies. It's the curse of old age that distant memories are more vital than those of the day before. We should just accept Bethia is dead and let things be.'

MacKenzie drank some wine. He knew men like Arran would abuse a woman without a moment's remorse. Was he one of those alluded to by Janet Dobbie? Had Arran forced himself on her? If that was the case, however, would she not have been protected by the family for carrying his bastard? She would have been removed to another house to give birth and supported elsewhere. Unless Arthur had caused trouble. Had he confronted Arran for abusing Bethia? Had Arran got rid of him? Arran would not have bothered unless the accusation was rape. He decided to move the conversation in a different direction. 'You have supported the old king in the past, my lord?'

Arran nodded. 'We all make mistakes. I spent a year in the Tower of London for it. I tread more carefully now. I've learned my lesson.'

MacKenzie got to his feet and stretched his back before packing his pipe with fresh tobacco and asking nonchalantly, 'What is the Cadzow Kiss, your grace?'

Arran smiled. 'I see you've been delving into our local customs. Just a little drinking club. They are not peculiar to Lanarkshire, you know. Such associations are found across the land, indeed the world. It's just some fun. Nothing more.'

'Are you a participant in the fun, my lord?' asked MacKenzie.

Arran laughed. 'I will not deny it. It's a little diversion when I'm back in the old country. A night of licence away from the prying eyes of elders. It keeps the men of the parish content.'

'Surely not all the men of the parish?' asked MacKenzie. 'Do Quakers or Presbyterians attend?'

Arran laughed again. 'Only those lucky enough to be asked. Are you seeking an invitation, MacKenzie?'

'I fear your mother would not look kindly on my presence there.' MacKenzie turned to Drummond. 'Have you attended, Mr Drummond?'

Drummond smiled. 'The Kiss is tame entertainment compared to the brothels of London or Paris.'

'I'm told the Kiss met in the old castle on the night Bethia drowned,' said MacKenzie, staring out over the trees.

Arran got to his feet and brushed the crumbs from his jacket and trousers. 'There was a meeting that night. I often combine a visit home with a gathering of… old friends. The Kiss is a good place to learn what's been going on. We sing and drink and dance and partake in daft rituals. In the morning, we wake up feeling worse for wear, but with a smile on our faces when we recall the night before.'

'Was Bethia in attendance that night?' asked MacKenzie.

Arran laughed and shook his head. 'You think she ran from the Kiss into the waters of the Avon? That is a little far-fetched. A girl like her was never seen near the Kiss. It's an association for men only. The women come from Glasgow and there's only one present at a time.'

'Could you tell me those who were there that night, my lord? One of them might have seen something in the woods beside the Avon relevant to Bethia's death.'

'It's a secret association. I cannot reveal the names. Drummond and I were there, as was a voluptuous girl from Glasgow whose name I cannot recall. It's against the rules to identify anyone. They would not name me. We are a loyal brotherhood. I doubt if any would remember anything anyway.'

'It's just that men were seen in the woods near the castle that night. Men described as being from beyond the parish, speaking French, some finely dressed.' MacKenzie decided to embellish Hugh Wood's account to provoke a reaction.

Arran shook his head. 'Complete nonsense! Who is your witness? A drunk! Some dress in their finery for the Kiss. Frenchmen work in the palace. Who is to say they do not attend?'

'I cannot tell you, your grace. The witness is mistaken?'

Arran guffawed. 'Are you suggesting French soldiers were at the Kiss? It's all a bit ridiculous. Some wear their old uniforms from days in the army or militia. It adds to the spectacle. Listen, MacKenzie, the girl lapsed and for some reason, which we'll never know, could suffer life no more. The sheriff-depute investigated the case. His judgement was suicide and murder of an unborn child.' The tone of Arran's voice changed and there was a hint of menace. 'I suggest you tell my mother you've found nothing. She must accept the explanation of self-murder due to moral lapse. It's best for everyone the matter is laid to rest. You should return to Edinburgh as soon as possible to tend your garden. You'll be compensated for your trouble.'

MacKenzie continued to stare out over the trees. 'There's something that unsettles me about it all. Like an itch under an old scar. I cannot give up these things. I will of course take guidance from your mother. I'll speak with her later and tell her my thoughts about the affair. If she wishes, I'll leave for Edinburgh right away and think upon the case no more. If she demands I continue with my investigations, that's what I must do.'

'So be it. I would prefer you left now. There's no word of Arthur?' said Arran, mounting his horse.

MacKenzie shook his head. 'My assistant has been looking for him in Glasgow. We might be able to clear up the history of her death if he's found. Do you not think, your grace?'

Arran shook his head angrily. 'You're wasting your time. He's probably out of the country already. He may be an old man by the time he returns to Hamilton. I'll speak to my mother as well. I'll encourage her to send you on your way. We don't want to waste any more of your time.'

Once MacKenzie had mounted his horse, he asked: 'Is Grinton the main financial beneficiary of her death?'

'Grinton benefits to the sum of a few hundred pounds,' said Arran. 'He has not the gumption to kill a cat, never mind drown his second cousin. He lives comfortably anyway. Why would he kill her?'

'I've heard someone else hoped to wed her,' said MacKenzie.

Arran laughed. 'That's news to me! Who is it?'

'I was hoping you could tell me, your grace.'

Arran did not reply and moved off ahead. Drummond steered his horse alongside MacKenzie. He spoke coldly: 'I would take my lord's warning seriously, Mr MacKenzie. It's best you are gone as soon as possible. It would be unwise to get on the wrong side of him. He's a powerful man. One day he may reach the top.'

Before MacKenzie could answer, Drummond turned his horse. MacKenzie dug his boots into his horse's sides. They caught up with Arran at the edge of the clearing.

'Did your brother Basil admire Bethia too?' asked MacKenzie.

'I would not be surprised if he did. She caught the eye of most men.'

MacKenzie smiled. 'I must take my leave, your grace. I've enjoyed myself immensely, although we have no kill. I'll leave you gentlemen to pursue the stag. I fear you'll make a better show of it without me. I have business at Grinton House this afternoon.'

CHAPTER 18

A Visit to the Gorbals

AS SCOUGALL READ another note from Mackenzie over breakfast, he regretted the two bottles of wine he had shared with Lawtie the night before. He did not usually drink so much and felt jaded. He still did not take to Lawtie, despite the doctor unexpectedly paying the bill. Lawtie, who was well known for being careful with his money, had no doubt hoped a few glasses would loosen Scougall's tongue so he could learn some gossip about MacKenzie. Lawtie had a sly comment about everyone: what did a bonnie lass like Chrissie see in a man like him? Had the old bat, Mrs Hair, lost her marbles yet? Why was MacKenzie not locked up as an inveterate Jacobite? They were all made with a smirk, suggesting he was only half serious, but Scougall was forced to drink glass after glass to smother his irritation. He did, however, glean a few details about Lawtie's life which he did not know before. Lawtie had trained as a doctor in Glasgow in the 1650s and moved to Edinburgh in the 1660s. He had suffered misfortune, losing his wife and son to plague; perhaps he was embittered by the experience. Despite feeling some sympathy for him, Scougall hoped to avoid him during the rest of his stay in the city.

In the late morning, after short meetings in Gibson's snug with a couple of merchants who sought small loans, Scougall walked down to the Clyde. The river was spanned by the biggest bridge he had ever seen in his life, its eight arches a wonder of construction compared to the short, humpbacked crossings over the Water of Leith in Edinburgh. He walked leisurely across, looking at the slow-moving water and recalling that Bethia Porterfield had drowned upstream. He thought of Chrissie and was touched by a feeling of loneliness. He closed his eyes and offered a short prayer to God that their bairn's arrival would wait until his return home, and that all would be well.

On the south side of the river, he took the road to the east which afforded fine views of Glasgow's towers and spires across the water. Soon he was in the small village of the Gorbals, just a few scattered dwelling places.

Turner's abode was a solid laird's house in a large garden, the most substantial one in the village, with a lovely view over the river. Scougall was anxious about meeting such an experienced military man who had led a glittering career in the armies of the Russian Czar. An old servant, who answered the door solemnly, showed Scougall into a room looking onto the garden through French windows. The chamber was crammed with an odd assortment of paintings, prints and exotic creatures frozen by taxidermy. Another old man sat at the fire, reading. Turner put his book down, took off his spectacles and rose stiffly to his feet. A large man, stooped by age and unsteady on his feet, he was wigless with a shock of grey hair sticking out from both sides of a bald head. With the help of a stick, he crossed the room and shook Scougall's hand warmly, before beckoning him to sit in the chair opposite him at the fire. In his fluster, Scougall forgot to test Turner's Masonic credentials.

Turner dropped back into his chair, painfully. 'Old bones, Mr Scougall! To what do I owe a visit from an Edinburgh notary. In my experience, a call from a lawyer is never good news.' He spoke in a deep, throaty voice, but his serious expression quickly broke into a smile and he laughed loudly. The laugh became a croaking cough.

Scougall waited for the coughing fit to subside. 'I'm sorry to disturb you, sir. I'm sent by my colleague John MacKenzie, advocate in Edinburgh. He's a guest at Hamilton Palace attending the legal business of the duchess. He's asked me to call on you about Arthur Nasmyth.'

Turner let out a deep sigh and shook his head. He sat up and called for wine from his servant. 'Why does MacKenzie want to know about him?' he asked gruffly, his face resuming a stern expression and his eyes narrowing.

'The duchess wishes to understand Bethia's death. I believe Bethia was the granddaughter of one of her ladies who travelled north with her during the civil wars.' Scougall repeated what he had learned from MacKenzie. 'And also, to locate Arthur for his mother, who is very worried.'

The servant entered with wine and filled two glasses. Sir James took a long draught, emptying his glass. He looked fiercely at Scougall for a moment, but his truculence melted and he smiled thinly. 'I'm aggrieved about the whole business, Mr Scougall. It has afflicted me acutely. His mother came to see me in an awful state to break the dreadful news. I knew Bethia well. She'd often come to the Gorbals with Arthur. I'm his godfather and very fond of him. He visited me every week when he was in Glasgow. He's like a son to me, for I have none of my own, having devoted myself to soldiering. When I was in better health, we walked in the country together, often down to Bothwell Castle. We liked to talk long into the night. He loved stories of my military days and, of course, any mention of his brave father. I read him extracts from my memoirs. I fear I've engendered a desire in him to be a soldier, although I always advised him the law would make a more sensible profession for a clever man like him. Nonetheless, I think he would make a good soldier. He doesn't mind being told what to do. I certainly don't think he has the right character for the ministry, as some have suggested. Bethia, however, was against him joining a regiment. I can understand why – the uncertainty and years of absence. It's not a life for a happily married man, although perhaps it is for an unhappily married one. You need to be independent, a loner, like me.' He smiled ruefully.

Scougall sipped his wine. 'Do you have any idea where he is, sir? I've learned he stayed at the Northern Sugar House for a few days after he came to Glasgow. He left in the company of an unidentified person. Since then, no one has seen anything of him, nor heard anything from him.'

Turner shook his head. 'I've not seen him since May, Mr Scougall. At least a month before Bethia's death. I fear he's taken ship or joined a regiment. I've sent my servants to search in Glasgow and the surrounding parishes half a dozen times. If I hear anything, I'll of course inform his mother and the duchess immediately.'

'I found this, sir. In the chamber in the Sugar Works where he was hiding.' Scougall handed him the crumpled pamphlet about the Carolina venture.

Turner examined it and nodded. 'This is the kind of thing he would be attracted by.'

'Do you think he's taken ship with the adventurers?'

'It's possible, Mr Scougall. It's the kind of rash decision a desperate young man makes. He was devastated by Bethia's death.'

'What do you think happened to her?'

Turner sat back in his chair and looked down at his large, scarred hands. 'I know no more about it than anyone else.' He hesitated for a moment. 'I've heard she was pregnant. I've heard the child was Arthur's and that it was not Arthur's. Some say she could not face the shame and drowned herself and her unborn child. It's dreadful she should be driven to such action. It's appalling the kirk should have such power over people. It supposedly promulgates Christ's message of love.' He hesitated again. 'They have such a rigid position on many issues. I believe the church has lost its way.'

'Do you believe that's what happened, sir?' asked Scougall.

Turner finished his drink and called for another bottle. He waited until his old servant filled his glass to the brim. He shook his head. 'It doesn't make any sense to me. None of it makes any sense. But sometimes tragedies happen. I don't believe she would kill her child, especially if it was Arthur's. Even if it wasn't Arthur's. After all, the child was completely innocent. I've wondered if someone forced himself upon her and she could not face the humiliation. Perhaps she could not bear life after being debauched. Perhaps she lost her mind for some reason. I would like to know the truth myself and, of course, where Arthur has gone. Perhaps he can be encouraged back from the Carolinas, if that's where he is. I miss the boy terribly!'

Scougall smiled. 'He's not sent you a letter or message since his disappearance?'

Turner shook his head. 'I received a note from him a couple of days before she died. It said little of interest. Let me find it anyway.' He rose and shuffled over to a desk at the back of the room which was covered in documents and papers. He rummaged for a minute and returned with a letter. Scougall looked down at it, noticing Nasmyth's neat hand.

10th June 1691
Nasmyth House

My dear Sir James,
It has been too long since we last shared a bottle and I heard some good stories from my dear godfather. I hope to visit you very soon, but some business has arisen out of the blue which will take up my time over the next few days in Hamilton. When it is resolved, I will visit the Gorbals on my way back to Glasgow and you may read me the latest instalment of your memoirs, which I look forward to very much.

Your beloved godson,
Arthur Nasmyth

Scougall read it again carefully, trying to commit the contents to memory. He noticed the unusual flourish under the 'y' in Nasmyth. 'Do you know what business he refers to, sir?' he asked.

Turner shook his head. 'I've no idea. It was unusual for him to write such a thing. I've never heard him refer to business in any letter he ever sent me. Most of his missives were very short indeed, usually little more than a few words, such as "I will call tomorrow or on such-and-such day at such-and-such time" or "I will drop in on my way to Hamilton to see you tomorrow afternoon." I cannot imagine what the business he refers to could be. It might be connected to the Nasmyth estate, although he showed little interest in it, or perhaps his future in the military or arrangements for his wedding.' Turner shrugged his shoulders.

Scougall suddenly had a thought. 'Could it refer to political business? There's much going on in Ireland?'

Turner looked puzzled and shook his head. 'Arthur has no interest in politics. He's neither strong for the old king or the new one. If he had to choose, I suppose he would support the old one, reluctantly, like many of us, who are shocked and surprised by the recent revolution in the government. He showed no interest in the rights and wrongs of the change. He is, however, very interested, like I am, in recent battles, in particular the Jacobite victory at Killiecrankie and the skirmishes at Dunkeld and Cromdale. We've discussed them often from a military point of view, in particular Dundee's use of a downhill charge of Highland troops. We never debated the politics of the business.'

'Do you know any of his close friends?' asked Scougall.

Turner thought for a moment and nodded. 'He's particularly close to Archie Weir and Robert Corse. Archie is the son of a sugar merchant. You've mentioned his father's concern already. He plays the fool most of the time, joking and boozing, but is not a bad lad. Robert is a school friend from Hamilton. They shared chambers in Glasgow. He studies for the church but is no fanatic, unlike his kinsmen. I know them both well and believe they would have informed me if they knew anything about Arthur's whereabouts.'

'Were there any others?'

'I've met a number over the years, mostly thin students. None stick in my mind. A few times his regent, Alexander Cruikshank, accompanied him on walks and called in here. They are all fine young men who liked a drink and a story, and I have a wealth of both. I would describe Robert as a steady figure, prone to doing and saying the right thing, a little too eager to please the powers that be. I'm not surprised he studies for the ministry. Archie had more of a twinkle in his eye. Both good men who loved Arthur well. I don't know how Robert will fare as a preacher. I suppose a man must do something with his life. Archie likes the bottle, I've heard, and is bored working with his father. He desires a different life, wanting to go to the Caribbean to work as a planter where fortunes can be made, but lives lost – the same as a military career.'

'What about Cruikshank?'

Turner shrugged. 'A good enough man. He has the condescending demeanour of the scholar. He seemed mighty fond of Arthur. He was always saying he was one of his best students.'

Scougall looked round the room while he was trying to think of another question. His eye was caught by a stuffed monkey on a shelf. It peered down at him mockingly. Above it was a huge, curved sword.

Turner noticed Scougall's gaze. 'A lifetime in foreign climes, Mr Scougall. The sword is a scimitar. I cannot throw anything away. They help me remember. They help me differentiate one skirmish from another. I've lived a lifetime of battles.'

'Can you think of anything else, Sir James, anything that has happened recently in Glasgow or Hamilton, anything out of the ordinary that might shed light on events?'

Sir James thought for a few moments, then emptied his glass again before replying. 'There's just one thing, Mr Scougall. A few days before the terrible event of Bethia's drowning, I received a visit from Archie Weir. Sometimes he would say hello to me when passing through the village. This time he came in and we shared a bottle.'

'What did you talk about, sir?'

'Oh, the usual gossip and tales of my army days. I do remember him asking if I had seen Arthur recently. He said Arthur was not his usual self of late and wondered if he'd confided in me. I told him he had not. It was unusual. I'd not seen Arthur in weeks. Archie said they had argued before he left Glasgow for Hamilton and he'd not heard from him. I asked what they argued about. He said it was nothing important and left.'

CHAPTER 19

A Walk by the Clyde

MACKENZIE TOOK A horse from the palace stables. He had sent a message to Grinton after breakfast that he would visit him in the afternoon. Grinton House, a somewhat decayed and ramshackle laird's dwelling, its construction dating back to the previous century, was a few miles south of Hamilton, accessed by a winding track through pastureland beside the Clyde. A large man standing at the front door raised a stick in welcome as MacKenzie dismounted.

'You received my message, Grinton?' asked MacKenzie, doffing his hat.

Grinton's red-cheeked face beamed brightly in the sunshine. MacKenzie was able to observe him more clearly than on their first meeting in the flickering candlelight of the palace dining room.

'It's a pleasure to spend some time with a gentleman from the north,' said Grinton, coming down the path stick first. 'It's a fine day, so let's not linger inside my stuffy abode. The path to the Clyde is this way. Let's enjoy the majestic river. There are many fine vistas, as you'll see.'

MacKenzie followed him across the road, over a style, which creaked under the laird's considerable bulk, and along a muddy track through marshland. As they rounded a clump of birch trees, a fine view of the river opened up, its brown water sparkling. 'A bonnie sight, Grinton,' said MacKenzie appreciatively.

'A fine one indeed, Mr MacKenzie. I enjoy it every day of my life. I walk by the river come rain or shine, summer or winter. I'm a creature of habit. I usually saunter by the river in the morning and stroll on the moor in the afternoon. I have changed by routine today for you.'

When the path reached the water, Grinton stopped and admired the view. MacKenzie stood beside him, looking across to the other bank where a horse and cart trundled by. It was a tranquil scene from a Dutch landscape painting. A blue sky beyond with perfect white clouds.

'Were you born in Hamilton?' asked MacKenzie.

Grinton smiled. 'I was born back there in Grinton House where I've lived all my life, except one foolish sojourn to Paris in my eighteenth year which I mentioned at dinner. I love the peace of the countryside. My father died not long after my return from France and I inherited the estate. Folk keep telling me to see something of the world. But I'm not ambitious like other men who huff and puff in the battle of life. I take things as I find them. I've no desire for public service. I don't wish to attend parliament in Edinburgh, nor pay homage to the king at court in London. I've no desire to meet whoever holds that position, nor the nobles who fawn around him. I do not wish to serve on the sheriff court nor the tedious kirk session with local worthies. I visit Glasgow a couple of times a year to buy wine and provisions. Otherwise, I'm content to tend my cows and grow my corn. I'm just a farmer with a few tenants scattered around and a couple of servants to serve me in my house. I attend the kirk on the sabbath as I'm expected to, though with no great relish. I'm glad to escape the place. I find ministers dreadful bores. My great delight is to dine with the duchess. There's no better company in the kingdom of Scotland. No more perceptive critic of the world than she. No kinder soul. That's enough social life for me. I'm really quite happy.' Grinton smiled at his own bulky reflection in the water.

MacKenzie nodded and returned the smile. 'I'm glad to find a contented man, Grinton. Not many can say so in these days of strife. Philosophers have provided many ideas for achieving happiness, but few have found it. I've attained it only fleetingly.'

Grinton turned to MacKenzie and looked him straight in the eyes. 'I'm sorry to hear that, Mr MacKenzie. I read a little philosophy myself in my youth. I remember little of it now, except some of the strange ideas of Diogenes. I believe the secret of happiness is quite simple and requires no great insight – a good walk each day for at least an hour with a fine view to enjoy, a good dinner with a bottle of claret, a good book when the weather is bad, a little company (not too much), a good night's sleep and, finally, as little speculation as possible about the reason we are here and the hereafter.'

MacKenzie chuckled. Grinton was not quite the buffoon he had appeared on first meeting. 'Your bedfellow is dead, sir?' he asked.

'Long gone, Mr MacKenzie. I was still a young man when she died. She left me no children. I've accepted it as God's will. I might have added the company of a good woman to my list,' Grinton laughed, 'but I believe that would be a bonus. A single life has its benefits.'

'You've not considered marrying again?' asked MacKenzie.

Grinton turned to MacKenzie, looking surprised. 'You know, sir, it has passed through my mind from time to time over the years, usually during periods of madness! I recently thought I might marry again. I don't know what came over me. I suppose something stirred within me. I made an offer to my second cousin herself, the tragic Bethia.'

MacKenzie was surprised by the revelation but tried not to show it.

'Just a few months before she died,' continued Grinton. 'Of course, she declined me immediately with a smile and I accepted her decision graciously. She had already received an offer from a younger man, the unlucky Arthur Nasmyth. I may make an offer to another woman if one catches my eye, although I hope I do not. I doubt if anyone will accept me anyway. I'm too old and the house too cold and there are too many dogs in my chamber at night. A dog is an agreeable bedfellow and much less expensive than a wife!' he guffawed.

'Were you not grieved when she turned you down?' asked MacKenzie.

'Of course, I was disappointed. But it wasn't unexpected. I'm hardly an exciting prospect. Some women are attracted by the security of a landed estate, many are not. They seek that mysterious thing called love. I don't know what that kind of love is.'

'So, you bore her no ill will?'

Grinton grinned widely. 'I rarely suffer ill will, Mr MacKenzie. Only when I'm forced to spend time away from my beloved Clyde. I'm easy, as they say. I was mocked for it as a schoolboy. I don't stir to anger easily. Some regard me as an eccentric who eats too much pie and sups too long at the nappy. When she rejected me, I shrugged my shoulders, kissed her hand and dined with the duchess that evening. I slept contentedly all night, much more deeply than if she'd accepted my proposal. That would have sent me into a commotion!'

MacKenzie nodded. It felt awkward to ask the affable Grinton such probing questions, but it was necessary. 'I believe you are a beneficiary of her death in monetary terms?'

Grinton nodded solemnly. 'As her nearest living kin, I'll inherit the little property she possessed. It will not change my life in any way, although I'll die a few pounds richer. If her death is confirmed as suicide, the escheat of her moveable goods will be purchased by some worthy adventurer no doubt. It will not be bought by me. It would all be too much bother. You cannot be suggesting I killed her for £200 Scots a year?'

MacKenzie shook his head and was forced to laugh. It sounded preposterous. 'As a lawyer, I must ask these questions. Have you heard anything about the escheat's progress?'

Grinton shook his head. 'These things get bogged down in the law. I heard David Crawford is considering it. As a local worthy, he'll benefit more than others.'

'What do you mean?'

'He has experience administering land. A small amount of legal work will be no burden for him. For anyone else, it would be an awful headache.'

Grinton stopped to wave at a man across the river, then beckoned MacKenzie to continue along the path. A heron stood motionless on the rocks on the far bank.

'What do you think happened to her?' asked MacKenzie, as the path turned away from the river and headed back towards the house.

Grinton stopped in his tracks and spoke more seriously. 'Many in this parish regard me as a fool. I'm different from other folk. I take each day as I find it and try to find some happiness in it. I am, however, a keen observer of my fellow creatures. I've come to learn most are complete fools. They chase their tails like puppies, their lives focused on pointless goals. Many are harmless, some are not. I see things when I'm out on my walks by the river or on the moor. There's no man in the parish who knows the hinterland better than I. I record what I observe in my diary. I note mundane things, such as the day of the year on which the first rose bloomed or the first lamb was born, how much rain there was and how much wind.' He stopped to emphasise what followed: 'I've heard and observed strange occurrences in the parish recently.'

'Please tell me more, Grinton,' said MacKenzie.

'Firstly, I've heard that special guests attended the last meeting of the Cadzow Kiss in June. You've heard of the association?'

MacKenzie nodded. 'I've heard about it from a few people. Special guests? What do you mean?'

'I've heard them described as foreign guests, speaking the French language.'

'Why would they be speaking French?' asked MacKenzie.

'I believe the question is why were they speaking French in Hamilton?'

MacKenzie smiled. 'Why were they here?'

'I don't know, Mr MacKenzie. There are a few French servants in the palace. I believe there's a Huguenot by the name of Gaspord Chambon.

It's possible it was him or one of the other French servants.'

'Were they perhaps smugglers or soldiers?' asked MacKenzie.

'That's possible, too,' replied Grinton.

'Were you at the Kiss yourself on that occasion?' asked MacKenzie.

Grinton smiled. 'I've not attended in many years. I was dragged along once or twice when I was a young man. I tired of its frolics quickly. It attracts those who want to rise in society, or who are worried about their status and seek to cling to the earl's interest. However, I hear about it as much as any other. I catch conversations when I take my cup of ale in the tavern every afternoon. My servants can be encouraged to divulge a little gossip after a glass or two of wine at the end of the day, or by the offer of a shilling or two.'

MacKenzie looked puzzled. 'Is it just a coincidence that the Kiss met on the night Bethia fell into the Avon? Or is there a connection between the Kiss and her death?' he asked. Grinton was proving a much more perceptive observer than he had expected.

Grinton replied: 'I don't know of any connection. But it's strange, would you not say, that she drowned on the very same night.'

MacKenzie nodded. 'Indeed. And what other occurrences do you refer to?'

Grinton placed his stick in the ground and leant against it. Sweat was dripping down his generous cheeks. 'The second occurrence is the recent attack on the Quaker burial ground. It's strange because Quakers have lived among us for years, indeed decades, and, as far as I know, have done little harm to anyone – indeed, they have done much good as honest and able workers and servants. The duchess employs a few in the palace and so do I, including my servant Richie Rae, a good, loyal man. Then their burial ground is destroyed. It was one of the most savage things I ever saw in my life.'

'You witnessed it yourself?'

Grinton nodded grimly. 'I was coming back from my walk on the moor in the gloaming. At first, I thought I had heard thunder in the distance, then I realised it was horses coming up the hill towards me. I was beside a rock where I often sit, looking across the moor. A group of the riders appeared at a gallop round the bend in the track. Worried that I might be seen, I ducked down behind to watch. I counted twenty of them, riding up the road from Hamilton to the burial ground at the top of the knoll. It was like a storm approaching, menacing, disturbing.

'As they got closer, I could make out a few faces under broad-brimmed hats and saw they carried weapons. They were mostly local ruffians from across the parish and beyond. They halted about ten yards from the wall of the cemetery. By then it was almost dark. There was only a ribbon of light on the horizon, just enough to see their black silhouettes. Suddenly there was a flare of orange as a torch was lit and from it another. One rider jumped the wall and rode across the burial ground to leap the wall on the far side. With torch raised, he rode back round, passing from tree to tree, setting them ablaze. The others moved forward one by one, leaping the dyke, and began turning their horses inside and moving back and forth, ploughing up the earth. Some dismounted and hacked at the stones of the wall, as if they worked in a quarry, smashing them to pieces, breaking it entirely in places, and throwing the stones to the four winds. Others dug the soil, throwing the few tombstones aside and the black earth everywhere, turning up the bones of the dead, who were not buried deep. Skulls were thrown between them like playthings. One was kicked like a football against the wall and smashed like a puff ball. Another was pulverized by a spade, then stamped on. The destruction was complete in twenty minutes. The graveyard looked like an ancient ruin or lonely sheepfold deserted by men long ago.

'When the riders had remounted, I heard one saying a prayer. Then they turned their horses towards the town, cantering at first, before galloping into the darkness. I came down from my hiding place, my stick probing the way until the burning trees provided light, and entered what was left of the holy ground. It was a place I had hardly considered before, having always passed it by as of little aesthetic worth. I wandered among the bones of the dead, the burning trees warming the air around me. It had been a day like any other. I had left my house in the early afternoon and walked for miles, happily. But I had witnessed an act of desecration. I made my way back home, troubled by the nature of men.'

'Who do you think was behind it, Grinton?'

'I believe an association called the Black Band.'

'The Black Band?' repeated MacKenzie.

'A group of fanatics with origins in the Covenanting years.'

'Can you name any of them?'

'I can only tell you what I've heard. The leaders are men like John Spreull, William Corse, Arthur Renwick and Archibald Cameron. They don't get their hands dirty but encourage others to commit acts of violence.'

'Do you mean the merchant William Corse? My assistant, Davie

Scougall, met with him in Glasgow.'

'None of them are well known to me,' continued Grinton. 'His nephew Robert is a different man. I've no time for hotheads who shove their religion in your face. They tried to persuade me to attend their outdoor conventicles, as they called them, countless times. I didn't answer the door when I saw them approaching.'

'What can you tell me about William Corse?' asked MacKenzie.

'He was imprisoned on the Bass before being sent to the Caribbean as indentured labour. He rose miraculously to become a rich planter and recently returned to Scotland. He's a man of wealth and power, but a thoroughly wicked individual who cloaks himself as a religious man. He has influence among the Presbyterian societies who were active in the recent revolution due to money gained from the plantation trade. He's the kind of man who does the world not a shred of good.'

'Why would he want to destroy the Quakers?'

'I can only tell you what I've heard. Corse has faced difficulties in recent voyages between Africa and the Caribbean. A ship he owned a half share in sank off Africa and another was taken by pirates. As a result, he cannot pay his debts, while those who owe him money refuse to pay him. There's another inexplicable thing about Corse. I've seen him in the company of the Earl of Arran. It was very surprising as they come from different political poles. Sometimes rogues drink from the same trough.'

'When and where did you see them?' asked MacKenzie.

'I saw them a few months ago. I was on the path beyond Millheugh on a walk on the moor. They were deep in discussion. Arran was with his two men and Drummond, his secretary. I could not hear what they said, but they were scheming about something. Why would an irreligious noble have anything to do with a Covenanting merchant? They sought to gain something from each other.'

'How do you regard Arran?'

'I don't like to speak ill of the duchess's children. However, Arran is not suited to lead the house of Hamilton. He spends huge sums of money in London. He plots, currying favour with both sides. There's a burning desire in him for acclaim. I fear he will undo all the good work done by the duchess since the palace was returned to the family after the fall of Cromwell.'

'He's been imprisoned in the Tower already,' said MacKenzie.

Grinton nodded. 'He views the Hamilton estates only as a source of money to fund his life in London and hopes a rich English bride will bail him out of his vast debts. He cares nothing for the Clyde Valley or Scotland. Once he has a sizeable estate in England he'll settle there. Hamilton is just the means of his own aggrandizement. He has not a thread of morality.'

The path turned away from the river back through the fields. Grinton House stood across the orchard in the sunlight. They had come full circle. At the gate, MacKenzie thanked Grinton for his time. 'If you learn anything more, please contact me at the palace. I must return to speak with the duchess.'

'Ah, you must make haste, Mr MacKenzie. She's a remarkable woman, a remarkable woman. I would do anything for her. A truly good soul. I've not met many of those in my life. I would do anything for her... it's a great shame,' he paused for a moment then continued, 'a great shame her eldest son is such a... rogue.'

MacKenzie nodded thoughtfully. He wondered about the relationship between Arran and Corse. Could Arran have used Corse to spread the story of Bethia's pregnancy? 'That's useful intelligence, Grinton,' he said. 'Just one final question about the family. What kind of man is Lord Basil?'

'Ah, our dinner guest. Young Basil is a good one, if somewhat naïve. A bit of a dreamer, always talking about trade and colonies and his desire to see the world because of his containment at the palace. I wish he was the heir and not his elder brother. Sadly, Basil worships his brother and is prone to copy him.'

CHAPTER 20

The Road to Hamilton

SCOUGALL SETTLED HIS bill and caught the coach for Hamilton outside Gibson's Tavern. There was already a man and young woman inside. The woman was wearing a shabby dress and shawl. She smiled at him as he climbed in. When the man looked up from his book, Scougall realised it was Simon Gilly, the chaplain he had met in the snug.

'Ah, Mr Scougall we meet again,' Gilly said, moving across to give Scougall room to sit beside him just as the horses took off and the coach jolted forward.

Scougall had to apologise to the woman for standing on her foot.

'You're heading for the palace, Mr Scougall?' asked Gilly.

'I'm joining Mr MacKenzie there for a few days. Are you returning to Hamilton?'

'I'm on my way to the palace also,' said Gilly. 'I've heard the earl has returned. It might be a busy couple of days.'

Scougall recalled the debt owed by Arran to William Corse and Cruikshank's story about Arran being the father of Bethia's child. He stole a look at the young woman. 'Are you bound for Hamilton also, madam?' he asked her.

She smiled knowingly. 'Indeed, sir. Just for one night. Back tae Glasgow tomorrow.'

Gilly closed his book. 'Have you learned anything more about Arthur?' he asked.

'I've learned... a little.' Scougall hesitated before saying anything more. He did not want to divulge anything in front of the woman.

'Well, Mr Scougall, it's fortunate we're travelling together. I've learned something you may find interesting. The pamphlet you were reading about the voyage to the Carolinas. I've some information about the venture.'

'Please tell me, Mr Gilly.'

'The ship left Ayr on the 18th of June with a hundred and twenty colonists and provisions for a year. I heard this morning they have made land in a most promising location, only losing a small number to disease on the voyage.'

'That's good news, Mr Gilly,' said Scougall.

'Once the colony is established,' continued Gilly, 'I've some hopes of serving the community there. I'll keep you informed of news after your return to Edinburgh in case a second ship is sent. They'll need more men and women. I'm sure you would be favoured,' Gilly said knowingly.

Scougall wondered about Chrissie's reaction to such a voyage with a young child. He doubted she would look favourably on it. 'So, you think Arthur may now be in America?' he asked.

Gilly nodded. 'If he was on the ship from Ayr and did not succumb to disease on the crossing. I've an associate who travelled on the vessel. The son of a Glasgow merchant. He'll be able to tell me for sure. He said he would write once they made land in America. It may take a few weeks or months to confirm if Arthur sailed with them. But we'll eventually know for certain.'

Scougall sat back, pleased with what he had learned. 'You said you'll be busy now that Arran has returned?' he asked casually.

Gilly smiled. 'I'll not be particularly busy in the chapel… with religious services that is. The earl has little interest in such things. There will be a few… other events to honour his presence… gatherings of friends and associates and parties…it's always a time of excitement in the palace and town when he returns.'

CHAPTER 21

A Disrupted Dinner

ON ARRIVING AT the palace, Scougall was told dinner would be served in twenty minutes. As a result, he only had a short time to settle into his room on the other side of the palace from MacKenzie. He unpacked quickly and changed his shirt. MacKenzie told him they would have time to discuss the case in detail after dinner. As Scougall looked out his window over the gardens, he had to pinch himself. Here he was, a guest in the famous Hamilton Palace! A few minutes later, in a state of amazement and nervous excitement, he found himself sitting in the High Dining Room. His journey from a humble dwelling in Musselburgh to the table of the highest noblewoman in the land seemed incredible. The famous duchess, renowned Presbyterian, sat across from him between her sons, the Earl of Arran and Lord Basil Hamilton. MacKenzie was at his side. On MacKenzie's other side was Simon Gilly.

'How did you find Glasgow, Mr Scougall?' asked the duchess once she had said grace and the soup had been served.

'I found it very well, your grace. It's my third visit to the city. I find it thriving,' Scougall replied nervously.

'Your business is the foreign trade, Mr Scougall?' asked Lord Basil.

'Yes, partly, my lord. Domestic trade and, increasingly, foreign trade. Merchants trading with the Baltic, of course, also America and the Caribbean. Mrs Hair makes loans to a few merchants in Glasgow already, as well as many in Edinburgh.'

'I've a great desire to see something of the world, in particular the colonies of America, Mr Scougall,' Lord Basil mused.

'As have I, sir,' replied Scougall enthusiastically. 'I've never travelled beyond Scotland, yet.'

'Nor I.' Lord Basil smiled. 'It's time we both went on an adventure.'

'Your time will come, Basil,' said the duchess. 'Now, Mr Scougall, did you find anything of note about Arthur in Glasgow?'

Scougall nodded nervously. 'Just a couple of things, your grace. I learned he spent a few days in a secret chamber in the Sugar Works belonging to Archie Weir's father. He left in the company of someone as yet unidentified. They departed in the evening, heading northwards out of the city. The trail runs cold thereafter.'

'You have hardly discovered much then, Mr Scougall,' said Arran, looking up briefly from his soup.

Scougall was upset by the snide comment but managed to maintain his composure. 'I also found a pamphlet in the chamber promoting a colonial scheme to the Carolinas. The ship left from Ayr in June. Arthur must have been reading it. It's possible he was on board the ship.'

'I've a friend on the venture who will confirm if he was on the vessel,' added Gilly.

'I spoke to Mr Cruikshank at the college,' continued Scougall. 'Also, Archie Weir and Sir James Turner in the Gorbals, as well a few other merchants in the city. Unfortunately, there have been no further sightings of him.'

'It looks like he's left Scotland, mother,' said Arran, putting his spoon down beside an empty bowl. He turned to Scougall, smiling warmly. He could be charming when he wanted to. 'I would like to pick your brains, if I may, while you're here, Mr Scougall.'

Scougall nodded reluctantly.

'A young man like you will be able to provide sound advice on where to obtain... a supply of cash,' added Arran.

Scougall recalled Mrs Hair's warnings about lending to the nobility. However, he could not reject an earl to his face. 'I would be... pleased to guide you, your grace.'

MacKenzie reflected that he had been fortunate to avoid an interrogation by Arran on the ride earlier that day. The earl had found a more attractive prospect and one who was easier to influence.

Just before Arran replied, a servant entered the room and walked up to the table. Standing at Arran's shoulder, he held out a plate. A note rested on it. Arran took it without looking round. The earl's face hardened and his eyebrows dropped. Flinging it down on the table in disgust, he cried: 'My God, can a man not enjoy his dinner in peace! Someone has died in town, mother!'

The duchess looked at her son, fearfully. 'Who is it?' she asked. 'Surely not Arthur?'

'I don't know,' replied Arran. 'A body's been found in William Corse's house on the High Street.'

Scougall was surprised to hear the name of the merchant he had met in Glasgow.

'You'll have to excuse me, gentlemen,' said Arran. 'I have to attend to it. There must be a reason why Crawford has ruined my dinner.'

'May I accompany you, your grace,' said MacKenzie, dabbing his lips with his napkin, 'in case there is some connection to Arthur or Bethia?'

Scougall, who was ravenous after his journey, was disappointed that a bowl of soup would have to suffice. Scougall and MacKenzie bowed deeply to the duchess and Lord Basil, and followed Arran and his men out of the palace. Five minutes later they were on the High Street where a couple of other men stood guard outside a house. Crawford was waiting at the door, looking worried.

'He was found half an hour ago by his wife, your grace,' said Crawford. 'They had travelled down from Glasgow yesterday. I've sent her back to her sister's house. We've not touched him or moved him yet. I don't know what's happened. May I return to the palace? I have business to attend to.'

Arran nodded and Crawford scurried away. They entered the narrow hall of the house and turned into the living chamber on the right. It was a tidy dwelling, furnished with solid, if unflamboyant, oak furniture. A body lay on the floor beside the dining table. A black jacket covered a long back. A wig had fallen onto the floor revealing a bald head and long, grey whiskers. Arran kneeled down and rotated the head slightly to observe the features: 'My God, it's Corse himself,' he said in surprise.

Scougall recognised the old merchant immediately. 'I was with him in Glasgow yesterday!' he blurted out.

Arran continued: 'This is Corse's house. He hailed from Hamilton originally. I believe you've met his nephew Robert, Nasmyth's friend. What was your business with him, Mr Scougall?'

'He was seeking a loan to cover a voyage to Barbados,' said Scougall.

'Now you'll need another home for Mrs Hair's capital,' said Arran with a smile. He seemed little concerned that a dead body was lying at his feet.

Scougall nodded uncertainly.

'We'll speak tomorrow,' continued Arran. 'Mrs Hair would certainly benefit from an association with the highest house in the realm.'

'If I may examine the body, your grace? I have some experience in these matters,' asked MacKenzie, moving towards it.

'Examine all you like, MacKenzie,' replied Arran. 'Corse was an old man, not in the best of health. It's probably a seizure or stroke. Look, he was enjoying his supper.' A knife and fork lay on the floor beside an overturned chair. A plate of food was on the table, half eaten. A bottle of wine. A glass, half full. 'A seizure during dinner, perhaps,' he added.

'It looks like something interrupted his dinner,' said MacKenzie. He got down beside the corpse and examined the neck. 'I believe it was no stroke, sir.'

'What was it? I thought you were a lawyer, not a doctor,' said Arran.

'Look at these bruises, your grace. It would not take a doctor of much experience to determine he's been strangled. Observe the gorged tongue.'

Arran lost his composure. 'Killed! Murdered! In his own house! My God!'

MacKenzie nodded. 'If I may, your grace, I would like to examine the premises before the sheriff arrives. In case I find anything... pertinent.'

'It will be a considerable time before the sheriff is sober enough to get here,' said Arran. 'It may be days, rather than hours. I'll get Crawford to move the body to the tolbooth. Make your examination. I have business in the palace. Come to my chambers at nine o'clock tomorrow morning, Mr Scougall. We'll talk then.'

Arran turned on his heel, followed by his men.

Scougall looked dumbfounded. 'Corse was on the Bass Rock, sir. He was transported to Barbados as indentured labour. He worked his way up to being a wealthy man. To have survived so much, then perish in his own dining room... the Lord's ways are mysterious.'

'You can tell me all you know about him later, Davie. Let's search the house before Crawford drags the body away and destroys any evidence.' MacKenzie began to search through Corse's jacket and pockets. He removed a pair of spectacles, some coins, the stub of a candle and a crumpled note which he read quickly, then handed to Scougall. The short message said: 'Come to the palace at four o'clock.' MacKenzie put in his pocket.

'Should we not leave it for the sheriff?' asked Scougall.

MacKenzie shook his head. 'I'll pass it on when we're done with it, Davie.'

MacKenzie continued to examine the body. He discovered tiny fragments of material behind a couple of Corse's fingernails on his right hand. He took a pair of tweezers from his pocket and removed them, placing them in a handkerchief. He poked at the remains of the bread and cheese on the table and got down on his knees stiffly – it was becoming more difficult as he got older. He eyed the floor closely. It had been swept clean apart from a few crumbs which had fallen from the table. He looked under the table and chairs. He caught sight of something beside a chair leg and reached out for it. It was a small, brown button, unremarkable and slightly frayed. He went back to the body and checked Corse's jacket. None were missing. It might have been lying on the floor for weeks, even years, and be unconnected to the killing. Then again, the floor had been cleaned recently. It could have come from the killer's jacket, dislodged in the act of strangulation. He slipped it into his pocket. He went to the windows of the chamber, then passed round the rest of the building checking the other windows and doors. All were secure. There was no indication of forced entry.

They methodically searched the rest of the house, a two-storey dwelling with a kitchen and larder at the back and two bedrooms on the first floor. They found nothing else of interest. It was sparsely furnished and showed little signs of being inhabited. The presses in the bed chambers were empty and there was nothing in the larder except the remains of the loaf and cheese Corse had dined on. It seemed that he and his wife rarely visited the house.

'It looks like he let his killer in,' said MacKenzie. 'He or she was perhaps known to him. Who would want to kill him, Davie?'

Scougall thought for a moment and shook his head.

'He was a rigid Presbyterian was he not? You might say a fanatic?' asked MacKenzie.

'He was from the enthusiastic wing of the kirk. He might have enemies from his time in Barbados or among those who fought against the Covenanters.'

'Did he mention coming to Hamilton at your meeting?' asked MacKenzie.

Scougall shook his head. 'No, even when I asked him about Bethia.'

'Did you discuss anything else apart from business?'

Scougall thought for a moment. 'I asked him about the attack on the Quakers I witnessed in Glasgow. He said they should be run out of town as blasphemers who supported the old king. He had lost none of his strong feelings on religion.'

'I've also heard his name mentioned among enemies of the Quakers. He may have been behind the attack on their burial ground and the abuse of Bethia's corpse,' reflected MacKenzie.

'He was an old man, sir.'

'Not an active part. Perhaps pulling the strings.'

'Could a Quaker have killed him?' asked Scougall.

MacKenzie shook his head, looking troubled. 'The Quakers abhor violence, although often provoking it in others. However, any man or woman can be driven to kill, and they have received foul treatment. Let's pay a visit to his nephew Robert to see what he can tell us about his uncle. I promised I would share a bottle with him, although I didn't expect it would be under these circumstances.'

CHAPTER 22

A Bottle with Robert Corse

ROBERT CORSE'S HOUSE was on a vennel off the High Street, two minutes' walk from William Corse's dwelling. The divinity student opened the door, looking pale and drawn.

'I presume you've heard about your uncle?' asked MacKenzie.

Corse nodded. 'I'm in a state of shock. I heard from my aunt. She was here an hour ago. Please come in, gentlemen.'

MacKenzie introduced Scougall.

'I'm pleased to meet you, sir,' said Corse. 'I'm sorry it's on such a night as this. My aunt is devastated.' Corse ushered them inside and they followed him into a small living chamber containing a desk, a table and chairs, a bookcase and a couple of armchairs around a blazing fire. 'Take a seat while I fetch some wine,' said Corse, leaving the room. Scougall sat at the table where a book lay open. He leant over to read the title of Richard Ligon's *A True and Exact History of the Island of Barbados*.

MacKenzie, who was still on his feet, picked up the book and flicked through the pages. Inside was a sheet of paper which he unfolded. It was a map of the island with five estates circled in pencil – Rastsey, Chester, Goddon, Ashford and Tennant – perhaps the ones belonging to William Corse, thought MacKenzie. He replaced the map and returned the book to the table just as Corse entered with a bottle of wine. Corse found three glasses in a cupboard and filled them.

'Your health,' said Corse, handing them glasses. 'My aunt thought he suffered a fit or stroke.'

MacKenzie took a sip of wine and placed his glass on the table. 'We've just come from the house, Robert. I'm afraid he didn't die of natural causes. Your uncle was strangled.'

Corse dropped into one of the armchairs beside the fire. 'My God!' he cried.

'He was disturbed during dinner and strangled by an intruder,' added MacKenzie.

Corse closed his eyes and shook his head.

'Who would want to kill him, Robert?' asked MacKenzie.

Corse shook his head again. 'My uncle didn't care about upsetting folk, whether in religion or business. He always took the hard line. He could be cruel. Cruel men make enemies.'

'Would a Quaker kill him for the recent destruction of their burial ground?' asked MacKenzie.

Corse shook his head. 'I don't know, sir.'

MacKenzie waited for a few moments, then asked: 'Is there anyone you can think of?'

'As I said, he was a difficult man,' said Corse. 'Some took to him. Many did not. Many feared him.'

'Feared him?' repeated MacKenzie.

'He was feared as a wealthy man with power and influence,' said Corse. 'I don't know anyone specifically. He fought at Rullion Green and was politically active in the field preaching days. There could be many who viewed him as an enemy. Are you certain he was murdered?'

'There's no doubt. I examined him myself,' said MacKenzie. 'There's extensive bruising on his neck. I've seen it before.'

MacKenzie sat on the other armchair. They all sipped their wine. Corse looked disturbed by the news. 'Have you any word of Arthur?' asked MacKenzie. 'Davie's been on his trail in Glasgow.'

'Not a word, I'm afraid,' said Corse. 'Did you find anything, Mr Scougall?'

'I've traced his movements after he left his mother's house on the morning Bethia was found. He spent a few days in a secret chamber at the Northern Sugar Works.'

'I didn't know he was there,' said Corse. 'When did he leave?'

'He left while Archie was away on business,' said Scougall. 'Someone came for him and took him up the road to the north.'

'Do you know who it was?' asked Corse.

'I don't know. A man, I think,' replied Scougall. 'They were seen leaving together. But the trail then runs cold. I did find a pamphlet in the chamber. It suggests he may already be far away, in the Carolinas possibly.'

'A pamphlet?' asked Corse.

'A pamphlet encouraging colonists to the Carolinas. The ship has already left Ayr. Did he have much interest in such ventures?'

'He talked many times of going to America. Perhaps when I've finished my training I'll go myself, if that's where he is.' Corse gazed into the fire and sipped his wine. 'I miss him much. I thought he would contact me. I pray every day for his safe return. If he's headed west, he may write soon. It will take some time for him to settle in the Carolinas.'

'Why has he fled, Robert?' asked MacKenzie.

Corse shook his head.

'I think there might have been someone with Bethia when she went into the water that night,' said MacKenzie.

Corse turned to him. 'Who?'

'It might have been Arthur,' said MacKenzie.

Corse looked troubled. 'How do you know?'

MacKenzie continued: 'Arthur told his mother when he saw her that morning that Bethia had fallen into the Avon. O'Flaherty did not find her bonnet on the Avon until the afternoon. How would Arthur know where she had gone in unless he was with her? In addition, O'Flaherty thought there was more than one set of footprints beside the water.'

Corse looked confused. 'Do you mean he was there at the time she fell in?'

'I don't know. Could he have... killed her for some reason?' asked MacKenzie.

Corse shook his head vehemently. 'No! He was devoted to her.'

'What was his demeanour the last time you saw him, Robert? When you saw him at the palace gates after he'd seen her body.'

'How do you mean?' asked Corse.

'Did he say anything to you about what happened to her?' asked MacKenzie.

Corse thought for a few moments, then replied: 'I'm trying to remember. As I told you, I met him at the gates. He was in such a state he could hardly speak. Yes, I think he did mention the Avon to me then. He said she went into the Avon. He must've known she'd gone in there. I wish now I'd accompanied him to Nasmyth House. I could have persuaded him to remain there.'

MacKenzie sipped his wine. The only sound in the room was the crackle of the wood on the fire. 'When did you last see your uncle?' asked MacKenzie.

Corse stared intently at his wine glass. MacKenzie noticed faint smallpox marks on his gaunt cheeks. 'I've not seen him in weeks, maybe months,' said Corse. 'That's not unusual. We were not close. He rarely came to Hamilton. We didn't share the same... outlook on life. We've argued in the past on points of theology. He held rigid views. I couldn't see much of Christ's love in his religion. I didn't even know he was in the town until my aunt appeared at the door.' Corse put his glass down. 'My God! You cannot suggest I killed him, Mr MacKenzie!'

'Of course not, Robert. Please be calm. I make no such claim,' said MacKenzie, staring intently at him. He noticed Corse's hands were shaking as they had done on their first meeting.

Corse turned his gaze from his glass to the fire, then drank more wine. He continued: 'My uncle was one of the Covenanting leaders. I suppose anyone who fought against them might be viewed as his enemy. He didn't suffer fools gladly in religion or business. I've heard he was a hard task master in Barbados. He had an absolute belief he was favoured by the Lord. I don't know where such certainty came from. He believed his soul was saved for eternity. Such confidence easily becomes arrogance. If you are guaranteed a place in Heaven, why bother being nice to anyone in this world.'

MacKenzie nodded. 'A common enough tale among the fanatics. Do you refer to anything specific in the field of business?'

Corse downed the rest of his wine. 'I cannot think. He was experienced in the sugar trade and the traffic in negroes.'

'What about his time in the Caribbean?' asked MacKenzie.

'I know little about his days there. He returned to Glasgow rarely. When he did, he was always a dark presence, hardly a man to look forward to seeing. Not an uncle who returned home bearing gifts. He left Scotland as a young man before I was born and came back a rich one, but not a happy one. For all his wealth, he was always disgruntled. He was always angry about something.'

'All his money was made in Barbados?' asked MacKenzie.

'Yes. It was a hard life there – disease, violence, death. He no doubt made enemies there too.'

'Do you know who they might be?' asked MacKenzie.

Corse shook his head.

'Who is the heir of his estate?' asked MacKenzie.

'He has two sons in Barbados. They are the main beneficiaries. No one else will inherit much, apart from his wife.'

'Will you benefit yourself?' asked MacKenzie.

Corse stopped in his tracks before replying. 'He may have left me a small inheritance. But I've no need for his money. I'll have a stipend when I obtain a parish. I have my father's property. I'll be comfortable. I don't need his money.'

'You'll be an eligible minister, indeed,' added MacKenzie, smiling urbanely.

Corse turned back to the flames. 'I've had no time for thoughts of marriage. I'm still too young.'

MacKenzie continued: 'So you don't court a lass?'

Corse smiled. 'There's no one.'

There was silence again. Scougall sipped his wine. He was happy to let MacKenzie ask all the questions.

After a few moments, MacKenzie asked: 'How did you find Bethia, Robert?'

'Find her?'

'Did you find her attractive? Many of those we've spoken to describe her as a beauty.'

Corse was aggrieved by the question. 'There was nothing between us, if that's what you insinuate. She was a beauty, there's no doubting it. But I didn't have eyes for her. I would never betray my friend.'

'Is it possible a Quaker sought revenge for the attack on the burial ground?'

'By killing my uncle?' asked Corse.

'Revenge for the way they've been treated. Your uncle had a virulent hatred of them.'

Scougall finally interjected. 'Your uncle told me so in Glasgow. He was looking to borrow from Mrs Hair.'

Corse shrugged. 'It's not their way to resort to violence. But they have suffered much. Are you sure he was involved in the assault on the burial ground?'

'We have no evidence. Just what we've been told.' MacKenzie was silent for a few moments and then posed another question. 'A witness saw your uncle in the company of Arran when the earl came north in June. Are they not unusual bedfellows?'

'I thought he despised Arran,' said Corse. 'I've no idea why they would meet.'

'Why would your uncle attend a meeting at the palace... this afternoon?' MacKenzie handed the note to him.

Corse read it, then looked away. 'It makes no sense to me, sir,' he said.

MacKenzie picked up his hat and rose from his chair. 'One further question before we take our leave. Do you know O'Flaherty well?'

Corse nodded. 'Of course. He's lived in the palace for years.'

'What do you make of him?'

Corse thought for a moment and shrugged. 'An old rogue. He's full of tales about his exploits in the wars. But a fine harper.'

'Is he a Papist?' asked MacKenzie.

'I believe he was raised one. But he does nothing to promote the religion of his birth. There's no priest in Hamilton to administer the Mass. O'Flaherty is no Jesuit.'

'How did he get on with your uncle?'

'I don't know, sir. Why do you ask?'

'I know he has no love for men of the Covenant. He fought with Montrose in the civil wars.'

Corse smiled. 'O'Flaherty has strong opinions. He huffs and puffs against the world. How it gets worse every year. Though raised a Papist, I think he does not follow that heresy, rather ploughs his own field in religion. He once told me he had no belief in God at all, nor the spirit world. I think he said it to shock me. I cannot imagine why he would kill my uncle. He has the hands of a harpist, not a killer.'

'I was suggesting no such thing, Mr Corse,' said MacKenzie, 'only that your uncle was a man who provoked strong emotions. Come, Davie. It's getting late. It's time we returned to the palace.'

CHAPTER 23

Late Conversations

THEY WALKED BACK to the palace in the rain, seeing on the way some men remove William Corse's body from his house and carry it to the tolbooth. MacKenzie was deep in thought and said little as they made their way up the driveway. Scougall plodded on, tired and hungry. 'I know it's late, Davie, but we need to talk,' said MacKenzie as they entered the palace from the Back Close. They found a servant who showed them to Scougall's room and agreed to find something for them to eat and drink. They were glad a fire was already lit in the chamber.

'To think I was with him only yesterday. Thank God we didn't lend him any money,' said Scougall, blurting out the first thing that came into his mind. 'I should've taken more account of his age in my reports for Mrs Hair and, of course, I didn't know about his trading difficulties. Mrs Hair has been saved from much embarrassment.'

'A lucky escape for you too, Davie,' replied MacKenzie taking one of the armchairs at the fire. 'Now, put her business aside. Tell me everything about your meeting with him.'

Scougall recounted all he could remember about the meeting in Corse's office in Glasgow.

'Did you take any notes?' asked MacKenzie when Scougall was finished.

Scougall removed his notebook from his bag, found the relevant pages and handed it to MacKenzie. 'His cash book itemises payments by his creditors and to his debtors,' said Scougall. 'I made sure he had more cash coming in than going out each month. There's also a list of all the creditors and debtors. I didn't have time to make a full copy. However, two names stood out – the Duke of Hamilton and the Earl of Arran. They had borrowed the significant sums of 10,000 merks and £10,000 sterling. I was surprised to learn that Corse was a major creditor of the

Hamilton family. I also learned – or rather heard from Arthur's regent, Cruikshank – that Arran was the father of Bethia's child... although it is just rumour.'

MacKenzie took out his pipe and tobacco and began to smoke. 'Many stories circulate about the earl. He does have a reputation as a libertine. I wonder if the duchess knows about these debts?'

'I wish I could remember the other names on the list,' said Scougall. 'They were not familiar to me. I think they were mostly lairds and merchants from the west. There was a Crawford on the list of debtors for a smaller sum. It might be David Crawford,' he suggested.

MacKenzie nodded. 'Now, let's consider the killing tonight. Corse was having dinner. He was interrupted and strangled. He was an old man and couldn't resist. I found a small bloodstain on the floor beside the table, perhaps from him or the killer. Under a couple of his fingernails were tiny strands of fabric, possibly from the killer's clothing. I've a sample here.' He took the handkerchief and a pair of tweezers and held the tiny threads beside a candle. 'It looks like hodden grey. I also found this under the table.' He rummaged in his pocket and pulled out the small, slightly worn, brown button.

'It looks like a coat button, sir,' said Scougall.

MacKenzie nodded. 'It didn't belong to Corse. I checked his clothing. It could be from the killer's jacket or coat. Perhaps it broke off during the struggle.' MacKenzie leant forward and emptied his pipe into the fire, before saying: 'Strange is it not, Davie, that there should be a violent death in Hamilton just as we investigate Bethia's drowning. Could there be a connection between them?'

There was a knock on the door and John Timothy entered with a tray of food and drink.

'Ah, John. This is my friend Davie Scougall from Edinburgh,' said MacKenzie.

John Timothy nodded and gave Scougall a brief smile. He placed the tray on the table. Scougall was delighted to see a bottle of wine and two glasses with bread and cheese and a selection of autumn fruit from the palace orchard.

'Have you heard about the death in Hamilton tonight?' asked MacKenzie.

John Timothy nodded.

'What are the servants in the palace saying about it?'

John Timothy closed the door before answering. 'I have heard Corse was not a popular man, sir. He was rich and had enemies.'

'Could he have been killed by a Friend in revenge for the desecration of their burial ground?' asked Scougall.

John Timothy shook his head. 'No, sir. It's not their way. They would pray for the Lord to show him the light. Is there anything else I can get you tonight, gentlemen?'

MacKenzie shook his head and John Timothy left the room. Scougall drank a single glass of wine with the food while MacKenzie finished the rest of the bottle, ruminating on Bethia's drowning and Corse's murder as he stared into the fire. He was sure that the supposition of the duchess was correct. He felt in his bones that there was some kind of foul play. But as yet there was little evidence apart from the footprints beside the river. There was also the Cadzow Kiss. It kept coming up in conversations along with the strangers seen in the parish.

'I didn't expect to see a black servant in Hamilton,' said Scougall when he had finished eating.

'He's a slave from Barbados, Davie,' said MacKenzie. 'Won by the duke in a game of cards and sent to Scotland. You should speak to him. Learn something of that vile trade.'

Scougall was too tired to debate the topic further that night. He yawned loudly.

'Just one other thing before we retire,' said MacKenzie. 'Look at this letter I found in Bethia's house. It's from Arthur to her. Pay particular attention to the signature.'

Scougall read the letter. 'That's interesting, sir. Sir James showed me a note from Arthur. His signature contained the same flourish beneath the "y". Do you have your glass?'

MacKenzie searched in his pocket and removed a small magnifying glass. Scougall examined the signature beside a candle. 'I think I know what it is, sir. It looks like a small pentacle has been added under the "y".' He handed the letter back to MacKenzie who examined it under the glass. There was clearly a tiny, five-pointed figure.

'You're right, Davie. What does it tell us?'

Scougall shrugged. He thought for a moment. 'Arthur was interested in symbols. Perhaps he was a Mason. It may be his Mason's mark.'

MacKenzie smiled. 'I knew your membership of the craft would prove useful! Tell me all you know about such nonsense.'

Scougall was annoyed by the inference that all things connected to the Masons were nonsense. 'I don't know much more about it than that,' he said, yawning again. 'Some Masons add a particular symbol to their signature and seals. A symbol that means something to them. I don't have one yet.'

Scougall was glad to see MacKenzie rising from his chair and taking his hat.

'We have much to do tomorrow, Davie. I need to find George Harlaw who discovered Bethia's body and I want to speak with Arthur's teacher, Dalziel. We should also question William Corse's wife about the events of tonight and I want to take another look in Arthur's chamber in Nasmyth House. We may not have much time left in the west. Arran is keen to get rid of us. Good night, Davie.'

MacKenzie was not sure of the quickest way back to his own chamber and meandered through the corridors in a mellow mood. After a few wrong turns, he found himself in the Horn Hall. As he began to climb the stairs, the front doors burst open. Drummond entered and shook himself dry.

MacKenzie called over. 'You have late business tonight, Mr Drummond.'

Drummond handed a servant his coat and came over to MacKenzie. 'There's always business to attend to for the House of Hamilton. You'll take a nightcap with me?'

MacKenzie laughed. 'I've already had a few glasses with Mr Scougall, but I'll not refuse one more.'

'Then let's take it in the office,' said Drummond.

MacKenzie noticed Drummond's windswept appearance and his boots spattered with mud. He followed him to a door in the far corner of the hall which Drummond opened with a key. It was a small sitting room with low couches, a desk and bookcases. There were hangings on the walls depicting hunting scenes. The embers of a fire glowed in the fireplace. 'The earl and I use this room for business,' said Drummond taking a bottle from a cabinet and filling two glasses. 'Brandy. I have no whisky, I'm afraid.'

MacKenzie took a glass and they toasted each other. 'Have you heard the news from town?' he asked.

Drummond nodded solemnly. 'Corse has died of a stroke. He was an old man.'

'It was no stroke. He was strangled.'

Drummond did not speak. He sat on a couch and drank his brandy. MacKenzie sat on the other couch.

'I believe Arran and his father owed Corse considerable sums of money,' said MacKenzie.

'They owe considerable sums to a score of creditors. Managing their finances is the... hardest part of my work. They are now debtors of Corse's sons for the same amounts.'

'I was surprised to learn Corse lent to clients who did not share his... religious views.'

'Money trumps theology, MacKenzie. You of all people should know that.'

'What business took you out so late, Drummond?'

Drummond looked aggrieved by the question. 'My own business, MacKenzie,' he said sternly. 'Are you suggesting I had some part in Corse's demise? You are sorely mistaken. My business tonight was not in Hamilton. I had to ride to Glasgow. I was away all afternoon. I've just returned.'

'Then you had nothing to do with Corse's... death,' said MacKenzie.

There were a few moments' silence. Finally, Drummond said: 'I hope you'll take the earl's advice and leave soon.'

MacKenzie sipped the spirit. 'I've made some progress in my investigations... but there's still no word of Nasmyth.'

'So, you're heading home soon?'

'Soon, Mr Drummond. Once I have the duchess's direction I should do so. I'm to speak with her again tomorrow. The business of William Corse complicates matters. I don't like leaving loose threads.'

'Why should that be?'

'It's not clear if there's a connection between his death and the other case.'

'How could there be a connection between a girl's suicide weeks ago and the death of an old merchant?'

'There may be none. It's just the old lawyer in me.'

Drummond's expression lost any hint of affability. 'As I said before, it would be unwise to make an enemy of the earl.'

'Or an enemy of you?' MacKenzie smiled.

'There's nothing for you here. Leave before...' Drummond did not complete the sentence.

'Before?' repeated MacKenzie.

'Before the earl's anger is roused. He can be unpredictable. He has a temper.'

MacKenzie eyed him coldly. 'Am I being threatened, Mr Drummond?'

Drummond did not reply for a few moments. 'Let it not be said we didn't warn you. Tell the duchess you've made no progress and be on your way. I assure you the girl drowned herself. There's nothing more to it than that. There's no conspiracy. As far as Corse is concerned, perhaps an enemy from his past caught up with him. We don't want any trouble on the estates… at this time.'

'Are you planning something?' asked MacKenzie, getting to his feet.

Drummond shook his head. 'We plan nothing. I simply want a period of calm in the family's affairs after the problems caused by the earl's imprisonment. A period of calm so we can focus on securing money for the upcoming winter at court. We must obtain a good marriage for the sake of the house. That's what I'm concerned with. That is our vital interest. Not unearthing old legal cases.'

CHAPTER 24

Breakfast with the Duchess

MACKENZIE RECEIVED A note when he was dressing the next morning, requesting he have breakfast with the duchess in her chamber. She was sitting at a small table beside a window when he was shown in.

'Ah, Mr MacKenzie. Please have something with me.'

He bowed and sat at the table, which was laid for breakfast.

'It's a fine day, indeed,' she said briskly, looking out the window. 'Now to business. Tell me what you've learned.'

MacKenzie shared all he knew about the case but tempered the threats of Arran and Drummond. 'I believe they think there's nothing to be concerned about and would like to see me back in Edinburgh,' he told her. 'A few more days, however, may allow us to learn more. The killing of Corse is another matter, a fly in the ointment, as they say.'

'Do you think his murder is linked to Bethia's death?' she asked.

'We cannot rule out the possibility. I have some questions of my own, your grace.'

'Please ask away.'

'Did you know William Corse?'

'I've never met him. I know of him, of course. He was a well-known Covenanter and merchant who prospered in the Caribbean.'

MacKenzie removed the crumpled note he had found on Corse's body. 'I found this last night.' He handed it across the table to her.

The duchess looked troubled. 'I had no idea he was here. Who was he meeting?'

'I don't know yet, your grace. Was it perhaps Crawford or Drummond?'

The duchess shook her head.

'Tell me more about David Crawford, your grace.'

She thought for a moment. 'You cannot suspect Crawford of anything, surely? He is a loyal servant of this house!'

'I must leave no stone unturned, your grace.'

'He's served us for years. He's a careful man of business. A respected figure in the parish. An elder in the session.'

'Did he have eyes for Bethia?'

She thought for a moment. 'I've never noticed him interested in any woman.'

MacKenzie finished his plate of smoked fish. 'I have another question, your grace. It concerns... an association I've heard mentioned by a number of those I've questioned over the last few days... the Cadzow Kiss.'

She looked surprised. 'I thought it a relic of the past.'

'I believe it still meets intermittently.' He waited for the duchess to look up at him, before adding: 'There was a meeting at Cadzow Castle on the night Bethia died.'

'My God! I thought it had slipped into oblivion years ago. Do you think it is connected to her death?'

'I mean to find that out, your grace.'

'I've heard rumours about it over the years, but perhaps I chose to ignore them. Do you know who attends it?'

MacKenzie hesitated. 'I believe that remains secret. I'll continue to investigate.'

MacKenzie excused himself and headed for Scougall's room. On the way, he bumped into Janet Dobbie in the Horn Hall. She looked eager to get away from him as soon as possible, but he knew he could not let the opportunity slip. He took her gently by the elbow and directed her into a corner. He could no longer afford to be affable. 'Have you thought about what I said, Janet?' he asked brusquely.

She did not reply.

'You must tell me the names of the men who pestered Bethia. If you do not, I'll take you to see the duchess right away and you'll be answerable to her.'

The girl looked petrified.

'You'll have to explain things to the duchess rather than me.'

She was on the verge of tears.

'Tell me, Janet. For Bethia's sake. For God's sake, girl!'

Her head dropped and she began to weep. Then she moved closer to him and whispered hoarsely: 'She told me it was Mr Crawford, the earl and Lord Basil. I've also seen her leaving O'Flaherty's chamber in tears. I've heard she left the laundry in tears after meeting the black servant.'

CHAPTER 25

A Gift from Arran

AS SOON AS Scougall awoke, he remembered he had a meeting with Arran and was angry with himself for not being more prevaricating. He should have told him that he did not have the authority to negotiate on behalf of Mrs Hair. He dressed and asked a servant to take him to the earl's bedchamber. He was shown in to a huge, luxurious room. Arran was being dressed by a valet beside his vast four-poster bed. He called over to Scougall to take a seat at his desk.

Arran looked more at ease than he had the night before. He sat behind the desk and asked his man to serve breakfast. 'You'll join me, Mr Scougall?'

Scougall nodded reluctantly.

'Let's get straight down to business,' said Arran enthusiastically. 'I require a loan, a substantial one. I need as much as £10,000 sterling to see me through the winter in London.'

Scougall was shocked by the large amount.

'One more season in London and I'll obtain a bride,' continued Arran. 'A syndicate in Edinburgh will provide the loan. Mrs Hair may join it for the sum of £1,000. The sum will be secured on my future income when I'm duke in my own right and, until then, by the jointure from my marriage settlement.'

Scougall knew that Mrs Hair would not countenance making such a loan to Arran. However, he feared the earl's ire. He thought the best policy was to be evasive. 'Have you signed a marriage contract already, your grace?' he asked.

Arran did not look pleased. 'It's a question of the chicken and the egg. To obtain a suitable bride, and thus a settlement, I must spend time in London. Spending time in London is expensive and requires a loan. If I'm seen as parsimonious, I'll hardly attract the right sort of wife. I must have one with sound financial prospects. A bonnie one would be a bonus.'

'Who are the other members of the syndicate, your grace?'

'I cannot name them, yet. They are obviously rich merchants and lairds with sufficient capital. Think of it this way, Mr Scougall, and this is the message I wish you to convey to Mrs Hair when you return to Edinburgh. A loan will stand the House of Hair in good stead for the future. It will establish a strong bond with myself, the highest nobleman in the land, indeed some might say in Britain. You'll recall my family's claim to the throne of Scotland. We will prosper together.'

Scougall nodded again. He realised his attempt to stall had been unsuccessful. 'I'll convey that to her as soon as I return.'

Arran smiled. 'Now, a little present to cement the deal.' He rummaged in a drawer and pulled something out. He held up a ring between his thumb and forefinger. The blue gemstone sparkled in the morning sunshine. 'For your wife, Mr Scougall. A fine piece. A sapphire from the Indies, worth a hundred pounds. It's yours. There, take it.' He leant over and presented it to him.

Scougall was flabbergasted. 'I could not, sir. It's very generous, but I cannot take it. Mrs Hair would not look favourably on such a gift before a decision has been made about a loan. She does not like such marks of generosity before an agreement is made.'

'Come now, Mrs Hair does not have to know about it,' said Arran. 'It's between you and me. A present for your fair wife. A gift from Glasgow. A little security for her future. You would not deny her that.'

'I could not, your grace,' Scougall repeated. He felt his face redden and he was beginning to sweat.

'You would refuse a gift from the Earl of Arran?' There was anger in his voice.

Scougall did not know what to do. He could not please both the earl and Mrs Hair. He had a desperate desire to get away from Arran's presence. Exasperated, he took the ring.

Arran smiled. 'That was not so painful, was it? I expect to hear from Mrs Hair soon after you return.'

CHAPTER 26

A Meeting with David Crawford

AFTER HIS CONVERSATION with Janet Dobbie, MacKenzie found Scougall in his room looking troubled. 'The earl gave me this, sir. He wouldn't accept my refusal,' said Scougall, holding up the ring. 'I shouldn't have taken it. I didn't know how to say no.'

'It's difficult to say no to a man like Arran,' said MacKenzie.

'I fear Mrs Hair will be disappointed with me.' Scougall looked despondent.

'Let the matter rest for now, Davie. We need to move swiftly.' MacKenzie told Scougall the names he had obtained from Janet Dobbie.

They went straight to Crawford's office. When he looked up from his desk, it was clear he was not pleased to see them. 'You again, MacKenzie.'

'A few words, Mr Crawford,' said MacKenzie. 'This is my assistant, Davie Scougall. You may have seen him last night.'

'Do I have any choice?' asked Crawford, putting down his quill.

MacKenzie and Scougall came into the room. MacKenzie took out the note he had found on Corse's body. 'Did you write this to William Corse?'

'That's not my hand,' Crawford scoffed. 'Look at my entries here in the ledger.'

Scougall came forward to compare the hands. 'They are not the same, sir,' he said.

'Whose hand is it, Crawford?' asked MacKenzie.

Crawford shrugged his shoulders.

'Did you know Corse?'

Crawford shook his head. 'Not well.'

'You share the same outlook in religion?'

'What of it, MacKenzie?'

'You lent the man money, Mr Crawford, but you hardly knew him?'

Crawford was taken aback. 'I admit I leant him a small sum. Drummond arranged it. I went to Corse's office in Glasgow. I handed over the cash and signed a bond. That's the only time I've ever spoken to him.'

'Is it not strange that Drummond should be arranging a loan for one of the fanatics?'

'The loans to Arran and the duke were made when Corse's finances were stronger,' replied Crawford. 'He is, or rather was, experiencing some difficulties. The House of Hamilton provided him with short-term relief. The earl and duke could not redeem their debts, so other clients of the family, like myself, were asked to help him out.'

'Were you happy to provide support for Corse?' asked Scougall.

'I would not say I was happy to support Corse. I'm always happy to do my duty for the House of Hamilton.'

'So, the note to Corse was from Drummond?' asked MacKenzie.

Crawford did not reply immediately, then finally said: 'Yes. There were ongoing financial negotiations. Both parties faced the same problem. They both have plenty of assets but cannot liquidate them. They are therefore without access to ready cash. They had to come to an accommodation.'

'Perhaps Corse decided to call in the loans made to Arran and his father,' said Scougall. 'Perhaps he had no choice in the matter after one ship went down and another was taken by pirates.'

Crawford shook his head.

'Was Corse killed so he would not call in these loans?' asked MacKenzie.

Crawford said nothing.

MacKenzie continued: 'Was he killed to delay the loans being called in?'

Crawford suddenly blurted out: 'That's nonsense, Mr MacKenzie! You slander the earl.'

'I do not slander him. The earl was dining with us at the time. But Drummond was out on business last night. He only returned near midnight.'

Crawford shook his head.

'Will you be paid your interest, Mr Crawford?' asked MacKenzie.

'I'll receive payment when Corse's properties are sold and other debts are redeemed.'

'A murky business indeed,' said MacKenzie. He walked over to the window and looked out on the Back Close, then turned and asked: 'How did you really get on with Bethia?'

'What do you mean?' asked Crawford.

'I've heard you were besotted with her. I've heard you tried to abuse her,' said MacKenzie grimly.

'Nonsense!' shouted Crawford, rising to his feet. 'You slander me!' Crawford's face was bright red.

'You've been named among her abusers!' shouted MacKenzie. 'Did you accost her, then kill her when she denied you?'

Crawford glowered at MacKenzie. After a few moments, he gathered himself together and sat back shaking his head. 'It was nothing. A trifle. I tried to touch her once or twice. It was nothing more. I didn't think she took it badly. She just ran off and nothing more was said about it.'

'Where were you on the night of the 13th of June?' asked MacKenzie.

'I was in my house in Hamilton. What do you insinuate?'

'Can anyone vouch for you?' asked Scougall.

'My man will vouch for it.'

'Did you attend the Kiss that night?' asked MacKenzie.

'I've told you I have nothing to do with it. You think I pushed her into the river for refusing me? You think I would risk everything I've worked for all my life for a moment's madness? Nonsense! I'll tell you something, MacKenzie—'

'What?' asked MacKenzie.

'I saw O'Flaherty the morning her body was found. Just after dawn. I was walking from my house to the palace. He was ambling by the Clyde. Why was he out so early? Did he not find her bonnet? How did he know where to look for it?'

'What do you mean, Crawford?' asked MacKenzie.

'The bonnet was the sole piece of evidence that she fell into the Avon. The bonnet was found by him. She may have gone into the water up the Clyde where he was walking that morning. I've seen the way he looked at her. He was teaching her the harp, apparently, composing songs about her. Did he get beyond himself? Could he not resist her? Did he lay his old hands on her and, when she rejected him, drown her?'

Through the window MacKenzie noticed Lord Basil preparing his horse in the Back Close. 'That's all for now, Crawford,' he said. He led Scougall out the room, down the corridor and into the courtyard. 'Good morning, my lord. Are you off somewhere?' he asked.

Lord Basil smiled. 'To Glasgow for the day, gentlemen.'

'May we ask a few questions before you leave, if you have time?' asked MacKenzie politely.

'Of course, come this way. We can sit in the garden.'

He gave the reins of his horse to his servant and led them through an archway into the gardens.

When they reached the Statue Garden, Scougall's attention was drawn to the sundial. He examined it and observed the strange symbols, including pentacles, carved on it. MacKenzie turned to Lord Basil. 'How do you find Crawford as a mentor?'

'I suffer two hours each day in his office writing instruments and learning bookkeeping.'

'What career do you hope to follow?' asked Scougall, recalling the long days he had spent doing the same thing.

'My brother Archibald is in the navy,' said Lord Basil. 'My brother George is in the army. That's the kind of life I want. There's not much for a young man round here. I'd take the chance to sail on a scheme like the one that left Ayr for the Carolinas.'

MacKenzie nodded affably, then his expression soured. 'How did you really get on with Bethia, my lord?'

Lord Basil looked at him in surprise. 'I got on well with her. Why do you ask?'

'We've been told you had... strong feelings for her,' said MacKenzie.

Lord Basil was silent for a moment. 'I liked her, Mr MacKenzie. She was a beautiful... woman.'

'You thought her a beauty,' MacKenzie repeated slowly.

Lord Basil was flustered. 'I would have married her, but...'

'You had thoughts of marriage to Bethia?'

'Just a silly fantasy, I suppose. I mentioned it to my brother. He said it was the most ridiculous thing he'd ever heard. He told me to go to a brothel in Glasgow instead.'

'Did you tell your mother about your thoughts of marriage?'

'No. I could not.'

'Did you tell Bethia of your feelings for her?'

Lord Basil looked out across the gardens and was lost in thought for a few moments. 'I tried to tell her many times, but she was always keen to get away somewhere. I tried to... kiss her once. She didn't like it. I could not speak to her after that.'

'Did you try to kiss her again?' asked MacKenzie.

He shook his head.

'Did you ever lay your hands on her?'

'Never, sir.'

'Did you ever debauch her?'

Lord Basil shook his head angrily.

MacKenzie kept his gaze fixed on him. 'Who will you marry, my lord?' he asked.

'My brother is to draw up a list of suitable candidates. I doubt if any will be as fair as her. You must believe me when I say I was distraught when she perished. She was... very dear to me. I'm just sorry I was never dear to her.'

'Where were you on the night of the 13th of June?' asked MacKenzie.

'You insinuate I killed her?'

'I have to ask the question.'

He shook his head.

'Were you at the castle that night?'

'The castle?' repeated Lord Basil.

'The Cadzow Kiss met in the castle that night,' said Scougall.

He shook his head. 'I know nothing about it, sir.'

'Arran has not invited you to attend?' asked MacKenzie.

'He did not. I suppose he does not trust me.'

'Where were you that night?'

'I was at home here all night. I had dinner with my mother and then went to my chambers.'

MacKenzie raised his voice. 'Did you drown her in the Avon after she rejected you?'

Lord Basil's fists were clenched in anger. 'You think I would throw her into the Avon for that reason.'

'Were you jealous of Arthur? He was beneath you in standing but she only had eyes for him. He was to wed Bethia while you, a member of the Hamilton family, were scorned.'

Lord Basil was trying to smother his anger. 'You misjudge me, gentlemen. Now, excuse me,' he said in disgust and stormed off.

CHAPTER 27

The Warrander

MACKENZIE AND SCOUGALL returned to the Back Close. The warrander's office was in one of the outhouses. They entered the small room without knocking. Strange objects were hanging from the ceiling. It took a few moments to identify them as rabbit furs. A lean, swarthy figure lounged beside a stove smoking a pipe. He looked up at them with a smiling face. 'Mr MacKenzie, is it not?' he said. 'I'm George Harlaw.'

'I'm glad to find you at last, Mr Harlaw,' said MacKenzie.

'I'm a busy man, Mr MacKenzie. I heard you were looking for me.'

Scougall introduced himself and Harlaw indicated they should join him on the wooden chairs beside the stove. MacKenzie removed his tobacco pouch and was soon puffing away. The smoke of two pipes filled the cramped interior, making Scougall feel nauseous.

'I look after her grace's cattle and sheep... and I control the rabbits,' said Harlaw, pointing to the furs above. 'I presume you're not here about estate matters?'

'We're investigating the drowning of Bethia Porterfield for the duchess,' said MacKenzie.

Harlaw nodded. 'I found her body in the river that morning.'

'Tell me what happened,' said MacKenzie.

'I'm always up early, usually before dawn,' began Harlaw. 'My job demands it. I walk the path beside the river every morning from my cottage. That day I noticed something lying in the water. When I got closer, I was shocked to see a body. I waded out and pulled it on shore. It was only when I turned her over I realised who it was. She was badly bashed up and her face bloated, but I knew it was her. I pulled her out and went to get help in the palace.'

'Can you remember how she was dressed?' asked MacKenzie.

Harlaw closed his eyes to concentrate. 'A blue dress. Black leather boots.'

'Was there anything else about her? Tell me exactly what you saw.'

Harlaw thought for a few moments. 'I remember one other thing. Something was wrapped round her wrist. It was a cord handle. She gripped a bag not much larger than a rabbit's head in her hand. I didn't touch it. I noticed it was gone when I saw her laid out in the palace later. I thought it must've been removed when she was attended.'

'Who looked after her corpse?' asked MacKenzie.

'Margaret Cassie, the nursemaid. She has experience in such matters. She prepared the body for burial.'

MacKenzie nodded thoughtfully and offered Harlaw some more tobacco.

'Have you worked here long, Mr Harlaw?'

'All my life, sir.'

'Did you ever see Bethia troubled by any man in the palace?' asked MacKenzie.

'I've seen every maid troubled by... some man. I think she was bothered by...' he stopped himself for a few moments before adding, 'David Crawford... yes, he upset her.'

'Did you ever see O'Flaherty bother her?' asked Scougall.

'Jago was no trouble to her. A good man is Jago,' replied Harlaw.

'What about Lord Basil?' asked MacKenzie.

Harlaw did not answer.

'Lord Basil?' MacKenzie asked again.

'I don't... think so,' said Harlaw hesitantly.

MacKenzie waited for a few moments, but Harlaw did not add anything. He continued with his questions. 'Did you know William Corse?'

'I know his family. I've little to do with them.'

'What are folk in the palace saying about his death last night?'

'That he deserved it... folk were not pleased to see him back here after all these years.'

'Why would they say that?' asked MacKenzie.

'Those who knew him before he was imprisoned in the Bass said he was a cruel man.' Harlaw emptied his pipe into the stove. 'I had no liking for him. I may have voiced my opinion about him a few times in the tavern. I don't share his grim view of life. However, I would never raise my hand against an old man.'

MacKenzie sucked on his pipe for a few moments then asked: 'What do you know of the Kiss, Mr Harlaw?'

'The Cadzow Kiss?' asked Harlaw.

MacKenzie nodded.

Harlaw smiled. 'It's a few years since I last attended. I can tell you little about it now, sir.'

'Has it always been used for... political purposes?' asked MacKenzie.

'Let me say this,' said Harlaw. 'It's always been attended by those who supported the king, if you get my meaning. By those who care little for ministers and kirk sessions and the Covenant. It's always attracted... free-thinking men.'

'Have you seen any foreigners in the parish recently?'

Harlaw shook his head.

'What about smugglers or gypsies?'

'There are few gypsies in these parts. As for smugglers, it's too far away from the sea.'

'Do you know John Timothy, the black servant?' asked MacKenzie.

'I've seen him about. He helped to carry her body back to the palace.'

'What do you make of him?'

'He's serious and quiet. Keeps himself to himself.'

'We've been told he may also have pestered Bethia,' said Scougall.

'I've heard nothing about that.'

'What about Arran?' asked MacKenzie.

Harlaw turned to MacKenzie. His face adopted a more serious look. 'What is it you want to know, Mr MacKenzie?'

'Is he involved in her death. Did he debauch her?'

Harlaw looked like he was choosing his words carefully. 'The earl had nothing to do with it.'

'What did happen to her?'

'If you ask me, Arthur Nasmyth was responsible.'

'Why do you say that?'

'Because such cases are always connected to affairs of the heart.'

CHAPTER 28

The Nursery

THE PALACE NURSERY was on the third floor, a large, bright room with high windows. Wooden toys were scattered across the floor. Scougall recalled the small chamber he and Chrissie were preparing for their son or daughter in Edinburgh. Margaret Cassie was standing beside a tiny bed. Just as MacKenzie was about to address her, she raised a finger to her mouth and pointed at the sleeping child. She smiled and indicated they should follow her into the adjoining room. She carefully shut the door when they were all inside her chamber.

'I'm sorry, gentlemen,' she said. 'An hour's peace. Her ladyship has plenty of smeddum, as they say. She'll be in no good mood if she's woken early. Now, how can I help you?'

MacKenzie introduced Scougall and told her they had a few questions about Bethia.

Cassie nodded. 'I'm quite new to the palace, sir. I was employed by the child's mother only last year, just before she died. I didn't know Bethia well. I found her a friendly lass, kind with the child, happy to play with her.'

'Did you attend her body after it was found in the river?' asked MacKenzie.

'Yes. I cleaned and prepared her the best I could.'

'How was she when she was laid out?'

'A terrible sight. Badly knocked about and swollen from the drowning. I'd seen a couple of similar cases before. I cut off her wet clothes, washed her down and put her in a white linen shift. She remained in the lower hall until she was buried a few days later. I presume you've heard about the dispute over where she should lie.'

MacKenzie nodded. 'I don't like having to ask this. Was there any indication she was with child?'

Cassie lowered her voice. 'I saw none, sir. Her belly was as flat as an iron. Only she would have known if it was so. If she was with child, it must have been very early.'

'How would the worthies in the parish know about it?' asked MacKenzie.

'They would not know unless she told someone. There was no physical sign.'

'Mr Harlaw mentioned a cord wrapped round her wrist and a bag she held when she was taken out the water.'

'Ah there was,' said Cassie. 'I'd forgotten. The handle of a small linen bag was round her wrist. She grasped a purse in her hand. I unwound it, prised her fingers apart and placed it on the dresser beside the table where she lay. I meant to look inside it later.'

'What happened to it?' asked MacKenzie.

'I don't know, sir. I'd forgotten about it until now. It may still be there.'

'Could you show us where?'

She went into the next room to check on the child, then led them down through the palace to a long, low-ceilinged hall in the basement. She went to the dresser on the right side of the room. 'This is where I put it, Mr MacKenzie. Down here on the dresser. It's gone.' She looked around, then opened the drawer beneath. 'Ah, it's been tidied away. It's in here.' She handed the small, misshapen object to MacKenzie.

The fabric was hardened by its soaking in the river. MacKenzie pulled it open carefully. He emptied six dice onto the dresser. 'What are these?' MacKenzie asked her in surprise.

She shook her head.

'What do you think, Davie?'

Scougall examined them closely. 'There are symbols on the faces… or are they letters?'

MacKenzie took out his glass and looked at one of the dice under it. 'Greek letters,' he said. He thought for a few moments. 'Why would she have these with her if she planned to kill herself?'

CHAPTER 29

Investigations in Hamilton

'WAS SHE WITH somebody that night, Davie?' asked MacKenzie as they walked briskly down the driveway into Hamilton. 'Crawford, Lord Basil and Arran no doubt have convenient alibis. We'll have to question O'Flaherty and John Timothy later.'

The door of William Corse's house was answered by an old woman dressed in black. She looked grief-stricken and disorientated. 'Margaret Corse?' asked MacKenzie.

She nodded vacantly.

'I'm sorry for your loss, madam. I am John MacKenzie, a lawyer working for her grace. This is Mr Scougall, my assistant. I wonder if we might ask a few questions?'

She looked at them suspiciously.

'I'm acting for the duchess, madam,' continued MacKenzie. 'She, as you might expect, is very concerned about your husband's death. She's asked me to make some enquiries before the sheriff's officer gets here, to help his investigation.'

'Come in,' she replied with little emotion. They followed her into the room where they had found her husband's body the night before. 'Take a seat, gentlemen. I'm forgetting myself. May I get you something?'

'We're fine, Mrs Corse,' said MacKenzie. 'We'll not take up much of your time. You must be in a state of shock.'

'He's gone to a better place, sir. But I'll miss him. We were married fifty years. We lived a hard life. Now his struggle is over. He's found glory at last.'

'You have two sons, Mrs Corse?' asked MacKenzie.

'Two sons alive. A son and two daughters dead as children. And a stillborn babe, a boy also. God's ways are mysterious.'

'How are your sons?'

'Well, sir, although I see little of them since we came back to Scotland. They remain as planters in Barbados where we lived for many years. They'll be shocked by their father's death.'

'How did your husband rise from indenture to riches?' asked Scougall.

'He worked hard. And the Lord shone on him. The Lord provided a bountiful harvest each year and a rising sugar price.'

'How was life in Barbados, madam?' asked MacKenzie.

'It's a hard life. There are many diseases. The climate is harsh. The negroes will kill you without a second thought. My husband managed his estates well and we prospered. We were lucky in life... until last night.'

'Why did you return to Scotland?' asked Scougall.

'Managing sugar plantations is a job for the young. The last rebellion was a difficult time. Many planters were slain.'

'Rebellion?' repeated Scougall.

'A slave rebellion,' she said.

'When was the rebellion?' asked MacKenzie.

'Five years ago, in 1686. After it was crushed, we decided to return to Scotland, though my husband continued to work hard, too hard, in Glasgow.'

'When did you last see your husband?' asked Scougall.

She thought for a moment. 'I prepared his meal in the kitchen. Our servant did not travel with us from Glasgow, so I'd taken a little food. I left him in the house about eight o'clock to visit my sister. When I returned an hour later, he was lying on the floor. I thought it was a natural death. He has suffered much strain and ill health recently. But I'm told by Mr Crawford he was slain. Strangled by an intruder. I fear Satan walks the streets of this town.'

'Why were you here, madam?' asked MacKenzie.

'William had business in town.'

'Business at the palace?'

She nodded.

'Did he say what the business was?'

She shook her head.

'Did he often have business there?'

'No, sir. We do not return here often. It no doubt concerned some purchase, perhaps sugar or rum or some transaction. My husband did not discuss such things with me.'

'Did it concern his loans to Arran and the duke?' asked MacKenzie.

'I don't know, sir.'

'Did your husband receive any threats recently, Mrs Corse?' asked Scougall.

'Threats?' she repeated.

'Is there anyone who bore him a particular grudge? Who wanted to harm him?' asked MacKenzie.

She shook her head. 'He was an honest merchant.'

'No one from the Covenanting days in his youth? They were violent times.'

'He took up arms for the Lord. Maybe some bore him a grudge. It's over twenty years ago. They've waited a long time to seek revenge.'

'Your husband opposed the Quakers vehemently,' said MacKenzie.

'They are agents of the Antichrist who serve the imposter James Stuart,' she replied. 'That sinner tried to turn this realm into the plaything of Rome. My husband rightly opposed them with vigour. Now I think of it, I saw one of them on the street when I left the house last night.'

'Who did you see?'

'I think he was one of Hugh Wood's sons. A large, burly, fair-haired man. You could not mistake him. I thought nothing of it at the time. Do you think he killed my husband?'

'The Quakers are usually peace-loving people,' said MacKenzie. 'Did you know their burial ground at Shawtonhill was destroyed?'

'I heard it, yes.'

'Was your husband responsible for the attack?'

Mrs Corse shook her head. 'He was no rioter. Just a devout servant of the Lord. He thought the parish should be cleansed of blasphemers. He was too old to ride up to the moors at night.'

'Did he encourage others to attack the burial ground and abuse the corpse of Bethia Porterfield, the young girl drowned a few months ago?'

Mrs Corse was silent for a few moments, eyeing them closely. 'He followed the Lord. He did everything with his eternal soul in mind. The Porterfield girl took her own life. By doing so, she sinned. She killed her unborn bairn. Such a sinner should not be buried in hallowed ground. The Quakers are heretics. Why should we welcome them here?'

'So, he did call for their persecution?' asked Scougall.

'He was active in the cause of righteousness and one of the beloved elders of the movement, a man highly regarded by all the faithful. A shining light has been snuffed out.'

'Can you think of anyone else who might have wished him harm?' asked MacKenzie.

She paused again. 'There are a couple in this parish who despised his honesty and who were chastised by him for their transgressions.'

'Who were they, madam?'

She thought for a moment. 'The Papist harper at the palace slandered my husband to his face as he walked down the street in this town, calling him a filthy usurer. The warrander Harlaw did likewise. My husband had good reason to call these men out as great sinners before the Lord.'

'What had they done to him, madam?' asked Scougall.

'O'Flaherty is a Papist devil. He practiced the Mass in the palace and fought with the traitor Montrose against the Covenant. My husband declared his presence was a stain on this town. Harlaw belongs to a family of inveterate Jacobites. My husband called him out more than once as a traitor.'

MacKenzie felt despair wash through him. There was a web of hatred in the parish. Scotland was a land bitterly divided.

There was a knock on the door. She left them to answer it and returned with Robert Corse. 'My nephew has come to see me, gentlemen.'

'We'll leave you to your grief, madam. Just one question, Robert. We've found a letter from Arthur to Bethia. There's a small symbol attached to his signature. See here.' Scougall took the letter from his bag and handed it to Corse.

Corse read the letter and examined the signature. He sighed deeply. 'It pains me to see my friend's writing, not knowing where he is. The symbol is nothing… just an interest of his. He was always drawing such things, copying them from the old books and manuscripts his father bought overseas. His father was a Mason, although we are not meant to talk of such things.'

'Is there a lodge in Hamilton?' asked Scougall.

'There is one. I'm not part of the craft, gentlemen. I'll no doubt join… sometime.'

'What about Arthur?' asked MacKenzie.

'He was not a Mason. I'm sure he intends to follow in his father's footsteps… in the future… wherever he's bound. Now, I must comfort my aunt.'

MacKenzie and Scougall returned to the palace and found Hugh Wood down on his knees in the vegetable garden, digging up carrots. When he saw them, he rose stiffly. 'Ah, Mr MacKenzie, how do your investigations proceed?'

MacKenzie sighed. 'I've uncovered a can of worms in Hamilton, Hugh.'

'Well, we have our problems in this parish, as you know,' said Wood.

'I'm sorry. It's your son Andrew I seek,' said MacKenzie. 'Margaret Corse says she saw him near their house last night. I need to find out what he was doing there.'

'Are you suggesting he killed Corse?' said Wood angrily. 'He would never do such a thing. We are peace-loving folk.'

'I know, Hugh. I'm sorry for it. William Corse may have been a leader of the fanatics who attacked your burial ground.'

'We believe you should always turn the other cheek,' said Wood.

'We need to speak to him, Hugh. I'm sorry, just so we can exclude him.'

Wood shook his head. 'You'll find him at the mill on the Cadzow Burn.'

The watermill was on the outskirts of town. Beside the wheel, a young man was moving sacks of grain onto a cart. He was a large, brawny figure in a broad-brimmed hat. He would have no trouble strangling an old man like Corse, thought MacKenzie.

They introduced themselves. 'Andrew Wood?' asked MacKenzie.

He nodded. 'My father has mentioned you as a friend of our people, Mr MacKenzie. I'm pleased to meet you both.' He lifted the sack at his feet onto the cart and shook their hands.

'You'll know from your father we investigate Bethia's death,' said MacKenzie.

Wood nodded. 'I knew her well, sir. It's a tragedy.'

'And now the killing of William Corse last night. Did you know him?' asked Scougall.

Wood shook his head. 'No, sir. I never spoke to him in my life. I knew who he was. I know what he's done. He has done our people much evil.'

'You were seen outside his house just before he was murdered,' MacKenzie stated plainly.

Wood dropped his eyes to the ground. 'I heard he was in town. I don't know why I went there. I thought I would challenge him. Make him repent his sins. But I didn't have the courage. I saw his wife leave the house. I was about to go to the door when someone appeared from the direction of the palace.'

'Do you know who it was?' asked Scougall.

'I couldn't say. It was dark and the person was wearing a cloak. I'm sure a man, from his size. He went up to the door and knocked on it. Corse answered and after they shared a few words, he let him in. I turned and went home.'

MacKenzie nodded, then moved closer to him. 'Are you missing any buttons from your jacket?'

Wood looked down and examined his jacket, then shook his head.

'Thank you, sir. I'm glad to clear this up,' said MacKenzie. 'I'm sorry we had to meet like this. Your father has been good to me. I hope to see your people compensated for what's happened to your burial ground.'

'I hope you find out what happened to Bethia, Mr MacKenzie.'

'What do you think happened to her, Andrew?'

He shook his head. 'She was like a sister to me. We played together when she was a girl. I don't believe she would kill herself. There was one thing she told me not long before she died which has remained fixed in my mind. She said Arthur was not the man she thought he was. She said it wistfully and the next minute she was gone. But I remember it clearly.'

'What did she mean by that?' asked Scougall.

Wood shook his head.

They followed the path back to town. Near the first house, MacKenzie stopped and turned to Scougall. 'Do you believe him, Davie? Or is he another man who desired her?' he asked.

Scougall thought for a moment. 'I believe him, sir. There must be some good men in this place.'

CHAPTER 30

The Dominee

THEY REACHED THE schoolhouse on the High Street of Hamilton just as the children were leaving. They waited for the line of youngsters to file out, then approached the old schoolmaster William Dalziel who stood at the door. He was dressed in a dusty black jacket and held a stick in his hand. They introduced themselves and MacKenzie explained why they were in town. Dalziel invited them into the schoolroom, a good-sized chamber with a table at the front and rows of wooden desks. A blackboard and a few maps were on the walls. MacKenzie was transported back to his own school in Fortrose where he was first forced to speak English.

Scougall stood beside the blackboard while MacKenzie wandered round the classroom, looking at the drawings and illustrations on the walls. A roughly sketched map of the Atlantic Ocean showed the British Isles, the Caribbean and the east coast of America.

'The children enjoy learning their geography, Mr MacKenzie,' said Dalziel.

'Glasgow looks to the west, indeed,' said MacKenzie, noticing a few of the islands in the Caribbean. He turned to face Dalziel. 'Did you teach Arthur Nasmyth?' he asked.

Dalziel smiled. 'From the age of seven until he passed to college in Glasgow at fourteen. He learned the Latin tongue in this room.'

'What kind of boy was he?'

'A quiet one. No trouble in class. Hard working. An exemplary pupil. His head was always down over his books. I never had to tawse him in all the years he sat in my class.'

'There was nothing particular about him?' asked MacKenzie.

Dalziel thought for a moment. He took a duster from his desk and began to clean a list of Latin verbs off the blackboard forcing Scougall to move out of his way. 'He was clever,' Dalziel continued. 'A very able linguist. Most accomplished in Latin and Greek.'

MacKenzie nodded. 'Is there anything else you can tell me about him?'

'It's sometimes difficult to think of anything particular about the able pupils, sir,' replied Dalziel. 'Those who struggle with their lessons can cause disruption that sticks in the mind. There is one thing I remember, Mr MacKenzie. Arthur was bullied a bit when he was younger, perhaps at the age of nine or ten. You know what children are like. He was picked on by a couple of boys for being studious and quiet. I had to thrash them once for it, but otherwise I cannot think of anything.' The description of bullying took Scougall back to his own schooldays. He had been persecuted by a couple of his schoolmates. He reflected with satisfaction that they had remained in Musselburgh as artisans while his career had taken him to the dining table of the Duchess of Hamilton.

'Who were the boys who bullied him?' asked MacKenzie.

'One was Robert Corse.'

'I thought they were friends?'

'They may be now. They were not then. Robert could be cruel when he was younger. He grew up and they settled their differences. By the time they left this room they were firm friends.'

'What became of the other boy?'

Dalziel did not reply.

'The other boy, Mr Dalziel?'

Dalziel looked reluctant to answer. Eventually he said: 'The other boy was Lord Basil Hamilton.'

'Did you have to tawse his lordship for bullying Arthur?'

'Of course, I treat all my students the same.'

'How did Lord Basil and Arthur get on thereafter?'

'I don't think they ever took to each other.'

'What do you make of Lord Basil?'

'He has become a reasonable man, but he was petulant as a boy. Spoilt as only the children of the nobility are. He also had a cruel streak. He thought he should be the centre of attention.'

'Was he cruel to other children?'

Dalziel hesitated. 'I don't think so. Like Robert, he calmed down as he matured.'

MacKenzie sat on the edge of one of the desks. Dalziel remained standing beside the blackboard. 'Did you know Bethia?' asked MacKenzie.

Dalziel nodded. 'Of course, it's a small town. I often saw her and Arthur together.'

'What did you think of her?'

'I knew her parents. She was known as a friendly girl.'

MacKenzie noticed the shape of a heart had been scrawled on the seat of the desk he lent against. 'What about the Cadzow Kiss, Mr Dalziel?'

Dalziel looked surprised by the question. 'I'm just an old schoolmaster, Mr MacKenzie,' he said.

'Have you ever attended?'

'I have not. My wife would... disapprove. When I came to the parish thirty years ago, I was asked if I wanted to go. I declined.'

'I've heard it still meets regularly?'

'From time to time... we hear rumours about it... why are you so interested in it, Mr MacKenzie?'

'I believe there was a meeting in the old castle on the night Bethia drowned.'

'I didn't know that,' said Dalziel.

'There are accounts of strangers being seen... some in uniform, speaking French.'

Dalziel looked troubled. 'There's one sure thing about the Kiss. There's always plenty of rumours spread about it, especially by those drinking in the tavern. I would think that's what you've heard. There are always stories about apparitions and ghosts in the woods... and of course Auld Nick himself appears now and again... it's the same in every rural parish in Scotland.'

'That is possible, sir,' replied MacKenzie.

'I'm a believer in reason, Mr MacKenzie,' continued Dalziel. 'Unless I see something with my own eyes, I don't believe it. In thirty years in Hamilton, I've never seen one ghost or witch. Nor have I ever encountered the Devil! They are the creations of our imaginations. Your French soldiers are no doubt the same.'

MacKenzie smiled. 'You've been here a long time. Did you teach the earl as well?'

Dalziel smiled. 'He was a handful indeed. His grace had no liking for Latin verbs.'

'What do you make of him?'

Dalziel hesitated. 'I must watch what I say. He'll be Duke of Hamilton one day.'

'Would you trust him, Mr Dalziel?' asked MacKenzie.

Dalziel smiled and shook his head.

'Thank you for your time, Mr Dalziel.'

CHAPTER 31

Nasmyth House

IT WAS LATE in the afternoon by the time MacKenzie and Scougall reached Nasmyth House. Isabella welcomed them expectantly when they were announced by her servant. She was disappointed when MacKenzie told her there was no news about her son and left them to search his room.

'What are we looking for, sir?' asked Scougall as they entered the chamber.

'I'm not sure,' said MacKenzie. 'Anything connected to the dice or Arthur's interest in symbols.'

Scougall looked round the room. His eye was taken by the portrait of Montrose and the weapons scattered everywhere. 'Did he use these?' he said without thinking. 'Did he use one on Bethia?' It had not occurred to Scougall until then that Arthur might have killed her. 'Why did he collect them?'

'I think his father brought them back from his campaigns,' said MacKenzie. 'Mementos of a life in the army. Get down on your knees and search under the desk and at the back of the press, Davie.'

Scougall looked under the desk. He did the same with the press. MacKenzie focused on the bookshelves. He began removing books to feel along the back. On the bottom shelf he noticed some flakes of wood. He took a small dagger from the wall and began to prise out a piece of wood. It gradually came away and he was able to pull it away. In the wall behind the bookcase was a small compartment, about three feet long by a couple of feet deep. Inside was a pile of leather-bound volumes, manuscripts and notebooks. He took them back to the desk and laid them out. He called Scougall over.

Scougall looked down on them curiously. 'Why did he hide these, sir?' he asked.

'The content must be...,' MacKenzie searched for the right word, 'contentious.' He opened a volume. It was a 1533 edition of Heinrich Cornelius Agrippa's *De occulta philosophia*. There were other books in different languages, including works in Spanish and Italian, as well as a pile of handwritten notes and manuscripts. 'Arthur's interests extended well beyond regular philosophy,' said MacKenzie. 'Some of these texts are forbidden. Many authorities would burn them.' He took up one of the manuscripts. 'Ah, look, Davie.' It contained a series of drawings of dice with Greek letters on their faces. There were explanations in Latin about how they should be used. 'They are divining dice!' he cried.

Scougall looked perturbed. 'Predicting the future is witchcraft, sir,' he said. 'Was Arthur a warlock?'

MacKenzie scoffed. 'There's no such thing, Davie! However, this is a substantial collection of illicit literature,' he replied.

'Why did Bethia have the dice with her when she drowned?' asked Scougall.

MacKenzie shook his head. 'Did she share Arthur's interests in the occult or was she looking after them for him? Or did she find them by accident?'

Scougall looked puzzled.

'We'll take the books and papers with us,' said MacKenzie. 'Put them in your bag. Isabella Nasmyth will not know they are missing.'

Scougall hesitated. He did not like the idea of carrying such works. What if he was caught with them? He might be accused of witchcraft himself.

MacKenzie sensed his nervousness. 'Give the bag to me, Davie. I'll carry them.' He returned to the bookcase and replaced the wooden slat and the books he had removed. 'We can study them in detail at the palace,' he added.

CHAPTER 32

The Cadzow Kiss

A NOTE WAS waiting for MacKenzie when he returned to his room written in the spidery hand of Jago O'Flaherty. The Kiss was meeting that night at Cadzow Castle. MacKenzie found Scougall asleep in the library; his head lay on one of the manuscripts they had found in Arthur's room. The thought of going out so late displeased Scougall, but he pulled on his boots and took his cloak and hat to join MacKenzie and O'Flaherty at the Back Close just after eleven o'clock.

The town was quiet as they passed down the High Street, just a gentle murmuring of subdued conversation and the odd guffaw at a drunken joke from the inn. They followed the path along the Cadzow Burn out of the town and were soon among the trees. O'Flaherty led the way slowly, with stick in hand, along a path which ascended into the woods above the Avon Water. Another winding path led higher up the slope through thicker undergrowth. By the time they came out of the trees, the mist had cleared and a full moon made torches unnecessary, although it was difficult to avoid tripping over stones and tree roots.

Cadzow Castle's ancient and decayed battlements soon loomed above them. The castle was a crumbling fortress from another age, constructed when ten-foot-thick walls were essential for defence. They stood for a few moments, gathering their breath, looking up at the huge structure.

'The family's abode before they built the palace a hundred years ago,' said O'Flaherty.

After a further steep climb, they finally reached the castle walls. Suddenly, there was a distant cry – a high-pitched squeal of laughter. It stopped them in their tracks. Then another, then silence again. They followed O'Flaherty through a decayed doorway hidden behind ivy which led to a narrow stairway. The stairs were uneven and worn. They ascended slowly to emerge on a rampart about a hundred feet above.

They stood for a few minutes in the darkness gathering their breath again. They could now hear muffled voices – laughter rising and falling on the wind. O'Flaherty ducked down onto his knees and indicated they should do likewise. They crawled along the side of a low wall. About ten yards along, it was partly breached and provided a place to view the courtyard thirty feet beneath, a large open space where a fire burned. The sound of laughter, coming from inside the castle, began to grow louder. It was a long, cold, uncomfortable wait. Scougall's mind drifted to his warm bed in Edinburgh.

Finally, after about twenty minutes, hooded figures began to emerge from a doorway accompanied by laughs, burps and sniggers. They spread themselves out over the courtyard, forming a semi-circle. The sniggering continued for a minute or two until one of them moved forward and raised their hand to quieten the others. Silence was established for a couple of minutes until another figure emerged from the doorway, came towards them and stopped in front of them. A cloak suddenly dropped to the ground. Scougall was shocked to see a woman's body in the flickering firelight, her long black hair on her bare white back. She began to lean provocatively towards the hooded figures as a fiddler struck up a jig from the darkness, a strange, disjointed tune. From a distance of a few yards, she offered her breasts to them, her smiling face caught briefly in the firelight. At first, Scougall was not sure what was happening in the half-light. When he realised, he was shocked. One figure moved round the semi-circle, waiting for a short while beside each person, holding what looked like a plate or platter waist high in front of them before moving onto the next, each time met with cheers and cries. The woman followed, moving before each figure, squeezing her breasts, saying words that could not be heard from the battlement. Her presence was accompanied by frantic movements and sighs.

'The Cadzow Kiss,' whispered O'Flaherty. According to the kirk, self-abuse was a sin, thought Scougall. Performing such an act in public was surely a grave transgression. He looked disapprovingly at MacKenzie, but he was concentrating on the figures in the darkness, trying to identify them. It was difficult from where they were hiding – he just caught flashes of faces for an instant. But he thought he recognised a few.

The fiddler stopped playing and the revelry dissipated. The woman moved back into the shadows at the side of the courtyard. Her cloak was returned to her. A figure came forward to stand in front of the others. The person removed a scroll from his cloak and began to read in a deep voice. They could just catch the odd word which seemed to make little sense. He spoke slowly and rhythmically until another figure emerged from the castle, leading another by a short piece of rope. 'The initiate,' muttered O'Flaherty.

The initiate, who was swaying slightly, stood in front of the semi-circle and the rope was unfastened. The person with the scroll began to read again. A bottle was handed round and swigs taken by everyone. The woman re-emerged from the shadows. She stood directly in front of the initiate, just a few feet away. Her cloak dropped again. She turned round and bent over, revealing her buttocks to him. The man with the plate came forward and a cheer went up, followed by a couple of minutes of nervous silence as she continued her provocative gestures. Finally, the man holding the plate shouted something and another cheer rose as they all cried out loudly: 'May prick nor purse never fail you!'

More bottles were passed round. The fiddler struck up a jovial tune. The figures began to dance. 'We should leave now, just in case we're seen,' whispered O'Flaherty. 'They'll dance and drink until dawn and then stagger home, but some may leave early.' They crawled back along the battlement and descended to the path through the undergrowth to reach the Avon Water and follow the Cadzow Burn back to Hamilton. Once inside the palace grounds, they stopped to rest in the gardens.

'Why were they doing it?' asked Scougall, unable to hold back his disgust.

O'Flaherty looked at him the way he would a fool. 'They spill their seed on the platter, Mr Scougall. It's a ritual. They swear to follow the rules of the Kiss. Few have witnessed the ceremony without participating in it themselves.'

'Who was the woman?' asked MacKenzie.

'A whore from Glasgow,' replied O'Flaherty. 'She was probably brought down yesterday. She'll go back tomorrow. There's no shortage of volunteers. She'll be paid well and it's easy work.' Scougall recalled the young woman sitting opposite him in the coach whose foot he had stood on.

'Did you recognise anyone, Jago?' asked MacKenzie.

O'Flaherty thought for a moment. 'It was difficult to see in the dark. I can name a few who were there. George Harlaw, Archie Weir and the French servant Chambon. Cruikshank, the regent from Glasgow. And Simon Gilly.'

'The chaplain!' exclaimed Scougall.

'The palace chaplain, Mr Scougall,' said O'Flaherty.

'I met him in Glasgow and in the coach to Hamilton... he seemed such a good man!'

'Do not judge the Kiss in that way,' said O'Flaherty.

'I thought I saw Crawford,' added MacKenzie.

'Crawford denied attending. He's an elder in the kirk for God's sake!' exclaimed Scougall.

'I think the initiate was Lord Basil,' said MacKenzie.

O'Flaherty nodded. 'You are observant, John.'

'Lord Basil swore he had never attended!' cried Scougall.

'It was his first time,' said O'Flaherty.

'What about Arran and Drummond?' asked MacKenzie.

O'Flaherty shook his head. 'I didn't see them.'

'You're very knowledgeable about it all, Jago,' said Scougall.

Jago laughed. 'I've attended many times in the past. I must confess the first time was something of an ordeal. A bottle of rum helped! As a newcomer to Hamilton, it was a good way to make... friends. Now I'm too old to crawl up to the castle to frig in the cold!'

'It's a disgrace!' Scougall blurted out. 'I should have words with Robert Corse or the duchess! It should be stopped!'

O'Flaherty shook his head and smiled: 'It's a harmless caper in the scheme of things, Mr Scougall. A bit of excitement. It doesn't harm anyone. Compared to the slaughter of war, it's nothing, a trifle of fluff. The lass will be well paid for her trouble.'

Scougall was recalling the admonitions of the kirk. He was lost for words.

MacKenzie turned to O'Flaherty. 'We need to identify more of those in the castle, perhaps the lass might help. If there were strangers present, she might know?'

'They'll sleep late after tonight's debauch, said O'Flaherty. 'The girl will go back to Glasgow by coach in the late morning.'

'Does the duchess know about it?' asked Scougall as they headed off to the palace.

'Everyone knows about it, Mr Scougall. She no doubt turns a blind eye.' said O'Flaherty. 'But the date and place are secret. It only becomes gossip after the event. I'm sure the duchess, like all women in the parish, does not approve, but what can she do? Trying to prohibit it would cause disquiet. It helps to secure the loyalty of certain men for her son and so her house.'

'How does it do that?' asked Scougall.

'They sing and dance and drink together and friendships are made in the secrecy of common debauch. They feel a little guilty in the morning as they stagger back to their manses and wives. That is until the next time they receive a message, then the excitement rises in their blood. It makes them feel special, as if they belong to a singular association or club. Unlike Arran and Drummond, they can't visit the fleshpots of London or Paris. But they can attend the Cadzow Kiss!'

'It's not unlike the Masonic craft, Davie. Though perhaps more fun,' said MacKenzie with a wink.

Scougall recalled his own initiation ceremony, only a week before. It was nothing like the Masons. He had a sudden feeling of nausea at the falseness of the world; beneath the surface, all was greed and lust. Those who attended the Kiss were surely sinners of the first rank.

'I presume the fanatics are not represented?' asked MacKenzie.

O'Flaherty shook his head and laughed. 'They would not attend such a joyous occasion! They condemn it as sin, but they don't have all the power in the parish.'

MacKenzie's face lost its playfulness. 'Before we retire to bed, I've one last question for you, Jago. I'm sorry I must ask it. A witness saw you returning to the palace just after dawn on the morning Bethia was found.'

O'Flaherty stopped in his tracks. 'You think I killed her, John?' His eyes flashed with anger.

'I didn't say that, Jago. What were you doing out so early?'

'I'm an old man,' said O'Flaherty. 'I don't sleep well. The battles in which I fought still haunt my dreams. I often walk by the river to watch the sun rise. It's the most beautiful part of the day. It's the best time for composing music.'

'What about your relationship with Bethia?' asked MacKenzie.

'I've told you. I've known her since she was a bairn. There was nothing... unsavoury about it. Don't believe all you hear from the parish gossips, gentlemen. Now I must bid you goodnight.'

'She was seen leaving your chambers in tears, Jago,' added MacKenzie.

'As I told you, I was teaching her the clarsach. I played her laments I composed about the wars. She was a sensitive girl. She often left in tears. Not for the reason you insinuate.'

'I'm afraid there's more, Jago,' continued MacKenzie. 'Corse's relict claims you were his enemy?'

O'Flaherty shook his head in disbelief. 'You think I killed them both.

You have me down as a monster. I thought you were my friend, John.'

'I must ask these questions, Jago,' said MacKenzie. 'We must get to the bottom of it.'

'Corse was a rogue,' said O'Flaherty. 'Years ago, I saw him denouncing an old Quaker woman on the street. I told him to his face he was an arrogant bully. He didn't like it. I will always stand up to the likes of him. But I'm too old to strangle an old man in his house. Goodnight to you, gentlemen.'

CHAPTER 33

A Coach to Glasgow

'I CAN MAKE little sense of these, sir,' said Scougall the next morning as he sat at a table in the library. The books and manuscripts they had taken from Nasmyth House were laid out in front of him. 'A manuscript with notes on how to divine with dice. Notes on how the pentacle can be used as a Mason's mark with a detailed discussion of its symbolism. I got nowhere with the Italian book because I don't read the language. The rest of the manuscripts are incomprehensible.'

MacKenzie came over to the table from the window. 'Pass me the Italian one, Davie. I know a little of the language from my days in the country,' he said.

The small, leather-bound volume was a second edition of *L'Alcibiade fanciullo a scola* published in 1651. MacKenzie tried to translate the title. 'I think it means "Alcibiades the schoolboy", Davie. It looks like a dialogue of some kind.' His eyebrows rose as he translated a few passages from the text to himself. He chuckled. 'This is quite a notorious book. It's a justification of sodomy.'

Scougall stopped reading from a manuscript, looking alarmed. Arthur Nasmyth's literary taste was worrying.

MacKenzie slowly translated a few passages: 'Actions are natural when nature inclines us to them... to call sodomy a vice against nature is ridiculous... that such a sweet delight should not be called "against nature" – and indeed is not "against nature" – is clearly demonstrated by the law of nature itself.'

'What does all this tell us, sir?' asked Scougall.

'Arthur was a devotee of arcane knowledge... symbols and divination... and he was interested in sodomy... Robert Corse hinted at his fascination for new fields of thought.'

Scougall shook his head. 'I don't like where this is going, sir.'

MacKenzie nodded. 'I agree each subject is problematic. The pentacle points to philosophical ideas which some might call heresy. Certainly, the enthusiasts would. Divination is a crime against God regarded as witchcraft by the kirk. Sodomy is a sin punishable by death.'

Scougall finally asked the question that was troubling him. 'Do you think Arthur is a sodomite, sir? Is that why he's fled?'

MacKenzie shook his head. 'The books are not necessarily evidence he's either a heretic, warlock or sodomite. He does, however, savour the occult.'

'It could be the reason Bethia told Andrew Wood she felt he was not the man she thought he was,' suggested Scougall.

MacKenzie nodded.

'Why did she have the dice with her?' asked Scougall.

'Did she find these books and papers in his chamber? Did their discovery alter their relationship, rather than his thoughts of joining the army? Was she worried about Arthur's interest in the occult... and sodomy? Did she have the dice with her to challenge him? But surely such a discovery would not drive her to kill herself?' MacKenzie thought for a moment, then asked: 'What time is it, Davie?'

Scougall proudly looked at his watch. 'Ten thirty, sir.'

MacKenzie smiled. 'Good. We have time to catch the coach to Glasgow.'

The coach left Hamilton at eleven o'clock from the tolbooth. There were three other passengers on board: a middle-aged man and woman sitting together, and a young woman with dark hair, her head resting on the window. She was snoring gently. MacKenzie and Scougall sat opposite her.

She woke now and again during the journey, yawning each time and then going back to sleep. Scougall recognised her as the woman he had shared a coach with and as the alluring figure in the courtyard of the castle. He could not stop looking at her long hair and remembering it on her bare back. The image of her large breasts and buttocks would not leave him. He felt himself becoming aroused. He cursed himself and closed his eyes. He felt his face burn red and prayed to God to turn his mind from such illicit thoughts. Finally, he forced himself to imagine Dr Lawtie sitting naked in the snug in Gibson's Tavern. The picture made him laugh out loud and eased his ardour. Thereafter, he kept his eyes fixed on the view outside the coach. He was relieved when they stopped at the Mercat Cross of Glasgow and they all disembarked. They followed her down the Trongate and caught up with her. MacKenzie called her to stop.

'Are you looking for something, gents? You saw something you liked on the coach?' she said, yawning. A flash of recognition passed across her face as she looked at Scougall.

'Were you in Hamilton last night, my dear?' asked MacKenzie.

'Yes, sir. What of it?'

'We have a few questions. What's your name?'

She smiled. 'Mary Scanlon.'

'What happened in the castle last night, Mary?' asked MacKenzie.

'I don't know what you're talking about, sir.'

MacKenzie opened his hand to reveal a silver coin. She stared at it and her eyes lit up. 'What is it you want to know?'

'Was it the first time you've… attended the ceremony?' asked MacKenzie.

'No, I was there a couple of years ago. I knew what to expect. It's just a bit of fun for the gentlemen.'

'We want to know who attended last night,' prompted Scougall.

'It's meant to be secret, sir.'

'Who employed you for the night?' asked MacKenzie.

'Who are you gentlemen?'

'Lawyers from Edinburgh investigating the death of a young woman,' said MacKenzie.

'Who?' she asked.

'Bethia Porterfield. She drowned a few months ago,' said Scougall.

'Ah, the one who did herself in.'

'Who employed you, Mary?' asked MacKenzie.

'The man from the palace,' she said. 'He's called the master of ceremonies. He met me a few days ago in Glasgow to arrange it.'

'What man from the palace?' asked Scougall.

'The man who looks after the livestock… the warrander.'

'George Harlaw?' asked MacKenzie.

'Yes, that's him. He's often in Glasgow looking for girls.'

'Did you see the Earl of Arran and his man Drummond in the castle last night?' asked MacKenzie.

She went to pick up the coin, but MacKenzie closed his hand.

'Were you watching us?' she asked. 'I can arrange an evening with a few girls if that's what you like.'

'Just the information, Mary,' said MacKenzie. 'There were at least ten men in the courtyard, as well as the initiate. I'm sure you know who they were?'

She nodded. 'The earl, I know. He wasn't in the courtyard. He was inside the castle. In a room with a few others. But not the ones outside. Those outside were all from Hamilton. I recognised a few faces. I don't know their names though. The new boy was Arran's brother Lord Basil.'

'What about William Drummond?' asked Scougall.

'I don't know what he looks like, sir.'

'He would be finely dressed. The man who attends the earl,' said MacKenzie.

'A number inside the castle were dressed finely. A few dandies among them. They never joined in the fun outside.'

'You don't know any of their names? You can't think you deserve any money for that.' MacKenzie withdrew his hand.

She thought for a moment. 'I'm sorry, sir. I wasn't introduced to any of the gentlemen inside. They kept themselves to themselves. They were having a good chat together.'

'There was a group of them?' asked MacKenzie.

'It was different from the first time I attended,' she continued. 'Last night, there were ones outside doing the frigging. I think they were all locals. There were others inside who didn't come out at all. I only saw them in a room when I was getting ready. I glanced through a doorway before Harlaw came for me. They were real gentleman, dressed like dandies, and a couple of others, who looked different, were in uniform, soldiers maybe. When all the business was done outside, I came back inside to gather my stuff. I opened the door of the room where I'd seen them earlier, but the room was empty. They'd all gone.'

'When was that?' asked Scougall.

'Maybe two o'clock.'

MacKenzie handed her the coin. 'Thank you, my dear. If you think of anything else, there are more of these.' She left them with a wave and a smile and was lost in the crowd on the wynd.

MacKenzie took out his pipe, packed it with tobacco and lit it. He stood looking down the wynd deep in thought. At last, he turned to Scougall. 'Let's make the most of our afternoon in Glasgow, Davie. Take me to Corse's office.'

Scougall knocked on the door, waited a couple of minutes and knocked again. There was no answer. MacKenzie knocked harder. Still nothing. MacKenzie looked furtively up and down the street, then leant heavily into the door with his shoulder. It did not give. He stepped back and brought his weight to bear on it. It broke open easily.

'Sometimes, a little force, Davie,' he said.

They entered the anteroom where Scougall had met Lawtie a few days before.

'Corse's office is through there, sir.' The door was unlocked. 'What are we looking for?' asked Scougall.

'We've a few hours until the coach returns to Hamilton. Let's examine as many documents as we can. Where did you get your list of debtors and creditors? I want you to make a copy.'

Scougall found the ledger, sat behind Corse's desk and set to copying it. Over his shoulder, MacKenzie read the names and loans on the list:

Debts owed by William Corse: David Crawford £100 sterling, Abraham Weir £100 sterling, John Spreull £200 Scots, Gilbert Lamb £150 Scots, John Butler £150 Scots, Hector Spence £100 Scots, David Cunningham £100 Scots, John Peacock £100 Scots, James Cruiks £50 Scots, Robert Kennedy 50 merks, John Lang 50 merks, Charles Balfour £20 Scots.

Debts owed to William Corse: Duke of Hamilton 10,000 merks, Earl of Arran £10,000 sterling, Lord Basil Hamilton £1,000 sterling, Robert Blackwood £1,000 sterling, William Drummond £1,000 sterling, William Woodrop £500 sterling, William Ardbuckle £500 sterling, John Anderson £500 sterling, Sir Francis Montgomery of Giffen £500 sterling.

'Abraham Weir is Archie Weir's father,' said Scougall.

MacKenzie nodded. 'I recognise a number of these names – David Crawford, of course. The Duke of Hamilton is in London. Arran returned recently with Drummond. Lord Basil, we know. Blackwood, Woodrop, Ardbuckle and Anderson are Glasgow merchants. John Spreull is Bass John himself. I don't know the rest. What do you make of all this, Davie?'

Scougall put his quill down and turned to MacKenzie. 'Corse is owed large sums by nobles, merchants and lairds. His own debts are much smaller than the amounts he's owed. The snag is that calling in those loans may not be possible. His problem is a lack of ready cash. The news of his recent trading difficulties will have intensified his liquidity problems.'

MacKenzie studied both lists carefully again. 'It's strange, is it not, Davie, that a man like Corse should lend to the likes of them?'

Scougall nodded. 'He lends and borrows from anyone, not just the

Godly. The sum he sought from Mrs Hair, I fear, may have been to pay off some of these smaller debts, rather than invest in a voyage. In other words, it was to stave off his lack of cash. I've allowed my view of him to cloud my judgement.'

'It might have left other lenders aggrieved they had not been fully paid back,' added MacKenzie.

Scougall nodded.

'But could this have turned any into killers, Davie?'

'Killing Corse would not provide money in the short term,' said Scougall.

Scougall removed the cash book Corse had shown him from a shelf. It provided details of payments going back over years. He began to study it.

While Scougall worked on the accounts, MacKenzie searched the rest of the office. He noticed the large Bible on the desk open at the Book of Deuteronomy. He opened the drawers of the desk and examined the contents, mostly quills, ink and paper. On the shelves were Corse's correspondence books. He began to peruse them; they provided a detailed history of his business all the way back to the 1660s. There were letters to and from merchants in Barbados, Belfast, Glasgow and London. It would take days to go through them all. He took down the volume covering the year 1691 and flicked through the pages. He noticed a letter dated the 12th of May from Captain Robert Hodge asking if Corse wanted to subscribe to the venture leaving for the Carolinas and selling its virtues. He showed it to Scougall.

'A possible connection with Arthur, sir,' said Scougall.

After a couple of hours, MacKenzie picked up his hat from Corse's desk. 'I think we're done here, Davie. Where's Lawtie staying? I've a job for him.'

They found Lawtie in the snug in Gibson's, nursing a cup of ale. 'My God, is it not the auld Jacobite himself!' Lawtie said as they entered. MacKenzie would normally have countered with a barbed reply of his own, but he did not want to annoy the doctor. 'I spent an entertaining evening with Mr Scougall a couple of nights ago,' continued Lawtie. 'You lawyers are not as dull as you seem!'

MacKenzie called for a bottle of wine and they joined Lawtie at the table.

'What news of your investigation, MacKenzie?' asked Lawtie, putting his cup of ale aside.

'We make some progress,' said MacKenzie. 'There are still a few loose ends. I seek your expertise, Lawtie. I've a job for you in Hamilton.'

'How much is the fee?' Lawtie did not seem concerned about the nature of the work.

'Twenty pounds Scots for the task, with accommodation for a night at the inn in Hamilton,' replied MacKenzie. 'Half paid now and half on completion.'

Lawtie looked delighted. 'A generous sum. I'll delay my return to Edinburgh for a night or two, gentlemen.'

CHAPTER 34

A Lonely Resting Place

SCOUGALL WAS EXHAUSTED by the time they set out for Hamilton later in the evening. Having seen Lawtie settled in the inn, they only had time for a quick meal and change of clothes in the palace. The thought of a warm bed was enticing. Instead, they were out in the cold again, leaving a little after nine o'clock to meet Wood, his two sons, Andrew and Jacob, and Lawtie at the Mercat Cross. They crossed to the kirk and walked through the kirkyard to a wooden gate which led into a field sloping down to the river.

'This way, gentlemen,' said Wood, raising his torch.

'I cannot believe I agreed to do this, MacKenzie,' said Lawtie in disgust, looking down at the mud squelching round his boots. 'If I'd known I would have to plod through a field in the middle of the night, I would've asked for another £10!' A thick fog from the river had enveloped them, exaggerating the sounds of the mud and reducing visibility to a few yards.

'You're being paid well, Lawtie,' replied MacKenzie. 'And I'll be in your debt. You may need my help someday.'

Scougall walked behind them silently. He felt that their excursion to the west was turning sour. He vowed to have no more to do with such investigations in future. His life was moving in a different direction and it was time he concentrated on his family.

They came to an area of flat, boggy ground near the river. They could hear the water but could not see it through the fog. Wood and his sons stopped beside a small mound of earth and placed their torches on the ground. 'Poor Bethia lies here, gentlemen,' said Wood, gesturing to his sons to begin.

Their spades made quick progress through the soft earth. The others stood in silence as the pair sank deeper and deeper into the ground and the pile of earth rose. Scougall had serious doubts about what they were doing. It was sacrilegious to dig up a corpse. The Quakers had suffered desecration of their burial ground. Now here was more sin. Bethia had been raised from her resting place to be dumped here. She was now being disinterred again. What on earth had she done to deserve such treatment? The sound of the spades slapping into the wet earth seemed to go on for ever.

At last, Andrew Wood looked up. 'Here she is.'

MacKenzie looked down on the corpse in a few inches of water. They looped ropes round her and raised her out, laying her on the ground. It was a piteous sight. The decayed body of a young woman in a linen shift – the beauty of youth food for the worms. The long, dark hair evident in her portrait was still visible among the dirt.

Lawtie opened his bag with a sigh. He removed an apron and instruments wrapped in a cloth. He put the apron over his head and tied it behind his back. Scougall turned away and wandered into the blackness. He could not bear to look at the doctor bent over the corpse. He walked a few yards further into the fog. When he turned, Lawtie was gone, but he could still hear the disgusting sounds of his knife.

Wood offered up a prayer, shaking his head. His sons stood beside him with heads bowed. MacKenzie watched Lawtie hunch over the remains of Bethia, his hands moving quickly across the cadaver. MacKenzie despised the task, but they had no choice.

At last, after about ten minutes, Lawtie rose stiffly to his feet. He turned to MacKenzie. 'There is no child here.'

MacKenzie nodded solemnly. Wood's sons lowered her into the grave. The wet soil was shovelled over her in silence.

They retraced their steps through the kirkyard. On the High Street, Wood's sons headed home. 'Let's return to my fireside for a drink,' Wood said as they walked through the town.

They sat in Wood's living chamber drinking toddy. 'Two parts whisky to three parts water, with a spoonful of honey,' said Wood. MacKenzie, Lawtie and Wood were soon puffing away on their pipes. Scougall sipped his toddy and yawned. He had to admit he preferred the taste to whisky.

MacKenzie finally spoke: 'No unborn bairn accompanied Bethia to the grave. Someone cooked up the story to blacken her name and deflect attention from the real cause of her death. I believe she did not take her own life.'

'Then you think she was slain, John?' Wood asked, staring into the flames of the fire.

'Even if it was an accident,' replied MacKenzie, 'it's been covered up for some reason. There was some kind of foul play. Someone wanted her death to look like suicide and they concocted a reason for it.'

CHAPTER 35

A Letter from the Carolinas

THE FOLLOWING MORNING, they sat pondering what they had learned the day before over breakfast in the High Dining Room. The duchess appeared with a letter in her hand which she handed to MacKenzie. It was a request from Isabella Nasmyth that he should come to see her as soon as possible.

MacKenzie and Scougall mounted horses in the Back Close and rode to Nasmyth House. They were shown into the living chamber by a servant. Isabella entered a few minutes later, looking elated. 'I have word from him at last, Mr MacKenzie! I have word from him, thank God for it,' she beamed. 'It's such a weight off my mind to know he's alive. That he's settled somewhere. I had feared the worst. Now I may encourage him to come home.'

'I'm glad of it, madam,' said MacKenzie.

She took a letter from the table beside her chair and handed it to MacKenzie. 'Read it for yourself.'

MacKenzie introduced Scougall, then read the following:

William's Town
South Carolina
10th of August 1691

My dearest mother,
 I am sorry it has taken me so long to write to you. I was in a state of deepest grief when I left you suddenly in June. I continued in that state until my arrival here a few weeks ago. Since then, my condition improves; I find I am returned a little to my old self and at last able to write.
 I took ship for Carolina from Ayr a few days after I last saw

you. The voyage was arduous and long. I suffered terrible grief. I did little but wander the deck in a daze, lie in my chamber and think of Bethia. I fear I may never know the reason my beloved took her life. She must have been seized by a fit of madness.

I'm glad to say this land has brought about a recovery in me. The warmth improves my humour and I am taken by the lush variety of life. I have hopes of buying a small tract of land.

I intend to make a life for myself among the colonists. I know it will be a hard one, but the profits should be substantial. When I have made enough money, it will allow me to return now and again to my homeland to see you and spend some time in our beloved house.

Please tell my dear Robert and Sir James that I am well and I will write to them soon.

I will write again when I am properly settled.

Your loving son,
Arthur Nasmyth

MacKenzie smiled. He noticed the small pentacle attached to the 'y' in the signature. 'I can see why you are relieved, madam,' he said. 'He's far away, but at least well. He'll maybe come to terms with her death eventually. You must be pleased he's not joined a regiment. Sadly, he doesn't provide any more intelligence about her demise.'

'Thank God for it, sir,' she said. 'I now have something to live for when I thought all was lost. He may marry the daughter of a colonist after a reasonable time has passed and return to Scotland someday. I may even take ship to America to visit him. Ah, here's the wine, gentlemen.'

MacKenzie handed the letter to Scougall and took a glass.

'Tell me something of yourself, Mr Scougall. Are you married?' she asked.

Scougall smiled, looking up from the letter. 'Not long, madam, I was married last year. We have a child on the way.'

'I congratulate you, sir.' She raised her glass and they toasted her son.

Scougall read the letter while MacKenzie and Isabella chatted about gardens and roses.

'We must return to Hamilton, madam,' said MacKenzie after finishing his wine.

'How do your investigations proceed?' she asked.

'There's one definite thing we've learned,' said MacKenzie. 'I ask that you don't share it for now. We've established Bethia was not with child when she died. You did not lose a grandchild. The story of her pregnancy was a smear to cover up something else. What that is, I don't know... yet.'

Isabella nodded. 'I'm relieved by it, sir. I hope you find who is responsible for the vile slander of an innocent girl. And now we have the death of Robert's uncle in town.'

'You knew him, madam?' asked MacKenzie.

'He had little to do with us. We, or rather my husband, belonged to the opposing political faction. It's amazing Robert has managed to stand against his family. I know he had little love for his uncle.'

'Was there hatred between them?' asked MacKenzie.

'I believe so. He was unkind to Robert's mother. William thought his brother had married beneath him and showed her little sympathy near the end of her life when he returned from Barbados. I think Robert bore a grudge against him for that.' She suddenly looked flustered. 'I don't mean to imply he did anything to harm his uncle, just that William was a cold man. Few will be sad about his death.'

When they were outside the gates of the house, Scougall turned to MacKenzie: 'There's something about the letter, sir.' He looked troubled.

'What do you mean, Davie?'

'I told you I examined the note Arthur had written to Sir James,' said Scougall.

'What is it, Davie? Spit it out, man!'

'I made a close study of it. I've a good image of it in my memory. There's something that strikes me about this letter. It's a close match to the hand, but I don't think it's Arthur's. I would have to check it carefully against the note sent to Sir James to make sure. It may not be the same hand.'

MacKenzie turned to Scougall. 'It could be a forgery?'

'I cannot be certain until I compare them. It's just a supposition.'

'I'll write to Sir James right away,' said MacKenzie, 'telling him of the letter, although I'm sure Mrs Nasmyth will already have done so, and asking him to send examples of Arthur's hand to the palace.'

'I may be wrong, sir,' said Scougall nervously. 'I had to voice my doubts.'

'Of course you did, Davie.'

'Should we ask her for the letter?' asked Scougall.

'I fear it would deeply upset her that we doubted its provenance. Let her be happy for now. I've just thought of something... wait here.'

MacKenzie gave the reins of his horse to Scougall and went back into the house.

He emerged five minutes later. 'As I suspected, she had retired to rest after the wine. I told the servant I'd left my pipe in the chamber. The letter was lying on the table where she left it. I don't like such subterfuge, but sometimes it's necessary. We'll return it later if it's not a fake.'

They mounted and set off for Hamilton. 'Why would anyone forge the letter?' asked Scougall.

'To imply Arthur is far away and well, when in fact he's not. If it's a forgery, I have grave fears for him.'

CHAPTER 36

A Meeting in the Park

THEY DISMOUNTED AT the palace gates and walked their horses down the drive. A man appeared in the distance from the Back Close. As he got closer, Scougall realised it was Arthur's regent, Alexander Cruikshank.

'Good day, Mr Cruikshank,' said Scougall.

'Ah, Mr Scougall,' said Cruikshank nervously.

'I am John MacKenzie.'

'It's a pleasure to meet you, sir,' said Cruikshank as they shook hands.

'You've been visiting the palace?' asked Scougall.

Cruikshank looked awkward. 'Seeing to a little business, gentlemen. I must catch the coach for Glasgow. Have you made any progress in your search for Arthur?'

MacKenzie interrupted Scougall who was about to give something away about the letter: 'We're making some progress… nothing definite as yet. What business brings you to Hamilton, Mr Cruikshank?'

Cruikshank smiled sheepishly. 'Nothing of importance, just visiting a few friends. It's terrible news about Robert's uncle.'

'Who were you visiting in the palace?' asked MacKenzie.

Cruikshank did not answer right away but eventually said, 'Mr Drummond, the earl's secretary.'

MacKenzie smiled. 'We know the real reason for your visit, Mr Cruikshank.'

Cruikshank was unnerved. 'What do you mean, sir?'

'You were attending the Kiss, Mr Cruikshank,' said MacKenzie.

'Whatever gave you that idea?'

'There's no point denying it,' said MacKenzie. 'We have witnesses who saw you there.'

Cruikshank was lost for words. 'There's no law against it… I admit it… just a little diversion…'

'Did Arthur ever attend?' asked MacKenzie.

Cruikshank shook his head. 'I believe he was asked... but refused.'

'Did Bethia know he was asked?'

'I don't know... I doubt he told her.'

'Was he under pressure to attend?' asked Scougall.

'Of course not... you cannot be forced to go.'

'What about Robert Corse?' asked MacKenzie.

'Robert has no desire to attend,' said Cruikshank. 'He's training to be a minister. You appear to know a lot about it, Mr MacKenzie.'

'What about Archie Weir?' asked MacKenzie.

Cruikshank did not answer.

'Our witnesses saw him there as well,' said Scougall.

'A merry little get-together indeed,' added MacKenzie.

'I must catch my coach, gentlemen,' said Cruikshank.

MacKenzie moved in front of him, blocking his way. 'There was another meeting inside the castle that night... the night Bethia died... as there was the night before last.'

'I know nothing about that,' said Cruikshank angrily.

'A meeting of a completely different nature,' said MacKenzie.

'You're mistaken, sir.'

'I thought you were a supporter of the Revolution, Mr Cruikshank?' asked Scougall.

'My first loyalty is to the House of Hamilton. Arran could be king one day. Think of that, Mr Scougall. That's where my loyalty belongs. I must be gone, gentlemen. I'll miss my coach.'

'Did you attend the Kiss on the 13th of June?' asked MacKenzie, raising his voice.

Cruikshank was unnerved. 'The last meeting. Yes.'

'The night Bethia drowned,' said Scougall.

'There's no connection,' said Cruikshank.

'What about the other gentlemen who met at the same time?' asked MacKenzie.

'I don't know what you're talking about.'

'When did you hear about Bethia's drowning?' asked MacKenzie.

'In the morning, like everyone else,' replied Cruikshank. 'I went to the palace for news after hearing about it in town. I met Arthur himself on his way out. He was distraught.'

'Where did you meet him?' asked MacKenzie.

'At the Back Close. He'd just come out of the palace. He was taking the path which leads from the close through the north woods out of town. It's another, longer way to Nasmyth House. He said he could not face speaking to anyone. I watched him run off that way.'

'He said nothing more about Bethia?' demanded MacKenzie.

Cruikshank shook his head. 'He had just seen his beloved… drowned. What could he say? Now I really must be gone, gentlemen.'

'Just one other matter,' said MacKenzie. 'Was Arthur interested in arcane knowledge?'

'What do you mean?' asked Cruikshank.

'We've found dice and a manuscript about divining in his library with other documents,' said Scougall.

'He never mentioned such things to me,' replied Cruikshank.

'Why would Bethia have divining dice in her bag the night she died?' asked MacKenzie.

Cruikshank shook his head, exasperated by the questions. 'You'll have to excuse me. I'll miss the coach.' He set off at a brisk pace down the drive.

CHAPTER 37

Comparing Hands in the Library

A BUNDLE OF letters arrived from Sir James a few hours later. MacKenzie left Scougall in the library to compare them with the letter taken from Nasmyth House. He went to the High Dining Room for dinner. The duchess was not in attendance. A servant told him she was eating alone in her chamber. The only diners were Lord Basil and the Laird of Grinton, accompanied by Simon Gilly.

'It's a pleasure to see you again, gentlemen,' said MacKenzie taking a seat.

Gilly gave MacKenzie a nervous nod.

Grinton smiled warmly. 'It's a great shame we miss the company of her grace this evening, Mr MacKenzie, but I'm pleased you're here to entertain us with some Highland tales.'

'I hope you're not here to make any more accusations against me,' said Lord Basil.

MacKenzie ignored Lord Basil's comment. 'We make progress, gentlemen. Mr Scougall is working on some documents at this very moment.'

Grinton stopped eating. 'I have some intelligence for you, MacKenzie,' he said. 'Yesterday, I decided to walk the northern boundary of my lands, a lonely area bordering the Nasmyth estate where I rarely go. In the glen above the Cloverhill burn is Crookedstane Tower, a ruined tower house. It was severely damaged during the civil wars and has been uninhabited for fifty years. It was late in the afternoon by the time I got there and beginning to get dark. I'm sure I saw candlelight inside the tower. It's a desolate spot where nobody goes. I said to myself, I must tell Mr MacKenzie about that. I've never seen anyone in the tower since I was a boy.'

'Did you investigate yourself?' asked MacKenzie.

'It's a long walk to get there,' said Grinton, 'perhaps two miles down an extended slope and over a burn. There's no brig, so you must wade. I decided to head for home. It may just have been a shepherd taking refuge for the night, but it's noteworthy. I've recorded it in my diary.'

'Thank you for telling me, Grinton,' said MacKenzie. 'Perhaps we'll ride out tomorrow to take a closer look. It may only be a shepherd, as you say, but we should check, just in case.'

MacKenzie turned to Lord Basil who was taciturnly munching his food. 'I have a question for you, my lord.'

Lord Basil looked at him sourly.

'I believe last night was an important one for you?'

Lord Basil spoke angrily: 'What do you mean?'

'I believe you were initiated into... the Cadzow Kiss!'

Grinton laughed. 'It happens to us all!'

Lord Basil looked embarrassed. 'It's meant to be a secret association.'

'I just hoped you might confirm who attended in addition to yourself, my lord,' said MacKenzie. 'Not those in the courtyard, but those inside the castle... who met with your brother.'

'I don't know what you're talking about. You must excuse me, gentlemen.' Lord Basil rose abruptly, throwing down his napkin and storming out.

MacKenzie turned his attention on Gilly, who also appeared awkward. 'You were also seen in the castle, Mr Gilly.'

Gilly looked round nervously, making sure no servants were in earshot. He nodded. 'It seems you have a good source, Mr MacKenzie. It's just a little harmless entertainment.'

'For a clergyman?' asked MacKenzie.

Gilly was about to answer when Scougall entered the room. He went to MacKenzie and whispered in his ear: 'I've found something, sir.'

MacKenzie excused himself. Once in the library, Scougall spoke excitedly: 'It's a fake! I'm sure of it. It's a close copy of Arthur's hand, but there are subtle differences.'

MacKenzie took out his pipe, filled it and sat beside the fire. He was soon puffing away. After a few minutes, he came back to the table and examined the forged letter again. He read it closely and smiled ruefully: 'Of course, Davie. I see now.' He shook his head. 'It breaks my heart,' he continued. 'I don't think anyone will see Arthur Nasmyth alive again.'

CHAPTER 38

Discovery on the Moors

SCOUGALL MADE A sketch in his notebook of the route to Crookedstane Tower from an estate map in the library. It was a fifteen-mile ride from Hamilton and would take a few hours to get there on horseback. Fortunately, the weather was fine and they reached their destination in the late morning. The tower was a traditional keep: centuries old, a massive stone block with thick walls and arrow slits rather than windows. It was in a state of decay; part of the roof was missing and the stonework was badly worn.

MacKenzie opened the low, wooden door and entered a hall. The two rooms off it were empty except for dust and cobwebs. He had to duck as they climbed the stairwell to explore the first and second floors. Again, the rooms were cold, damp and empty. On the third floor, a door was slightly ajar. There was a peculiar smell inside the small chamber, different from the rest of the tower: a mixture of food and stale urine. The room contained a wooden table and chair, and a box bed in the corner. On the table were a couple of sheets of paper and a quill in a stand.

'Someone's been here recently, Davie,' said MacKenzie.

'Who did Grinton see here... a passing shepherd?' asked Scougall.

MacKenzie shrugged his shoulders. 'When did the adventurers sail from Ayr, Davie?'

'Weeks ago, sir. But why would someone fake a letter from Carolina?' asked Scougall.

'It's possible Arthur was here after returning from Glasgow. Someone would have to supply him with food,' said MacKenzie.

'His mother? Or Corse? Cruikshank or Archie Weir? Or someone else?' suggested Scougall.

They descended the stairs into the darkness of the cellar. Scougall took a candle from his pocket and lit it using his tinder box. It was one large room used in the past as a prison and wine cellar. MacKenzie lit another candle and they began to search. Scougall found a pile of empty wine bottles in a corner. MacKenzie located a long, wooden table. The top was stained in places. He looked under it and saw another large stain on the floor. There were also numerous flecks on the wall behind the table.

He rose stiffly. 'Look, Davie. I think these are bits of flesh. And bloodstains on the table and floor. Something's been butchered down here. I hope to God it was a deer!'

Scougall joined him at the table and raised his candle. He observed the stains on the table and floor, and the tiny flecks on the wall.

MacKenzie grimly shook his head. 'Where would you dispose of a body?' Suddenly he had an epiphany. 'Come, Davie. We need to make haste.'

Clouds had descended by the time they emerged from the tower, smothering the moors and hills in a grey blanket. It had begun to rain. They took another path down the slope towards the burn and up onto the moors in the direction of Grinton's estate. Scougall had never spent so much time in the saddle in his life and his whole body was aching. He had an overwhelming longing to be back in Edinburgh with Chrissie. MacKenzie dug his heels into his horse's sides, and Scougall reluctantly followed suit. It was a hard, wet hour's ride. They dismounted at the top of a rounded hill. There was little to be seen of the surrounding countryside because of cloud cover.

'Shawtonhill burial ground,' said MacKenzie. Scougall was shocked by the scene of destruction.

'Why are we here, sir?' he asked.

'We have another grisly task, Davie. We're looking for human remains, the remains of a young man, the body parts of someone recently dead.'

MacKenzie directed Scougall to search the east side of the burial ground. Scougall reluctantly climbed through the wall and wandered among the debris of earth and bones, his eyes pinned to the ground. After a few minutes, he saw something that made his hair stand on end. It was a hand recently cut from an arm. He called to MacKenzie that he had found something.

'Mark it, Davie,' MacKenzie shouted back.

Scougall removed his cravat and ripped off a piece of the material. He tied it round a finger of the hand. He noticed blue ink stains on a few of the fingers. He continued to search. Near the centre of the burial ground, there was a large heap of earth. It took a few moments to discern it was a human torso without arms or legs. A jacket was still visible under all the muck. He shouted to MacKenzie and tied another bit of cloth to a stick to mark its position.

MacKenzie had also found something. A head was lying beside a pile of bones, a bloody stump where it was severed from the neck. MacKenzie noticed a small scar, crescent-shaped, on the side of the face. 'Arthur Nasmyth,' he said solemnly.

'My God, sir! How do you know?' asked Scougall, who had moved round beside him.

'The scar on his cheek. I've seen it in his portrait. We need to find the rest of him and get the remains back to town.'

They spent another hour in the burial ground, but only found an arm. It was starting to get dark, so they stacked the body parts outside the wall. MacKenzie examined them all carefully.

'I'll get Hugh Wood to send a cart. I'm afraid we'll have to take this with us as evidence, Davie.' MacKenzie put on a glove, lifted Arthur's head by a clump of matted hair and placed it in a sack. 'I want Lawtie to look at the remains.'

'What do you think happened, sir?' asked Scougall.

'I think he was killed in the last week or so. He was dismembered in the cellar. Grinton probably saw a candle lit by the killer.'

'Who did this, sir?'

'I want to wait to see what Lawtie can tell us about the manner of death.'

In the early evening, the remains were deposited in the tolbooth. Lawtie made a quick examination before his coach left for Glasgow. 'Death was caused by a blunt instrument to the back of his head. He was then butchered,' said Lawtie. 'There's not much more I can say. Death probably occurred within the last few days. Now I must be on my way, gentlemen. I've certainly earned my fee in the west!'

CHAPTER 39

Questions for John Timothy

THEY WERE EXHAUSTED by the time they got back to the palace. Scougall was exasperated when MacKenzie told him they had one more task to complete that day which was essential to clarify things. He rang the servants' bell. A couple of minutes later, there was a knock on the door and John Timothy entered. MacKenzie asked him to close the door behind him.

'I've a few questions for you,' began MacKenzie, 'about… Bethia.' He waited for a reaction, but John Timothy did not flinch.

'I've been told she received unwanted attention from men in this house,' said MacKenzie.

John Timothy did not reply.

'I need to ask you about a meeting you had with her. A witness told us she left in tears.'

John Timothy still said nothing.

'She was seen leaving the laundry looking distressed. She was seen talking to you there.'

'What am I being accused of?' asked John Timothy, finally.

'Do you deny this happened?' asked MacKenzie.

'No. She was upset when she left the laundry. Not long after I arrived at the palace.'

'She was a bonnie woman,' said MacKenzie. 'I'm sure you are a lonely man. Did you make advances towards her?'

John Timothy shook his head vehemently. 'No, sir. I never touched her!'

'Then why was she leaving in tears?'

'We had talked of things.'

'What things?'

'She told me her troubles. She feared Arthur did not love her anymore.

She thought things had changed between them. She could not tell the duchess about it. I don't know why she told me. I think she had to tell someone.'

'Why did she leave in tears?' asked Scougall.

'Because she had a good heart, sir.'

'What do you mean?' asked MacKenzie.

'After I sympathised with her about Arthur, she asked me about my life. Not many people care to do so. They are afraid what they might learn. I told her... something of my existence as a slave. How I was taken suddenly in Africa as a boy. How I never saw my mother and father again. How it happened out of the blue on a fine summer day. How my life was changed for ever in an instant. How my wife and daughter were taken from me after a slave revolt. She began to cry.'

'You must tell me the truth,' said MacKenzie adamantly.

'It is the truth, sir.'

'How do we know it's the truth?' asked MacKenzie.

John Timothy was sweating. 'I could not...' he began but stopped mid-sentence.

'Please continue,' said MacKenzie.

'I... I could never debauch her... I could never debauch any woman...'

'What do you mean?'

'I mean... I'm not able to...'

'How are you not able?'

'I was punished in Barbados... I was punished... after the revolt.'

'How were you punished?'

'I was... I was castrated!' he cried out.

MacKenzie shook his head. 'I'm sorry you've suffered such vile treatment.'

Scougall stood like a statue, not daring to move.

MacKenzie's tone softened. 'I must ask that you show me, John. I'm sorry. I need to know for certain.'

MacKenzie went to the door and locked it. John Timothy lowered his breeches and pulled down his undergarments. Scougall looked away and stared at the darkness outside. MacKenzie observed the mass of scar tissue between his legs. He turned away shaking his head. John Timothy pulled up his trousers.

'I'm truly sorry I had to put you through that. I had to eliminate you,' said MacKenzie.

John Timothy was breathing hard. 'Is there anything else, sir?'

MacKenzie walked over to the window and reflected for a few moments. 'Did Bethia name those who were troubling her?'

John Timothy shook his head. 'Only that she hoped it would end when she became Lady Nasmyth.'

'Is there anything else you can tell us about the people in the palace that might explain what happened to her?'

'I cannot say anything, sir,' said John Timothy. 'I would not be treated well if I accused anyone. I've never been treated well by... white men.'

MacKenzie nodded. 'I understand. I understand why you would not trust us, but if there's anything you can say.'

'Only that she showed me some sympathy and that's a rare thing.'

CHAPTER 40

A Confession

MACKENZIE AND SCOUGALL returned to the library the next morning. MacKenzie looked down at the collection of books and manuscripts from Nasmyth House laid out before them. 'So many lies, Davie,' he said turning away.

Scougall nodded.

'A secret society encourages lying,' said MacKenzie.

Scougall wondered if he was also referring to the Masons, but before he had time to say anything, MacKenzie continued: 'All is secrecy. All is lies. Crawford lies. Arran lies. Drummond lies. Cruikshank lies. Lord Basil lies. Does O'Flaherty also lie? There are too many liars. What about Gilly and Weir? Does anyone tell us the truth here?'

Scougall shook his head.

MacKenzie began to pace round the room. 'What do we know for sure, Davie? Bethia was pulled from the Clyde on the morning of the 14th of June. We know she was not pregnant. We know she was later smeared. If we believe O'Flaherty, she fell into the Avon Water. I'm willing to believe him. It's possible another person was with her. This could've been Arthur. Or was it one of her abusers? Or was it more than one person? We also know the Kiss met that night and there were strangers attending it. We don't know of any direct connection between the Kiss and her death. We know Arthur was interested in the occult. We know Bethia had his divining dice with her when she died.' MacKenzie stopped for a few moments. 'We've found out what the duchess desired of us. We know Bethia did not drown herself and we know she was not with child. But that's not enough for me. How do we string it all together, Davie?'

'I must admit I'm bamboozled, sir,' said Scougall.

'I've just remembered something. Is there a copy of Ford's map of Barbados in the library?'

Scougall thought for a moment. He went to the collection of maps in a press. He was sure he had seen a few of the Americas and the Caribbean. He came back with the map of Barbados.

MacKenzie looked at it carefully, making some measurements between places with his fingers. He nodded to himself, folded it and put the map in his pocket. 'In a case like this,' he said with a slight smile on his face, 'we may never link all the evidence together. Another approach is called for. Let me call it my degree of truth tally. We'll see how it works out.'

MacKenzie took his hat and cloak. Scougall did not understand what he meant but followed him out of the palace and into the town in the rain, all the way to Robert Corse's door. There was no answer for a few minutes. At last, Corse appeared, looking distraught. MacKenzie spoke calmly to him: 'A few words with you, Robert, inside if that's convenient. It's very important, please.'

Corse beckoned them into his living chamber where a fire sputtered weakly. On the table was paper, a quill and an open Bible. He was preparing a sermon. Once they were all in the room and the door was shut, MacKenzie turned to him. Corse stood at the hearth looking into the fire. Scougall was at the window.

MacKenzie spoke harshly to him: 'You've heard we discovered Arthur's body yesterday?'

Corse did not turn or reply but kept staring into the flames, breathing heavily. 'I cannot believe it... my beloved friend... I'll never see him again.'

'You've lied to me, Robert,' said MacKenzie.

Scougall was not sure why MacKenzie was being so callous to him. He felt himself begin to sweat.

'You've lied to me on three occasions, Robert,' MacKenzie continued. 'Once, I could perhaps let pass. We all twist the truth occasionally. Twice, caused an alarm bell to begin ringing inside my head. Can a man be trusted who lies twice in the space of two meetings? But three lies in three meetings revealed you were hiding something.'

MacKenzie paused for a few moments. Corse continued to stare silently at the fire.

'Firstly,' MacKenzie continued, 'when I met you at the Mercat Cross a few days ago you told me you had spoken to Arthur at the palace gates on the morning Bethia's body was found. This was contradicted by Mr Cruikshank, who told us he saw Arthur leaving by a different route from the Back Close.'

Still Corse stared at the fire.

'Secondly,' continued MacKenzie, 'when we spoke on the night of your uncle's murder you said you didn't know Arthur stayed in the Sugar Works after he fled to Glasgow. You had already told me you knew this, contradicting yourself! And thirdly, when we met the next morning in your aunt's house, you told me the symbol beneath Arthur's signature was nothing. I could hardly believe it meant nothing. The pentacle is a powerful symbol with multiple meanings. It was clear you sought to underplay his interest in such things. I recalled the estates you had circled on the map inside Ligon's history of Barbados.' MacKenzie pulled out the map he had taken from the library. He opened it and put it on the table. 'The five estates you circled form a particular pattern if we draw lines between them. Do you have a pencil, Davie?'

Scougall handed him one.

MacKenzie drew a series of lines on the map connecting the estates. 'Look – a pentacle! This surely shows you share Arthur's interest in esoteric knowledge.' MacKenzie held out the map, but Corse did not turn to look at it. MacKenzie raised his voice. 'Why would you lie so many times, Mr Corse? And you a man training to be a minister!'

Corse did not flinch. His eyes did not move from the point in the fire he stared at. Scougall examined the map in surprise and saw the estates did indeed form the shape of a pentacle.

'And then, Mr Corse,' continued MacKenzie, 'there is the letter you forged from Arthur. It was almost a perfect match. Only the sharp eye of Davie spotted it was a fake. The pamphlet about the Carolina scheme which Davie found in the Sugar Works was no doubt planted by you. A clever way to suggest that Arthur was already gone. Why would you do it?'

Corse finally turned to face MacKenzie. He was shaking and looked deathly pale. There was a look of mania in his eyes. He dropped into a chair. His head went down into his hands and he sighed deeply. Pulling himself up, he looked at the wall beyond them and said: 'Please forgive me. I didn't know what to do.'

MacKenzie waited for a few moments, then said: 'Tell us the truth, for God's sake, man. Tell us the truth about what happened to her. No more lies.'

Corse nodded and then spoke weakly in a hoarse whisper: 'I've kept certain things from you. For that I'm truly sorry. I beg for God's forgiveness. I've suffered for it. You'll see there are reasons for my lies.'

'I'm sure God demands the truth now, so speak up, man,' commanded MacKenzie.

Corse nodded seriously. 'I'll tell you what happened. I need to tell someone about that night. It's destroying me. Eating me up. I need to confess... to someone. I was with Arthur and Bethia that night.'

MacKenzie lowered himself into the chair beside Corse. Scougall remained standing at the window. Corse was shivering despite the fire being only a few feet from him.

Corse continued: 'The three of us had been out together for a walk that day. We were late returning to Hamilton along the Avon in the dark. I stopped to pass water behind a tree and fell behind them. They were about fifty yards ahead of me. I tried to catch up with them, when suddenly, I heard a commotion. There were shouts and cries. I saw torchlight in the trees. A group of men, a couple on horseback, were on the track beside them. By the urgency of the cries, I knew immediately something was wrong. I slipped behind a tree to watch.'

'Who were they?' asked MacKenzie.

'Some looked like nobles and others were soldiers. My eye was drawn to one man in particular – an important man from the way he was dressed and the way he held himself on his horse. At first, I thought King James himself had returned to claim his crown!

'I heard shouts of "No one must know!" then I heard a French name and something about Ireland. Arthur shouted at Bethia to run. He pushed one to the ground and ran off himself into the trees. A couple of shots rang out. Fortunately, they missed and he was lost in the darkness. Bethia stood for a moment, petrified, then fled in the opposite direction. A couple of them pursued her along the path by the river. I followed in the darkness. She ran upriver from the castle, back the way we had come. They soon caught up with her.' Corse stopped and his eyes filled with tears. He began to sob.

'I know this is difficult for you. Please continue, Mr Corse,' said MacKenzie.

'They had trapped her at a small clearing beside the river. I hid in the trees about thirty yards away. I heard her beg them to let her go home. Not just lives, but kingdoms were at stake, I heard one say in French. They could not risk that she would talk. She had to be silenced. She had seen the duke. I remember one saying that. She had seen the duke.' Corse hesitated again. 'I had no weapon with me. What could I do? I was frozen with fear. I should have called out to distract them. I should have run off to draw them away and give her a chance to escape. But my courage failed me. I could not move. They pulled her into the shallows and plunged her head under the water. I hoped they just meant to scare her. I thought they would let her up in a few seconds. There was splashing in the water as she struggled. It went on and on and on and on and they did not allow her up. Then there was an awful silence. One waded into the river with her body and let her be taken downstream by the current. I could not believe I had witnessed coldblooded murder. I should have acted to save her! I should have done something! I should have distracted them! But I could not.' Corse broke down in tears again.

MacKenzie waited for a few moments then said: 'Please continue.'

'I've suffered awful guilt since that night. I've asked God countless times why he did not let me act to save her. The only answer that appears in my mind is that they would have killed me as well and then no witness to her murder would be alive. I crouched in the woods until they were gone and then my mind turned to Arthur. Had they killed him also? I retraced my steps to the track, but they were gone. I wandered back to my house in town. I collapsed in bed. In the morning, I heard a body was found in the river. I had to speak with Arthur to tell him what happened, but when I went to his house, his mother told me he had been to see Bethia's body in the palace and fled.'

MacKenzie mulled over what he had heard. 'What has happened to Arthur?'

Corse did not answer him but continued to sob.

'Did an assassin find him and kill him?' asked MacKenzie.

Corse nodded and broke down again.

'Why were you in the woods that night?' asked MacKenzie.

Corse looked down at his hands. 'Arthur wanted to talk to me about his future. He was having doubts about marrying Bethia. She saw us leaving town that afternoon and followed us. She overheard us talking in the woods near the Avon. She heard Arthur say he wanted to break off the marriage and join a regiment. She ran off screaming when she heard it. We heard her cries. Arthur went after her and managed to calm her somewhat. I tried to catch them up after passing water. That's when they ran into the men.'

MacKenzie shook his head. 'You could not tell anyone? After what you had seen done to her. You remained silent. A man of God remained silent when witness to such evil?'

'I feared for my life. I feared for Arthur's life. I didn't know what to do. I feared if I said anything they would find me and kill me. If they had killed her like that, they would do anything.'

'So, you found Arthur in Glasgow,' continued MacKenzie, 'and arranged for him to come back to the tower until he could be smuggled out. You planted pamphlets and forged the letter to suggest he was already in America.'

Corse was in tears. 'I had to do it for him. He was ready to leave. I had arranged a horse for him to ride to Ayr. And then he was gone from the tower. I went there the day I met you at the cross. I had clothing for him in my bag. But he was not in the tower. I didn't know what had happened to him. I thought perhaps he had decided to flee without telling me. Now I know they found him. I know they killed him just as they had slain her. Now they will kill me!'

CHAPTER 41

A Conversation with the Duchess

MACKENZIE AND SCOUGALL returned to the palace. MacKenzie informed a servant he wanted to see the duchess urgently. 'Join me in the garden, gentlemen,' she said rising from her desk.

MacKenzie bowed his head and followed her out the French windows into the gardens. Scougall followed a few yards behind. They stood looking across the river. 'It's been a pleasure to have seen all this, your grace. I'll return home with many new ideas for my own gardens,' said MacKenzie.

'Are you leaving soon, Mr MacKenzie? Are your investigations complete?' she asked anxiously.

MacKenzie nodded thoughtfully. 'They are complete, your grace.'

She looked up at him expectantly.

'Firstly, as you suspected,' he continued, 'Bethia was not pregnant. Secondly, she did not take her own life.'

'I knew it!' she cried.

'What I have to tell you, however, will be difficult to hear,' he added.

A darkness came across her face and all she said was: 'Please leave nothing out.'

MacKenzie beckoned her to sit on a wooden bench. He remained standing and spoke calmly to her. 'The relationship between Arthur and Bethia was not as harmonious as many believed, your grace. From her side it remained strong, but Arthur was passing through a time of doubt, not just about the wedding, but his path in life. They had argued on the morning of the 13th of June in Bethia's house, witnessed by Janet Dobbie. Later in the afternoon, Arthur met Robert Corse to talk. Bethia spied them on the street and followed them. They went into the woods along the Avon. She overheard their conversation. Arthur did not want to go through with the marriage. She revealed herself and a row ensued.

She stormed off into the darkness. Arthur pursued her and they ran into a group of men who were there for an entirely different reason. A few seconds later and they would have passed them by and none of these tragic events would have unfolded. They were there for a particular purpose under the cover of the Cadzow Kiss which was to meet later that night in the castle. The group included an envoy from King James: one of his closest advisers, the Duke of Melfort. They thought Arthur and Bethia overhead something of importance and panicked. They killed Bethia in cold blood, drowning her in the Avon.'

At this point the duchess let out a long sob and began to cry.

Nevertheless, MacKenzie continued his narrative: 'They tried to kill Arthur, but he escaped into the woods. Robert Corse also got away but was not seen. Arthur searched for her all night but learned in the morning she was dead. Later, Bethia was smeared to make it look like she killed herself. An assassin was dispatched to hunt Arthur down. It took weeks to find him, but he was finally located at Crookedstane Tower. He was killed and his body was dismembered. He was dumped in the Quakers' burial ground... I've uncovered a series of the darkest deeds carried out in the name of politics with the aim of protecting the cause of the old king.' He paused for a moment. 'There is also the political position of your son to consider.'

The duchess looked shocked and disgusted. 'My God, Arran was involved!' she cried.

'The meeting with Melfort was engineered by him under cover of the Kiss. There was much secrecy around it because so much was at stake. Was Arran to support another effort to take back the throne for James Stuart in Scotland? I don't believe he was responsible for the killings. I don't know if he had any knowledge of the smearing of Bethia. But they must've had local knowledge to spread false rumours about her. I believe this was carried out through William Corse, probably at the behest of Drummond.'

She stood silently, staring across the gardens, tears on her cheeks. Finally, she turned to MacKenzie. 'Is there any evidence of this?'

'Robert Corse is the only witness of Bethia's murder. He'll not testify in court. He fears for his life. There's no evidence to suggest who murdered Arthur.'

The duchess shook her head, a painful expression crumpling her face. She had aged in a few minutes. 'What should I do, Mr MacKenzie?'

'I told you I would find out what happened to Bethia, your grace. I've determined she was killed by Jacobites. Melfort and his men are already back in France or Ireland. They are unreachable and unpunishable. It's your decision how you deal with your son and Drummond.'

She nodded slowly. 'Am I to bring down the House of Hamilton? I've worked ceaselessly to build it up from nothing. Is it to be brought crashing down again?'

'Justice is often unobtainable, your grace. At least you know the truth about Bethia. No one else knows what happened, except Corse. At least Bethia can be reburied in the kirkyard. A proclamation should be made that she was not with child and died tragically, not by her own hand. I'll leave for Edinburgh tomorrow.'

The duchess shook her head despondently. 'What about the killing of William Corse?' she asked, finally.

'That's another matter, your grace. William Corse was close to bankruptcy and desperate. Perhaps he was demanding too high a price and had to be silenced. Perhaps his death is not connected with Bethia and Arthur at all. It's an issue for the sheriff of Lanarkshire, not me.'

CHAPTER 42

Last Words with Arran

MACKENZIE AND SCOUGALL returned to their rooms and began to pack for the journey home. Scougall was delighted to be heading back to Edinburgh. MacKenzie was surprised to receive a message from Arran, requesting a meeting at Cadzow Castle. One of the earl's men escorted him. He left Scougall to his packing.

Arran was waiting on the ruined battlement, not far from the spot where they had crouched to watch the Kiss. In the daylight, the castle seemed a more benign place. Arran stared out across the Clyde valley; his usual arrogance was gone. He let MacKenzie gather his breath from the climb, then turned to him. 'I like to meet up here, Mr MacKenzie. It's a fine spot. A man can think up here away from the hubbub at the palace, away from... the influence of my mother. No one can hear us up here.'

'You'll be duke yourself one day,' added MacKenzie.

Arran nodded. 'My mother, how should I say this, has steel in her veins. I sometimes think she'll outlive me. She has a loyalty to the past I don't have. The world will change when she's taken by the Lord. Our house must look elsewhere for its vitality in the future. It must look south to England. That's where real power lies.' He paused for a moment and sighed. 'I've spoken with her this morning. She tells me you've discovered the truth about Bethia's drowning.'

'It's time I left Hamilton, your grace,' said MacKenzie. 'I want to see my daughter and grandson. Let me tell what happened.'

Arran nodded. 'I'll not interrupt until you tell me the whole sorry tale.'

MacKenzie provided the same description of events he had given the duchess. While he spoke, Arran continued to look out over the Clyde, his gloved hands holding the edge of the battlement. He listened attentively but began to shake his head. He did not speak until McKenzie had finished.

'An interesting explanation. But you're wrong, MacKenzie. You're wrong,' Arran said.

MacKenzie was surprised. 'Wrong she was killed by Jacobites?'

Arran took a deep breath. 'Jacobites did not kill or smear her, and they did not kill Arthur. Drummond accompanied Melfort to the castle that night and left with him. All went according to plan. There was no impromptu meeting with Arthur and Bethia in the woods. Drummond would not lie to me. Before I tell you the truth, I must ask that you don't divulge what I'm about to say to anyone.'

MacKenzie nodded, surprised by Arran's reply. 'By breeding and inclination, I'm a Jacobite,' Arran began, 'although sometimes my reason rages against the creed as the rashest in the world. However, I cannot accept a Dutch impostor on the throne of Scotland or England. You have surmised correctly that we use the Kiss as a cover for political activity. It's been a useful meeting place over the years, before, during and after the Revolution. A gathering of particular importance took place on the 13th of June. The Duke of Melfort himself – James Stuart's principal adviser – was here from Ireland. I cannot divulge our discussions. I'll only say they concerned how my house can aid the return of the true king. Melfort's party travelled in disguise and arrived at the castle in the late afternoon while it was still light, coming on the road from the west. They had taken a ship to the Ayrshire coast and were escorted here by Drummond. They were never in the woods after that. Following our discussions, they left the castle with Drummond at about midnight, just as the Kiss was in full throng. They took the road to the west again, back to Ayrshire. I accompanied them myself for the first few miles along the road. Surely long after you say they had run into Arthur and Bethia. Drummond guided them through the country to Ayrshire, where a ship was waiting to take them back to Ireland. They went in the opposite direction from the Avon. They travelled all night and the ship sailed at eight in the morning. Drummond returned the following day and gave me a full report. At Cantrae House, on the coast, certain documents were signed before witnesses. I have one here. Look at the witness list: it includes Melfort and Drummond. It proves they were all there to sail at high tide.'

MacKenzie raised his eyebrows. A Gaelic proverb came into his mind which simply stated once a liar, always a liar. He took out his pipe, filled it with tobacco and sucked hard on it. He had a sudden revelation. 'If what you say is true, your grace, I've been lied to, again. Thank you for being so frank with me. I apologise for implicating Drummond.'

'Speak to Drummond if you want. He'll corroborate my account.'

'I'll inform your mother I'm mistaken.' MacKenzie bowed his head and was on the point of leaving. 'Just one other thing, your grace. The ring you gave to Mr Scougall.'

'Ah, I had forgotten. Just a little gift as an introduction. Let us forget about it. He may take it as his fee for helping my mother. Let's leave it at that.' Having wrongly accused him, MacKenzie felt loth to pursue the point. The gift would no doubt resurface to haunt Scougall in the future, despite Arran's assurance.

CHAPTER 43

A Letter from Beyond the Grave

MACKENZIE RETURNED TO the palace and found Scougall had finished his packing. Scougall's hopeful expression disappeared when he found out that Corse had lied again. MacKenzie picked up Scougall's hat. 'We're not finished yet, Davie. I have a hunch.'

Scougall reluctantly followed him out of the palace to the Hamilton Tolbooth. The remains of Arthur were still in the cellar on a wooden table covered by a filthy sheet. The stench was overpowering. 'The ink stains on his fingers, Davie,' said MacKenzie. 'The paper and quill in the tower. Had he been writing something?'

MacKenzie lit the candles at the side of the room and removed the sheet. He put on his gloves and checked the pockets of Arthur's rotting jacket. They were empty. He removed his dagger and used it to pull back the sides of the jacket so he could search the inside pockets. They were also empty. He began to feel round the inside lining of the jacket. Scougall had to cover his mouth as a feeling of nausea swept through him. There was something in the lining of the jacket. MacKenzie cut through the material with the knife. He carefully removed a piece of paper. It was a badly soiled letter. The address was just visible. It was a letter for Sir James Turner. 'Arthur must have written this just before he died. Before he could get it to his godfather.'

Scougall could not contain his surprise. 'A letter from a dead man?'

MacKenzie nodded solemnly. He opened the letter and read the following:

My dearest godfather,

I write to you in a condition of deepest despair. First, Bethia was taken from me. Now I fear for my own life. In case the worst should happen, I have written this to you as both explanation and confession. I love you as a dear friend with all my heart.

I do not know if you have surmised my true nature. We have never spoken of it openly, but you may suspect it. I do not know why I was born the way I am. It was not my choosing. I have had a compulsion to sin all my life, especially as I grew from boy to man. I believe you above all men will understand me. It has haunted my waking hours and my dreams at night. I prayed to God, day after day, that I might be free of it. At times, I had hopes of freedom and thought I might live a happy life with Bethia. But my sinning nature always returned. There was nothing I could do to escape it.

The desire to sin became so intense in me at times that it drove me to distraction. I was forced to prosecute it secretly with abandon until it was assuaged, but its assuagement only magnified my desire to sin again and again. Thus, it went on and on, week after week, month after month, year after year. A story of illicit meetings, secrecy, lies and relentless fear of discovery.

My beloved friend Robert was both my easement and the source of my agony. As we grew into men, we sinned together, hesitantly at first, then with intensity. I can hardly write it, but it was almost as if we lived as man and wife together during those days at the college when we shared chambers in Glasgow. I would use the word love for what we shared, but I know the world would condemn us as sodomites who engaged in practices contrary to the natural order created by God. Robert argued with me often that we were as natural as any of God's creations and provided arguments from philosophers. But I could not help the deep feeling of sinfulness caused by our carnal relations which cast me down into deepest despair. I often contemplated self-murder as the only way of escape.

Bethia was always my closest friend as a child and as I grew into a man. But I could tell her nothing of my true nature. I dreamed of a settled life with her when I conquered my lustful, sinful feelings. We would live happily and raise a family. I prayed this might be so and at times it seemed it might happen, but I always found myself lapsing back into sinful ways. I could never tell her what was in my heart and the truth about my nature. However, in recent months she began to realise something was wrong. When she was taken in the river, I fell into a precipice of despair from which I could find no way out and the manner of her demise cleaved my heart. I pondered ending my own life every hour and was tempted to it night after night. She was an innocent creature who did not deserve to die. I see now her death was the price we paid for our sinning. It was no accident she met her end, nor did she have my child in her womb, or any child, as some have said, for we never lay together as man and wife. It was a terrible occurrence which still makes me shake when I recall it.

We had argued in the morning of the 13th of June in her house. She accused me of growing cold towards her. Later in the afternoon, she followed Robert and I into the woods around the Avon. She discovered our most secret hiding place, a location hallowed by us over the years that no one else knew about, a place providing secrecy and protection. When she witnessed what we were about in that enclave, she shrieked in horror. She cried us out as witches. She screamed she had found dice and a document on divining in my chamber. Was I not trying to divine the future? And now she found us engaged in an act so hideous it was as if she had seen Satan before her, as perhaps she had. She fled into the growing darkness. Robert and I gave chase. Robert is a faster runner than I. He caught up with her by the turn in the Avon beside the pool where we played as children. It was then the Devil acted. Robert tried to calm her, but she struggled with him in her anguish and revulsion. She backed away from him and slipped into the water. At that moment, he might have saved her by reaching down and pulling her out. But Satan paralysed him. He did not aid her, even though she called out to him. I arrived as she shrieked one last time and disappeared under the water.

As I reached the edge, she was not to be seen, the water having sucked her under. Robert called out she would have decried us both as sodomites and we would burn at the stake. I cursed him and went after her, running down the side of the water, trying to see if she had been caught somewhere. But in the darkness, I could not find her. It was the most hopeless night I ever spent in my life, passing back and forwards up and down both banks of the Avon to no avail. Hour after hour through that dismal night, I searched for her. I finally wandered back to Hamilton as the dawn rose and heard the awful news that she was pulled out the

Clyde downstream. I ran to the palace and looked down on her cold body. I shrieked in agony. I saw what my sinning nature had done. I went home in a demented state. I could not tell my mother the truth. How could I tell her? So I absconded, not knowing what I should do. I stayed in Glasgow for a few days in a secret location, cursing my life and Robert, and thinking I should end it. Robert eventually came to see me there. At first, I could not face the sight of him. But I relented and, after many long debates, he took me back to the old tower on our estate where he said I should stay until I decided what direction to take. Thoughts of my own demise haunted me constantly in that lonely place.

I had much time to think in the tower. I decided on countless plans which I rejected the next minute. More and more I had a desire, for the sake of my soul, to confess my manifold sins and take the punishment I deserved. But Robert argued vehemently against this, saying that he would hang for not aiding her and we both would burn for our sinful life together.

We have argued much in recent days. I see he no longer trusts me. He fears me. He fears I will blurt out everything to the first person I see. He looks worse and worse, afflicted with guilt, haunted by what he has done, gravely troubled in his mind with a dark look in his eye. I fear him now when he visits. I fear the look he gives me. It is no longer one of love, but of hate. And so, in case something should happen to me, I have written this confession which I sign with my own hand, and will have delivered to you, dear godfather, having left it at the inn in Hamilton, so at least someone will know the truth.

God forgive me.

Arthur Nasmyth, 21 September 1691.

MacKenzie passed the letter to Scougall who read it in horror.

CHAPTER 44

Hiding Place

NEWS SPREAD THROUGH the parish that Robert Corse was missing. It was the Sabbath and he had not turned up to give a sermon as part of his training for the ministry. A search was made for him across the parish. He was not in his house and could not be found anywhere in the town. MacKenzie and Scougall were also on his trail. In his house they found a collection of forbidden books and manuscripts hidden in his larder. After a few hours of fruitless searching, they sought O'Flaherty. MacKenzie asked him about the secret location mentioned by Arthur in his letter. O'Flaherty thought for a moment then told them to follow him. They passed along the Avon and into the woods upstream of the castle. Scougall cursed under his breath. He was fed up tramping around the countryside and wanted to get home. About a mile upstream from the castle, there was a narrow passageway between two rocks. It was partially blocked by an array of wood and debris which had to be moved to get through. Beyond the passageway was a courtyard created by a curtain of rocks. A ruined building overgrown with ivy, once used as a storehouse, was built into the side of the hill.

They entered and searched the rooms on the ground floor. They were empty. They climbed upstairs. In the room on the left, a figure sat on a chair staring forlornly at a picture held in his hand. He turned towards them as they entered. It was Robert Corse. He stood up as they arrived, looking like he was about to flee, then realised they blocked the only exit and slumped back down. Corse was painfully thin and pale.

'Then it's over, gentlemen. I'm glad of it. Thank God for it. I'll burn as I deserve. Take me now. I cannot face the deception anymore.' He held out his hands for them to shackle him. 'I thought I'd outwitted you,' Corse continued. 'But it would not matter anyway. I didn't kill her, but I didn't save her either. The Devil spoke to me by the river. The Devil told me what I should do to Arthur in the tower. That I should stave in the head of my beloved friend. That I should dismember his beautiful body. That I should load his remains on a horse. That I should ride to the Quaker burial ground and disperse the bits of him as if I was throwing lumps of meat to a dog. I killed her. I killed my beloved friend to save myself. I'm bound for Hell if that place exists.'

'How could you butcher him?' blurted out Scougall.

Corse screamed out: 'I was beyond myself! I had lost any sense of myself. Satan had taken me, or perhaps I was mad. My whole life has been deception, saying one thing and feeling another. I did not ask to be created like this and in moments we shared such joy, although always tinged with guilt. I thought I could rationalise my nature and live a secret life as some men do. I must now face the Lord for what I've done. I did not mean to let her die. I did not want to kill the man I loved. It was as if another man did it. It was a monster... not me!'

'What about slaying your uncle as well?' asked O'Flaherty angrily. 'Did you get a taste for killing, boy?'

'That was not me, I swear it, O'Flaherty!' cried Corse. 'On my soul, it was not me. I admit the vile treatment of my friends. I'll not admit to something I didn't do. I've no more time for lies.' Corse rose and took a couple of steps forward. 'I'll come with you now. I'll confess my sins to the session. My account will fill pages of their minute book. They'll revel in it as only those who judge the sins of others can gloat. But at least the truth will be known.' He took another few paces towards them. 'Come, tie my hands.' He put his wrists together.

'Why did you not help her?' cried O'Flaherty. 'And then spread lies about her which encouraged the fanatics to abuse her body?' O'Flaherty moved slowly towards him and for a moment stood in front of Corse, looking him up and down. He took Corse's hands in his as if he was about to bind them. Then it happened in a flash. He dropped Corse's hands. A dagger came from somewhere in his clothing and he lunged forward, stabbing Corse in the stomach, holding the blade deep inside him as the blood seeped out over his hands.

MacKenzie yelled for O'Flaherty to stop as Corse sank to his knees, holding onto his stomach. O'Flaherty took hold of Corse's hair, yanking it back and bringing up his chin to reveal his emaciated neck. He cut his throat from side to side. Two long, black wounds gushed blood. Corse collapsed on the ground. The miniature painting of Arthur fell beside him.

O'Flaherty turned to MacKenzie and Scougall. 'A little justice for Bethia!' he cried. He threw down the weapon. 'It's the first time I've used it since the wars. He deserved to die!'

MacKenzie shook his head. 'The law should have dealt with it, Jago. The courts should have considered the matter. The truth revealed to all the people in public!'

O'Flaherty moved towards them, then fell on his knees and cried out in despair: 'She was my daughter! She was my child! I could tell no one! Her mother was married to another man!'

MacKenzie recalled sitting in O'Flaherty's chamber, listening to the lament he had composed for Bethia and looking at the lost expression in O'Flaherty's eyes. He saw now it was a father's lament for his daughter.

CHAPTER 45

A Loose Thread

MACKENZIE TOLD SCOUGALL to return to his room and finish packing. He reassured him the matter of the ring was settled. He knew Scougall would continue to worry about it and did not mention his own suspicion it might resurface in the future. MacKenzie rang the servants' bell. He stood looking out the window on the grey sky and river. There was a chill in the air; winter was round the next bend. It would be good to get back to the Hawthorns before the weather turned. There was a knock on the door and John Timothy entered. 'How can I help you, sir?' he asked.

MacKenzie smiled. 'Please, come in, John. I'm getting ready to leave. I want to talk with you one last time. Take a seat beside me, by the window here.'

John Timothy looked surprised. He closed the door and walked across to the armchair at the window. He did not sit but stood beside MacKenzie, a serious look on his face.

MacKenzie took out his pipe and packed it with tobacco. He was soon puffing away. 'Do you smoke, John?' MacKenzie asked pensively.

'No, sir,' replied John Timothy.

'A habit I've long tried to rid myself of, but I keep coming back to it. A bit like my desire to see a puzzle solved. My work here is done. I hope things are settled for you after the misunderstanding around Bethia. I had no choice but to question you about her.'

John Timothy nodded. 'I understand, sir. Do you want me to pack for you?'

'No, John. I've something to tell you. I've learned the truth about the sad history of Bethia and Arthur. You'll no doubt hear some of the details from the other servants soon. Bethia will receive proper burial alongside her mother and father in the kirkyard. Arthur will be buried beside her. The duchess will compensate the Quakers for the desecration of their burial ground. I'm sorry to say O'Flaherty will hang for killing Robert Corse.'

'I've heard about it, sir. I cannot believe it,' said John Timothy.

'There's just one matter outstanding,' said MacKenzie. 'I'm not directly involved with it. It's strictly the business of the sheriff of Lanark, who, I hear, spends little time considering it.' MacKenzie waited to observe John Timothy, who stared intently at him with an emotionless expression. 'I refer to the killing of William Corse.' Again, MacKenzie was silent for a few moments, puffing away and observing him carefully, before continuing: 'I'll not say I understand everything about it, but I know who killed him.'

A bead of sweat was visible on John Timothy's temple. He said nothing.

MacKenzie continued: 'I'll tell you what I think happened to Corse. He returned to Hamilton that afternoon for an appointment in the palace with Arran on business connected with the debts owed by the earl. He went back to his house where his wife had prepared a meal. She left him alone to visit her sister. He continued to sup contentedly. During his repast, there was a knock on the door. He was annoyed to be disturbed. He was surprised to find a black man standing before him.' MacKenzie lowered his voice. 'It was you at his door, John. You said you wanted to speak with him. He let you in and you closed the door. From this point, what I say is conjecture. Perhaps he scorned you and laughed in your face, perhaps you mentioned something that happened in Barbados years before, maybe connected to the slave revolt of 1686. I don't know if you went to the house intending to murder him, but you lost control and your hands were round his neck. He was an old man. It was easy to strangle him to death. Some threads from your shirt got under his fingernails as he struggled and the button of your jacket broke off. I picked it up a couple of hours later from the floor under the table. I believe if I were to examine your bluff coat, a button would be missing and the fabric would match your shirt. I believe they are the only things linking you to his killing.'

John Timothy's head dropped. There were tears on his cheeks as he whispered: 'Lord, forgive me. Lord, forgive me. Lord, forgive me.' Finally, he raised his head. 'You must believe me, Mr MacKenzie. I did not intend to kill him. I went to his house to see if he recognised me, to see if there was a flicker of remembrance. At first, he had no idea who I was. But when I mentioned the island of Barbados, I saw there was recognition in his eyes. He told me roughly to be gone. He would have words with the duchess about my insubordination and he scorned me arrogantly. It was not this threat that made me do it, you must believe me, it was the sound of his laughter, his haughty, sneering laughter. It took me back to the island. I saw his face in the flames of the fire, watching my friends being burnt alive, burned as rebels, the stink of their roasted flesh in my nostrils. Burned on his orders.' John Timothy was silent for a moment before continuing: 'I do not regret killing him, sir. I'll stand to account for it before the Lord at the end of my days.'

'Tell me everything, John,' said MacKenzie solemnly.

John Timothy looked down at his hands as he spoke, emotionlessly. 'I've told you something of my life but not all the details. It's too painful for me. I was taken from my parents aged nine by slavers. I survived the dreadful sea crossing from Africa, although many did not. I cried for my mother every night in that dark hold. We came to a strange island where I was sold to a planter. I was given the name "John Timothy". I worked in the sugar fields six days a week, and each day was an eternity of despair. I missed my mother and father and brothers and sisters. I tried to talk with the other slaves, but we all spoke different tongues and we could not understand each other. And there was the relentless work and the viciousness of the master and his men, brute cruelty to men and women and children. The master was called William Corse, among the harshest on the island. The years passed. I survived somehow. I grew into a man. I learned the language of my oppressor. I met a young woman from another people, seized in Africa as a girl. We became husband and wife and had a child, although we could not officially marry. There was now something of a life amidst the torture. I had something to live for. There were moments of light in our lives, flashes of happiness. Then the Quakers came to Barbados. I heard George Fox preach. I saw not all white folk were devils and I found consolation in the words of God. I became a Friend of the Truth in my heart, although I could not reveal myself in the open. But Corse and other planters faced setbacks in their business as the price of sugar fell. They sought to make savings which caused great consternation in the plantation and ultimately precipitated a revolt. Strangely, it was a time of hope for us. We had a dream of breaking off our shackles and taking over the island and living as we wanted. We had heard about the Maroons who lived freely in parts of Jamaica. The rebellion was months in the planning, but it failed. We were betrayed by the treachery of other slaves and it was crushed ferociously.

The ringleaders were dealt with savagely. Some were hung, others burned alive, having been castrated. I tried to escape. I was hunted down by dogs and castrated, but I survived. I was sold and my woman and daughter also. The three of us dispersed to the wind like leaves across the sea.

'Years and years have passed since those moments before the fire in Barbados. I have lived in a trance. I was taken by a new owner to London and won by the Duke of Hamilton. I found myself in the Palace of Hamilton in a land called Scotland, a cold, northerly land. I became acquainted with Hugh Wood. I was delighted to find he was a Quaker who knew George Fox. Hugh was a good Christian soul who took me under his wing and encouraged me to study the Bible.' John Timothy looked MacKenzie in the eyes and then added. 'Then one afternoon I opened the palace doors for a merchant who was visiting Arran. I saw William Corse in front of me. He was older and diminished, but the same smirk, the same whiskers, now whitened by time, the same grim face, now lined with age. He looked right through me, as he did with all of us slaves, but I found out from other servants as much as I could about him. I learned where he lived when he was in Hamilton and each time he met Arran thereafter, I watched his door, until the night I saw the woman leave. I entered under some pretext and in his living chamber, as he finished his meal, I mentioned Barbados and the rebellion of years before. He stopped eating and examined my face. I knew then he recognised me. I also knew God had provided this opportunity for me. God had transported us both across the ocean from Barbados to Hamilton where I would have my revenge. For, mark my words, Mr MacKenzie, Corse was an evil creature, as evil as Beelzebub himself. He cursed me and told me to get out of his house, but he was no longer the robust planter who had whipped men and women in the fields. He was an old man with fear in his eyes. I seized him by the throat. I could not stop myself. I crushed the life out of him, staring into his terrified eyes as I did it. I would never see my family again, but the man responsible was sent to Hell. Where else could such a creature be bound? I stood in the room for a few minutes. I knew if his wife came back, I would be caught. I could not kill her, so I crept back to the palace. Now I must hang like my fellow rebels in Barbados. I'm ready to meet my death, sir.'

MacKenzie continued to puff on his pipe thoughtfully. 'Your narrative is a moving one, John. It does not excuse the taking of life, of course, even though I've no doubt Corse was an evil man. Perhaps you had no choice in the matter. It's impossible sometimes to turn the other cheek. I don't know what I would do to the man responsible for selling my wife and daughter and killing my friends. It's quite possible I would do the same as you. Tell me, do you know anything of them, you mentioned New York?'

John Timothy wearily looked up again. 'That's all I know. That's where she was sent. As for my daughter, I know nothing. She could be anywhere in the wide world. She could be dead.'

MacKenzie nodded. 'Listen to me, John. I've been able to work out who killed William Corse. But the evidence no longer exists.' He held the button between his thumb and forefinger, then handed it back to John Timothy. 'There are others suspects – Corse had many enemies. Your story will remain secret.'

John Timothy put his hands on MacKenzie's and thanked him.

MacKenzie continued: 'Say nothing more of his name ever again. Now, there's another matter. As part of my payment from the duchess I've received the sum of £100 sterling. A large sum of money. I've exchanged it for another asset. I've been given you as my fee. I despise the fact any human being can own another, but when I leave you must accompany me as my servant. We depart in an hour on the Glasgow coach. Now, I must find Hugh Wood who promised me some seeds and cuttings for my garden.'

John Timothy looked perplexed and uncertain.

CHAPTER 46

Scougall Returns Home

EDINBURGH LOOKED AND smelled the same as ever when they climbed out of the coach on the High Street. Scougall was exhausted by the time he ascended the stairs to his apartments. He had much to think about. MacKenzie had reassured him the matter of the ring was settled with Arran, but he remained unconvinced. He did not know if he should give it to Chrissie or not. He did not know what he should say to Mrs Hair about it. He would recount the story of John Timothy to her when he returned to the office. He thought it would be the best way to highlight the uncertainties he felt about the slavery question. He was now convinced the trade was immoral. He was moved by the humanity of the Quakers in opposing it. They had left John Timothy at the Broomielaw to board a ship for America. It was an emotional parting. MacKenzie had given him a document that Scougall had hastily drafted which bestowed his freedom. It was one of the shortest legal documents he had ever written, but the one he was proudest of.

He opened the front door of his apartment with his key, trying not to make any noise as it was late. As he came into the hall, his mother-in-law appeared from the living chamber. She was a small stout woman. 'Davie, it's you, son,' she said. There was a worried look on her face and his heart dropped like a stone down a well. Had something happened to Chrissie or the child while he was away gallivanting in the west? She was due to give birth very soon. He raised his hand to his mouth. But her face broke into a broad smile and a stream of laughter erupted from her as she came towards him with open arms. 'You have a healthy daughter, Davie! Chrissie is well! God be praised!'

She came up to him and he fell against her. He did not try to stop the tears that dripped onto her shoulders as he thanked the Lord from the bottom of his heart.

Epilogue

The Hawthorns, 5 January 1692

MacKenzie sat at his desk in the library at the Hawthorns. A fire was burning and there was a thin covering of snow in the garden outside; his old dog, Macrae, was snoring contentedly at his feet. He was finishing his correspondence, writing a note to Davie and Chrissie Scougall. MacKenzie smiled to himself. Chrissie had given birth to a healthy baby girl on the 30th of September, just as their coach trundled its way back to Edinburgh. MacKenzie was chosen as her godfather. He doubted the existence of a creator, but he would not disappoint Scougall by decrying the convention. The Christening was set for the following week in St Giles Kirk.

The door was suddenly flung open and his grandson Geordie, a youngster of two years, raced into the room, followed by Elizabeth. Geordie jumped onto his grandfather's lap. MacKenzie spoke to him softly in Gaelic, the words calming the child. He waited for a reply and smiled in satisfaction when Geordie uttered a few words in the same tongue. 'I'll make him a Gaelic speaker if it's the last thing I do, Beth.'

Elizabeth stood beside the desk looking down on them both. 'What good will it do him, father?' she said. 'What good will it do him speaking Irish when it's the English tongue that's spoken in every corner of the world. Gaelic is a language of the past.'

'He may get something out of it,' said MacKenzie with a smile. 'It's a gift I failed to give to you, lost as I was in grief after your mother's death.' Geordie jumped off his knee and went running out the way he had come, squealing in delight. Elizabeth placed a bundle of letters on the desk before following her son.

MacKenzie shook his head contentedly and rummaged through the pile. They were mostly written by hands he recognised: clients in the north, chiefs and clan gentry, his brothers and sisters, a litany of requests for advice and money. All these could wait. One letter stood out. It was written in a hand he did not recognise. He opened it and read with delight:

New York
25 November 1691

My dearest John,
 I arrived in this city four weeks ago. I have found work and a room to live in. I work hard and believe in this place I may make a life of some kind for myself. I will save money and begin the search for my wife and daughter. There is no word of them yet, but I pray to God every day that I might find something of their trail and we may be reunited again.
 There is a little community of free slaves in the city and a congregation of Quakers also. I have joined their communion. They all pray that through God's intervention my family may be reunited.
 I thank you again for all you have done for me and the money you provided for my passage back across the ocean to this city on the other side. I keep the document Mr Scougall drew up in my breast pocket, so it is beside my heart always. It is the sweetest thing I have received in this cruel world since I held my daughter's tiny hand on the day she was born.
 Please write telling me of the events in Scotland, about your family and Mr Scougall's. If fate should ever bring you to this new world, it would give me the greatest joy to see you again.

 Your loving friend,
 Quashee Eddoo

Acknowledgements

I would like to thank my wife, Julie, and all my family for their love and support. I would also like to thank Rachael Murray for editing the text and everyone at Luath Press.

I have found the following works of history particularly useful in writing this novel: George B Burnet, *The Story of Quakerism in Scotland 1650–1950* (2007); Richard S Dunn, *Sugar and Slaves: The Rise of the Planter Class in the English West Indies 1624–1713* (1973); Rosalind K Marshall, *The Days of Duchess Anne: Life in the Household of the Duchess of Hamilton 1656–1716* (1973); David Stevenson, *The Beggar's Benison: Sex Clubs of Enlightenment Scotland and their Rituals* (2001); David Stevenson, *The Origins of Freemasonry: Scotland's Century 1590–1710* (1988); Tom Betteridge (ed), *Sodomy in Early Modern Europe* (2002); John R Young, 'The Seventeenth Century', in *Exploring Our Past: Essays on the Local History and Archaeology of West Central Scotland*.

Luath Press Limited
committed to publishing well written books worth reading

LUATH PRESS takes its name from Robert Burns, whose little collie Luath (*Gael.*, swift or nimble) tripped up Jean Armour at a wedding and gave him the chance to speak to the woman who was to be his wife and the abiding love of his life. Burns called one of the 'Twa Dogs' Luath after Cuchullin's hunting dog in Ossian's *Fingal*. Luath Press was established in 1981 in the heart of Burns country, and is now based a few steps up the road from Burns' first lodgings on Edinburgh's Royal Mile. Luath offers you distinctive writing with a hint of unexpected pleasures.
Most bookshops in the UK, the US, Canada, Australia, New Zealand and parts of Europe, either carry our books in stock or can order them for you. To order direct from us, please send a £sterling cheque, postal order, international money order or your credit card details (number, address of cardholder and expiry date) to us at the address below. Please add post and packing as follows: UK – £1.00 per delivery address; overseas surface mail – £2.50 per delivery address; overseas airmail – £3.50 for the first book to each delivery address, plus £1.00 for each additional book by airmail to the same address. If your order is a gift, we will happily enclose your card or message at no extra charge.

Luath Press Limited
543/2 Castlehill
The Royal Mile
Edinburgh EH1 2ND
Scotland
Telephone: 0131 225 4326 (24 hours)
Email: sales@luath.co.uk
Website: www.luath.co.uk